The Bringer

by

Samantha Towle

*For Craig, Riley & Isabella. I love you guys;
and to quote the wise words of Buzz Lightyear -
to infinity...and beyond.*

Acknowledgments

First and foremost, I want to say a humongous thank you to my husband, Craig. I still can't believe you'd read a romance book for me - big props for that! You've given me sound advice, dare I say the best....you've believed in me, listened to me, championed me, and put up with my mood swings! Love you, babes.

Thank you to my beautiful babies, Riley & Isabella, for being born, for inspiring me every single day, and for been great sleepers! Love you, my darlings.

A big thanks goes to my, mum, Carol Towse. You've read everything I've ever written, even the rubbish stuff, and you still encouraged me to keep going. Love you.

Thank you to my girl, Nicky Oliver – for your crazy ideas, for making me laugh, even when you didn't mean too! You've been my cheerleader from the word go, love you honey – vodka's on me.

I also want to say thank you to the rest of my family and friends, you've all helped me immensely, in one way or another, probably without even realising, especially my mother-in-law, Sue Towle; those home cooked meals you send home for me so I can get on with my writing are a Godsend – just don't forget the chocolate cake next time! Also I want to say a big thank you to my online friends, some of the writing tips I've got from you guys has been invaluable.

And last but not least, a big thank you to my publisher Tim Roux. You've given me this amazing opportunity to get this story of mine heard and I can truly never thank you enough.

Ok, enough now of my ramblings – let the story commence.

Chapter 1

The Awakening

I stand by the doorway and wait patiently while she looks at what used to be her body.

Turning slowly, she brings her vivid blue eyes to look up at me. "Are you an angel?" she asks in a timid voice.

If I had a penny for every time I've been asked that - well not that pennies are of any use to me, but still.

I gently shake my head. "No. I'm not an angel. But I am the one who's here to take you to the angels." I add a friendly smile to make her feel more at ease.

She considers this for a moment, then turns back to look at her grieving parents who sit agonised by her bedside.

"Will I ever see them again?" I can hear the tremor in her tiny voice, sadness I know it to be.

"Yes. I don't know when, but one day you will see them again."

This I'm not privileged to have seen with my own eyes, but it is what the Elders tell us to be true.

I deliver humans to the door of Heaven. To their door into Heaven, but don't truly know what occurs when they pass through. But I do know it to be something wonderful, giving joy and happiness to all who go there.

I'm a Bringer.

It's what I do, and have done since I've existed. I'm here to guide, to make humans feel as comfortable as possible through their, mostly unwanted, transition from being alive to just being.

Humans struggle to leave behind the ones they love. And for their sake, I have to ensure they don't try to stay here on earth, trapping themselves for all eternity. Because once they walk away from Heaven, they will never, ever, be able to go there. Once their door closes, it never again opens.

I glance over at her parents. The mother is sobbing, clinging to her daughter's lifeless hand. The father has silent tears trickling down his cheeks as he desperately tries to comfort the mother. They both appear broken, beyond repair.

Humans always take the death of a child the worst. I think I understand why this is.

I have seen what these two people are feeling hundreds, of thousands, of times before. Have been told in vivid description by many humans who I've taken to Heaven how it feels, but have never felt it myself.

I don't feel.

Not in the physical or emotional sense. I have an awareness of feelings - sorrow, happiness, love, pain, compassion. I also note the sensation of touch. But I don't actually feel it.

I do comprehend the joy and beauty in things, such as the sun rising in the bright blue sky, or the sound of a songbird singing gaily in the morning. Just not in the same way as a human does.

I know of all the feelings that surround me every day, but they just don't attach themselves to me.

That's just how it is – Bringers don't feel.

I believe we were conceived like this, so we don't attach ourselves to humans in any way.

Often, though, I do wonder how it would be to feel.

With what I see in every single moment of my existence it obviously presses me to peruse the question which is worse - to feel the agonising pain of loss, or to have never felt it at all?

I have no concept of what it is like to love someone with such ferocity that it rips you to your very core to lose them. My imagination limits my understanding.

I just sometimes wonder, what if . . .

The child I'm here to take to Heaven – Amy Jones, as I know her to be called - takes one last look at her parents, at her body, then turns and tentatively walks toward me. Her movement slow, reluctant.

It's strange that humans have two names. Sometimes they have three, four, sometimes more. I have only one.

When Amy Jones reaches me, she slips her tiny hand into mine and looks up at me.

"You look like my mamma," Amy Jones says, inclining her head toward her mother.

I ponder that for a moment.

Interesting.

It intrigues me how I look to each human. They see me as whichever female human form makes them feel most comfortable. Like now, with Amy Jones, she chooses to see me akin to her mother, thus making her feel safer. They do this unknowingly.

I have never seen myself. I have no reflection upon which to do so. When I look down all I see is a solid mass of light, alike to the shape of a human body, which glistens and sparkles, just as the snow does when the sun is gently dancing off it.

Often I have wondered what my true appearance is, or if I at all have one.

I look at the mother again. To my eyes she looks to be visually pleasing. Hair the colour of ripe cherries, skin the colour of the pale moon, eyes the colour of emeralds.

Is this exactly as I look now?

I glance down at Amy Jones about to ask this very question, when I see a faraway look in her eyes, sadness covering her face. And very quickly, my question becomes incredibly futile.

"Are you ready to go?" I ask instead.

Her eyes glitter up at me. "What's your name angel?"

I smile to myself. Children never believe I'm not an angel. I think it somehow comforts them to think I am.

"Lucyna."

"Lucyna," she hums my name over her plump lips. "That's a pretty name. Am I going to Heaven, Lucyna?"

"Yes, Amy Jones you are."

"Will you be staying with me in Heaven?"

"No. I can only remain with you until we reach Heaven's door."

Her face saddens. "Then will I be alone?" The fear is so apparent in her voice, it practically tremors across the room.

"No, you will be with others. Many others just like you. You'll never be alone."

She mulls over my words for a moment. Her tiny lips trembling ever so slightly. She bites down on her lower lip.

"Okay, Lucyna. I think I'm ready to go to Heaven now." I sense her hand tightening around mine.

"Close your eyes," I say.

Her heavily lashed lids close slowly. I can sense her fear. Her apprehension of stepping into the unknown.

"You've nothing to fear Amy Jones, you're safe," I whisper.

I close my eyes and we're gone.

* * *

I've returned to Earth since taking Amy Jones to Heaven as I wish to spend some time at my favourite place – Hyde Park in London - before I take my next human to Heaven, my next 'bring' as we refer to it. London, coincidentally, is where my next human happens to be. Not that it would matter where I am, as it only takes me a matter of seconds to travel. I close my eyes, think where I want to be, and there I am.

I see my friend Arlo already here, sitting on our usual bench. He too must be waiting for his next bring. We Bringers have no need to sit, to rest, as we never tire. We do so, I suppose, in attempt to adapt to the environment around us.

I glance around Hyde Park. There are a few humans milling about, taking in the wonderful sights. This place fascinates me. Over time I have observed with interest the beautiful sights it has to offer. Year after year I have watched it travel through its seasons, noting how the trees sprout greening leaves that spiral around the willowy branches, creating the most incredible shades of greenery, for them to only turn to burnt amber as they succumb to wane, and fall unwillingly from their dwelling. Lastly they end their journey on the Earth's floor, leaving the tree bare, only for it months later to once again begin its cycle. And I am charmed by all the differing varieties, of colourful flowers. I watch as they explode into bloom. Then ultimately, and sometimes untimely, fade and die.

Just as humans do.

Arlo and I have been to places all over the world, seen all the extraordinary sights that God has to offer, but sometimes it is the simplest of things that can be the most captivating.

The bench Arlo is sitting on has a plaque with an inscription scribed on it. It reads –

'John, I'll love you always and I know we'll be together again one day. In the fields of Heaven, when God calls for me to come join you, where I know you'll be waiting patiently for me. Ava'

I always sit on this bench, one that has been marked by a human loss. It feels very much in time with who I am.

Humans always mark the death of ones they love. Whether it's a headstone at a grave or a bench very similar to this one. I think I understand why they do this. An expression of how much they truly meant to them.

They really do have some very strange ways, which is why I find them so fascinating. Arlo is also intrigued by them. We spend almost all our free time together watching humans, discussing them. Seeing how they interact with one another. We spend countless hours puzzling over them. How they think. How they feel. Why they behave as they do.

"How long do you have?" I ask as I approach Arlo.

He looks up at me, his yellow hair glowing in the light of the sun. "Eighteen minutes. And hello to you, Lucyna."

Arlo is always very precise and to the point.

"Hello, Arlo," I say with a smile.

Taking my seat beside him, I pause momentarily, hovering over a question that I have wanted to ask him for some time, a question which has now been piqued by my visit with Amy Jones.

"Arlo, may I ask you something?"

He turns to me. "Of course."

"How do I look to you?"

He looks at me puzzled.

I refresh my words. "I know our appearance changes according to each human, but for some time now I have wondered how I actually look to you?"

"Hmm." Arlo looks as though I have ignited a thought within him. "You have never wondered this before, Lucyna?" It almost isn't a question, but I answer anyway.

"Well, I have thought of it many times before Arlo, but have never asked you. Honestly, I'm not sure why. It's very curious to me."

I turn to look at him. His bright eyes are gazing upon me with seeming concentration.

"Well, what do you wish me to describe?"

I take a moment to think this over before answering. "What colour is my hair?"

"Black. As black as the night sky," he replies.

"And what is my eye colour?"

He ponders this for a moment, rubbing his forehead in thought. "Well, I would say they are like the colour of the waters that surround the Maldivian Islands. I would have to go back and check that I am correct in this, but that is what I believe to be true. I can go now if you wish -" His eyes close, readying to leave.

"No, Arlo, there is no need. I take your word on this."

He opens his eyes.

I now find myself even more curious. I thought by asking Arlo these questions it would end my wondering, but it now seems to have only furthered it.

How I wish I could see what Arlo sees when he looks at me.

"And I, Lucyna, how do I look to you?" Arlo says, breaking into my thoughts.

Putting aside my own contemplation, I turn and look at him even though I do not need to. I would know how Arlo looks even if my eyes were closed.

"You, Arlo, have the most glorious hair. It's the colour of the sun, and your eyes, well they are the colour of sugar snap peas."

His smile broadens at my words.

I glance back at the few humans around us, gliding through life. Completely unaware of our existence.

"Why do you think we cannot see ourselves, Arlo, as others do?"

But before he gets a chance to answer, my mind begins to fill with the name of my next bring. I'm always informed of when and where in good time, but I don't receive the name until two minutes before the human is about to leave their body for good.

"Sorry, Arlo. Time for me to go."

"Where to now, Lucyna?"

"Chelsea and Westminster Hospital, here in London," I say, as I prepare to travel. "We shall continue our discussion later?"

He nods in response.

"I shall see you soon, then."

I hear the beeping of machines and frantic commands of human voices before I even open my eyes.

Humans have ones they call doctors who take care of others when they are ill or dying. I do admire them. Their determination to cure and save is awe inspiring. But unfortunately for them, when a human is truly dying, when God has called that one to Heaven, no one, or nothing can save them.

The doctors are working tirelessly on the human I know to be called Maxwell Harrison, but I know that their tiresome work will not save him to his body. My being here says so.

He appears at the end of the bed where his body still lies.

Maxwell Harrison is an older human, but he hasn't died from old age. His death was meant to be when his when his heart ceased to work.

Positioned by the doorway, I begin my patient wait, allowing Maxwell Harrison the time he needs to come to this new realisation.

Suddenly he spins around, his eyes frantically searching the room.

He locks them onto me and visibly wavers at my sight. Then his eyes narrow in his glare. "Tell me ... am I dead?" I can see panic and fear gripping his face, not an unusual sight for me.

Some humans are prepared for death; they know it's coming. Some don't. These are the ones it hits the hardest. But all humans, though, however much prepared, will fear the unknown. It's inbuilt. It's in their nature to do so. That's just being human, I suppose.

"Yes, Maxwell Harrison you are," I answer with finality.

"And who are you – my angel?" I hear what I believe to be sarcasm adjoining his already gruff voice. " ... because listen to me, angel," he continues. "I certainly don't want to be dead. It's not my time."

"Unfortunately, it is your time." I speak candidly.

"And who says so – you?"

I decide not to answer his question with words, instead raising my eyes up to Heaven.

He laughs. A big raucous laugh, it bounces off the walls. "The big man upstairs? Give me a break! Trust me, he certainly wouldn't want an old reprobate like me in Heaven. I've definitely been no angel in my time." He nods at me. "No pun intended." There's a grave expression on his face, but a smile is curving the edge of his lips.

"I'm not an angel, Maxwell Harrison."

He looks at me with open surprise. "So, what are you then?"

"Just call me your guide to Heaven."

He hovers over my words for a moment before speaking. "So – guide, why don't you just put me back in my body, and we can forget all about this."

I slowly shake my head. "I'm sorry, that's not a possibility."

He shrugs his broad shoulders. "Well a guy's gotta try, huh." I catch a gleam in his eyes before he turns back to his body.

The doctors have finally given up trying to save Maxwell Harrison, and with much resignation they all quietly move around the room carrying on with their job in the aftermath of a human death.

One of the doctors begins speaking to another. This appears to prick Maxwell Harrison's attention.

"I'll go out and tell the son," the doctor says.

"James," he utters. His eyes follow the doctor to the door, just skimming past me, and his gaze remains there until moments later when a man enters the room.

The man is younger than Maxwell Harrison, but very similar looking. He has the same intense, deep brown eyes.

12

I watch him slowly walk over to the bed where Maxwell Harrison's body remains. Then all of a sudden, something unexpected and inexplicable hits me, almost knocking me off my central balance. It appears like a veil of shimmering light, wrapping itself all around me. And no sooner is it there, it's gone.

What on earth . . .?

The man's face crumples up with pain. "Oh, dad," he whispers, laying his trembling hand on Maxwell Harrison's chest. "What am I gonna do without you?"

I continue to watch the man as the shock of what just happened reverberates through me. Tears are tumbling down his cheeks, dripping freely onto his chest. He roughly wipes at his eyes.

Maxwell Harrison looks forlorn as he walks up to the man. He reaches his hand out to him, pauses, and turns back to me.

"Can I touch him?"

It takes me a moment to answer, to find the words, as my mind is spinning with confusion.

"Of course," I eventually say, "but know that he won't feel you."

He bows his head in submission and lays his hand tentatively on the man's back. "James, I'm here. It's okay."

Then out of nowhere I do something very out of character. I move from my stance by the doorway. This is not something I have ever done before. I don't even realise I've moved until I find myself there, standing at the other side of the bed, looking across at the human Maxwell Harrison calls James. And I mean really looking at him.

Of course I always observe humans, but never truly look at them properly. Usually, I only bother to graze my eyes over their external features, my interest only ever laying in their minds, their emotions, their feelings. But as I stand here looking at James, I appear to be looking for more as I attempt to absorb every fine, physical, detail of him. I'm intrigued by the structural shape of his face. The depth of brown that colour's his hair. His sun stained skin. The scar splicing his brow. His broad nose, and chiselled jaw line. His perfectly lined teeth and the full lips that adorn them. I watch with fascination as tears glisten on his lashes, sparkling against his intense, dark eyes.

And as I stand here, soaking up every microscopic detail of him, I'm suddenly struck by the shimmering light again. Only harder this time. It seems to grasp hold of me, wrapping around me, knocking me backwards, lingering slightly longer than before, then, once again, gone as if never here.

Quickly shutting my eyes I go back to the doorway whilst my mind begins to spill over with bewilderment. Maxwell Harrison doesn't even seem to have noticed my movement. He's still standing with James, his forehead lightly resting against his shoulder.

I am completely and utterly perturbed, and I very quickly decide not to go anywhere near James again, because every time I look at him that shimmering light hits me.

"Can you watch over him?" Maxwell Harrison says suddenly to me.

"I'm sorry?" I utter, not fully registering his words, still wrapped up in my own puzzling thoughts.

He turns to me, wavering ever so slightly. "James, he's got no one left. I'm his only family. We lost his mother, she died when he was still a baby. It's always just been me and him. He'll be all alone and I can't bear the thought of it. I know him, he won't take care of himself properly. Please, can you just watch over him? Take care of him. Make sure he's okay. Please."

Now he has my attention. This is not the first, or I imagine, the last time that I'll be asked this. The Elders have taught us well on how to handle this situation.

"Maxwell Harrison -"

"Max. Please just call me Max."

"- Max," I continue in a soft voice, "this is not something I can do." 'Or right now would wish to,' I silently add.

Max reluctantly leaves James' side and takes a few steps toward me. "Have you ever been human?" he asks.

His question throws me. Surprisingly, I have never been asked this before.

"No," I answer warily.

"Do you have a name?"

"Yes."

There's a long pause between us. Max looks at me impatiently. "What is it?"

"Lucyna."

"Lucyna. Can't say I've ever heard of that before. Is it some sort of special heavenly name?"

I smile. Max has a strange manner. Oddly, it makes me want to smile. I can honestly say I have never encountered anyone like him before in all my time.

"No. I believe there are some humans who also have this name, amongst their other names that is."

He takes a deep breath. I find this intriguing. A human soul has no need to exert for air, but as the body requires it, it becomes a natural thing for them to do, even when no longer required. So they unknowingly continue with the pretence of breathing.

"Look, Lucyna I'm not asking for much. Just every now and then check in on him, make sure he's doing okay."

My eyes trail down to the floor, away from Max's determined stare.

"Please, Lucyna," he implores.

As his pleading words swirl around me, my voice of reason is urging me to once again tell him that it's not possible. That it is most definitely not a possibility. It's very much a rule breaker. The Elders are very clear on this; under no circumstances are we to honour this request.

I have been asked to do this thousands of times before by other humans, and have never once had any difficulty in explaining to them how this is not a possibility. If I and the other Bringers were to look in on every human we were requested to, we would never have time to tend to our duties. Yes, we could lie to them, ease their pain, but deception is not a part of who we are.

And yet, knowing this to be the case, why can I not seem to be able to bring myself to once again say it now?

And honestly, I really do not wish to be around James because, for some unknown reason, he seems to bring this odd shimmering light with him that insists on striking me at any given opportunity. It's something I have never encountered before, or wish to again. And really, what could I do if James wasn't coping? Nothing, obviously.

But as much as I try, I can't seem to make my mouth convey the words.

I look back up at Max and can clearly see the hope on his face, as if written there in indelible ink, the very hope he is pinning on my response.

"I'll do my best," I hear myself saying.

Relief sweeps the breadth of Max's face. "Thank you so much, Lucyna. You don't know how much this means to me. I would kiss you right now, if it didn't seem really inappropriate to do so." He grins.

"Your thanks are plenty enough, Max." I return his smile, far from wishing to as my mind is nearly combustible with turmoil.

What am I doing? This is not something I can commit to.

I know I'm the one speaking but I don't know where these words are coming from. It's almost as if I've been taken over and someone else is now speaking for me.

Frantically, I try to search for the right words to take back my agreement with Max. Disappointingly, nothing comes to mind, or should I say nothing I find myself able, or more to the point, wanting to say?

"Max, you need to be aware that I won't be able to tell you how James is doing. Once I leave you at your door to Heaven, we will never again see each other."

His brows knit together. "Won't I see you in Heaven?"

I shake my head. "No. Unfortunately Heaven is not a place I am permitted to access. I take you there, but never pass through."

"Why?"

It's a good question, and one I don't truly know the answer to. So I say the only thing I can. "That's just the way it is."

Max begins pacing up and down. He appears to be mulling something over. After a moment he pauses, glances at me sideways, opens his mouth to speak, closes it again, then reopens. "Do I have to go to Heaven?" he finally says.

This is a question that is not very agreeable for me, but I'm never surprised when it occurs.

I take heed before answering. "No, you do not have to go," I answer truthfully, "but I wouldn't advise staying here on Earth. Once you take the choice to remain here, then you will be here for all eternity, unable to ever access Heaven. And, Max, eternity really is a long time to spend alone."

"But I'll be here with James." The hope is evident in his voice.

"And he will not know you're here. You'll be very much alone until the day he dies, and then what? On discovery, I believe James would also choose not go to Heaven and stay with you. Is that what you would want for him? For yourself? To be trapped on the plains, on the outside, always looking in at the world, but never able to once again be a part of it. Please trust me, Max, when I say that it's in your best interests to come with me and be a part of something that you now belong to."

With my speech over, Max turns from me and back to James. I know he's considering my words.

At these moments a distinct unease always settles around me. Even though I have never lost a human to this idea before, there is always the possibility that it could happen one day. If I had the need for breath, then I would be holding it right now.

"Okay," Max says after a long moment. He turns, bringing his dark eyes to meet mine. "I hear what you're saying." He pauses with some consideration. "Look, I'll come with you as long as you *promise* me that you will take care of James." The emphasis is on the 'promise' and he looks at me with heavy persuasion.

Please, not this again. Once more, if I could breathe, I would sigh right now. I have absolutely no idea why I have found myself committing to this.

"I promise to do my best, Max."

Why do I continue to dig myself further and further into this? It's like I can't stop myself. Making a promise now, a promise that is impossible for me to keep, a promise that if I do keep, will break the rules I reside by.

He raises his brows, creasing up his forehead. "Well . . . okay, if that's all I can get you to promise, then I guess it'll have to do."

"Are you ready to go now, Max?"

He gives me a sorrowful look. "No, but I guess no time is ever gonna be right, is it?" Reluctantly, he nods in assent.

"Take hold of my hand."

He slips his large hand around mine. "You know, Lucyna, you look really similar to my wife, James's mother. When I first saw you, for a moment there, I thought you was her . . . you're not, are you?"

"No."

He visibly contracts with relief. "Thought not." He shakes his head as though clearing his thoughts. "If you were my Maddy, she would have probably given me a good hiding the moment she laid her eyes on me after what I've been getting up to over the years since she passed." He grins, then it suddenly drops from his face. "Oh, boll . . . err . . . blast. She's gonna be waiting up there for me, isn't she?" He looks at me expectantly.

"Yes, Max. I would say she is in Heaven."

A look of discomfort passes over his face and he takes a deep breath. "She'll be fine," he mutters to himself.

I wonder what on earth he's been doing that makes him fear seeing her so.

"Okay, let's get this show on the road," Max says. "Best not keep God waiting." His nervousness is very apparent so I press an encouraging smile at him, hoping to offer some ease. But this smile I provide is one that is forced because something is nagging at my thoughts, fluttering around my mind.

"Close your eyes," I say, relaying my usual line.

Max takes one last look at James, as all my brings do, taking that one last look at how their life used to be, and I find myself unwittingly following his gaze to where James still stands, his pain clearly evident as he cries silent tears over Max's body. Then, once again, I'm hit by the shimmering veil strengthening in its intensity.

Pulling my eyes to a close, I instantly take leave, ensuring Max's passage to Heaven and getting myself away from James and this strange shimmering light he brings with him.

Chapter 2

The Promise

I'm confused, to say the least.

Puzzled. Perplexed. Bewildered. Yes, they seem more fitting.

I've returned home now, as I have some free time. Home is Pure Land. It lies on the Astral Plane between Heaven and Earth. It's where all Bringers live, alongside the Elders.

The wonderful thing about home is that it can be whatever I want it to be. For instance, if I want to be standing on a sandy beach whilst the bright moon glows down on me, then I can manifest that to be as I wish.

Which is exactly where I am right now.

I even have gentle waves lapping at the water's edge, for perfection, allowing the moon to reflect off them artistically, a beautiful sight for me to gaze upon whilst I nomadically wander up and down the shore line in a tireless attempt to work through my puzzled thoughts about James and his shimmering light.

I have been deliberating over many options of what it may actually be as I have never encountered anything like it before.

A thought suddenly strikes me. Maybe James is not human. He could be something otherworldly, something I know not of - but no - the thought is as quickly quashed as it appeared.

James is Max's son, and Max was very much human.

Maybe James's mother was otherworldly then? But again, no. Max himself told me the mother had died. She must have been human to have done so.

No mistaking it then, James is human.

Pausing, I sit down on the sand, push my legs into the water and try to imagine what it feels like. Is it warm or cold? How would it be to feel it wash up over my legs? Would it soothe or discomfort me?

I begin to trace my finger over the wet sand. It disappears and emerges, in and out, with my movement, making no indentation at all on the sand itself.

Suddenly, I have the urgency to want to make a mark. So I focus all my attention on trying to push my finger into those tiny grains. Unsurprisingly, it just passes through, as I'm fully aware it will.

Why on earth am I even trying to do such a thing?

I'm plagued. Everything I know is in turmoil. The calamity of all calamities, you could say.

James and his shimmering light. My promise to Max.

What in the world was I even thinking agreeing to this, or not thinking, as the case may be?

And there's no way I can go back on this as it would be wrong to renege on a promise, thus leaving me no option other than to fulfil it.

But I'll have to be beyond the realms of careful, because if the Elders ever discover what I have pledged myself to, then there will undoubtedly be consequences to my reckless actions.

What has become of me? Now I'm considering deceiving The Elders, the one thing I chose not to do to Max.

Why am I doing such a thing?

No, I shall not think of that now. There is enough for me to deal with in the here and now, I will address it later.

So, it's agreed I have to visit James, but I will not go and see him now. I'll wait maybe, say seven days, and then I'll just go to where he is, make sure all is fine and leave immediately after. By doing this I will have fulfilled my promise to Max.

Then again, maybe waiting is not the way. Perhaps I should go sooner?

A human's grief, after all, is the hardest for them in the initial period of mourning. Also, it might be best to get it over and done with, fulfil my promise to Max so the Elders shall never come to learn of what I have tied myself to.

Firstly, though, I must try and understand what the veil of shimmering light is before seeing James again, as it is with him alone that I experience it.

I know this is the case as I have been around many other humans since first encountering him yesterday, and not once did it occur, not once did the shimmering light appear and impose itself on me. So that proves, it's only when I'm in the company of James when it happens.

If I can understand what it is, then maybe I can somehow dispel it into the ether.

Lying back onto the sand, I stare up at the night sky, the sky we all share, whether we're ethereal or human. We all reside together in the same atramentous universe.

And what an amazing sight it is. Exquisitely beautiful. Utter blackness. It's very enthralling.

Black.

Exactly what Arlo tells me is the colour of my hair. If only I could see for myself.

Why am I now wondering these things to this extent? I'm filled with so many questions and have no certain way to the answers.

I trace my eyes carefully over the stars which adorn the sky, each one uniquely beautiful and standing majestic in its own right as I look for a distraction, any distraction, to keep me away from a thought that is consistently trying to present itself as an answer to James' shimmering light.

I'm reluctant to consider this possibility, because once I do I may not be able to walk away from it. And if this is what I discover to be the truth, then things are very quickly going to become incredibly troublesome for me.

But then, on the other hand, maybe I should consider it. I'm fairly sure it's not the case, so perhaps I should just think it, get it out in the open, and then I can lay it to rest.

Okay then.

Feelings.

Maybe the veil of shimmering light that struck me could possibly have been feelings. What hit me may have been a wave of emotion. Maybe that's how I would see feelings, how they would present themselves to me. I mean, I wasn't aware feelings could be a visual thing, but maybe James' grief was so overwhelming that it emitted from him in that form.

No, it just doesn't sound right as I say it in my own mind. I've

21

obviously encountered grief, in many different forms and have never had that, or any other emotion, present itself in that way.

Then a thought strikes me like a bolt of lightning.

Oh no. It couldn't be - could it?

Could this have been a feeling that I alone incurred. Nothing whatsoever to do with James.

My own feelings?

No. To choose that option, is – well, not an option. It's inconceivable. I don't feel. It's not possible. Bringers don't feel.

To consider that I had James' feelings somehow imposed on me, causing me momentarily to feel them is bad enough, but to consider that I am beginning to feel . . . no, it can't be.

I lift my hands up to look at them. They sparkle and shine against the night sky, just as always. Nothing different. I appear to be the same but, then again, how would I know what feelings are like to be able to distinguish between them? Or may it be possible that I'm not feeling physically, just emotionally?

Well it doesn't appear to be happening at the moment as there is no veil of shimmering light. It only presents itself when I'm near James. But why would I feel only in his presence? If that's what's happening - would it not happen all the time?

Oh Lord, what am I to do? I'm impounded by confusion. I wish I could ask for your unbiased help, for your guidance through this confounding time.

Maybe I should speak to Arlo about this; he is so wise and knowledgeable. He may know the answers I so desperately seek.

But, then again, if it is feeling that is happening to me, Arlo would have to tell the Elders of my problem, and then what would happen? Surely the Elders wouldn't let me near a human ever again, thus meaning I would never again take a human to Heaven. I would no longer be a Bringer. I'd never be allowed to Earth. I would spend my eternity in Pure Land. What would I do? What would become of me?

I can't let that happen. I'll just have to figure this out alone.

Well, as it appears to be James that causes this problem I'm having, then I will just stay away from him, problem solved, but oh no . . . my promise to Max. This, without a doubt, means that I will have to see James again.

It's not within me to break a promise, no matter how much I may wish it. 'Catch twenty-two', as they say.

Okay, so I shall fulfil my duty to Max and check upon James once, and once only, thus keeping my promise, though only in part, as going to see James once and never again is most definitely not 'checking in from time to time'.

What to do? What to do?

It suddenly becomes abundantly clear to me that the time for thinking has now passed. I have to take decisive action as my solitary thoughts are obviously getting me nowhere.

Rising easily to my feet, I turn from the water and walk across the sand, closing my eyes as I prepare to travel. The glorious beach slowly disintegrates in the wake of my departure as I now think of going to the only one who may be able to provide the much needed answers to my impatient, burning questions.

James.

And as quickly as I think his name, then no sooner are my eyes meeting with his.

He's sat on a sofa, feet up on a coffee table, a bottle of drink in his hand - alcohol I believe it to be.

I glance around, taking in my surroundings, and find myself in a house, what I assume to be James's house.

The television is on and I see that even though he is staring at it, his eyes look to be somewhere else, somewhere very far from here. He looks tired. His face is pale. His eyes are red and puffy.

I sit down on the coffee table next to where his bare feet are resting, fix my eyes to him, and brace myself for the inevitable light to hit me.

But nothing happens.

I wait a moment more. Still nothing.

I'm perplexed. Did the veil of shimmering light not happen? No, surely it did. It made itself abundantly known, not once, but thrice.

This is, yet again, incredibly confusing for me.

Maybe I was correct in my earlier thoughts after all and it was

James' overwhelming grief that thrust itself upon me in that hospital room and not my own feelings transpiring in his presence.

James shifts his position and brings his knees up to his chest. He wraps his arms around them and rests his chin on his knees. He sighs heavily and, as he does so, a stray tear glides down his cheek, which he quickly wipes away.

I'm drawn to the notable affliction shown in his movement, wondering just exactly what it is he feels at this precise second.

Is it sadness, grief, anguish? I assume it to be all these things. He will undoubtedly be suffering emotionally after the death of Max. And as my mind swims with thoughts of James, distracting my attention, I'm unexpectedly hit by the veil of shimmering light again.

This time it forcibly and ineptly presents itself. But unlike the other times, it appears not to be going away any time soon as it wraps itself all around me, enveloping me, and then disappears into my very being, becoming a part of me.

And even though it's incredibly strong, I do not allow it to knock me off balance. I remain there, eyes resolutely fixed on James, absorbing every fibre of his being whilst the light surges through me, taking me over, now knowing that even if I wanted to there's no way I'm able to escape its clutches.

And through this wondrous turmoil, the only thought dominating me is to wish that I could take James' pain away, ease his burden somehow, soothe him, be able to touch him.

I mentally shake myself. What am I thinking? I could never help him in that way.

That's what humans do for one another. Not Bringers. And to want to touch him is madness. I don't have the capability to do so, let alone ever wish to.

Why now? Why a human? And more to the point - why him?

I'm very quickly coming to the rationalisation that the shimmering light bestowing itself on me is without question feelings, feelings, which appear to be undoubtedly connected to James. Yet I still chose to return to him, knowing this to be a strong possibility.

Was I just hiding behind the promise I made to Max as to the reason why I came here, convincing myself I needed to discover what the source of this shimmering light is, when truly I did not?

Have I unwittingly come here and seen James for another reason, a reason unbeknown to me?

Then, without warning, the truth hits me almost as hard as James' light and certainty dawns upon me.

I feel for James.

My feelings are for him.

Oh no.

My new reality fast becomes apparent, stretching itself formidably and staggeringly out in front of me.

Words escape me as a hundred different scenarios quickly flash before my eyes.

This is happening too quickly. What I am supposed to do with these - feelings? I believe they are filled with complexities that far outreach my knowledge or capability.

Suddenly everything about me seems wrong somehow.

Feelings.

The word sounds out of place. It's rattling around my mind like an unwanted guest, an enemy invading on unwelcome territory.

Why is this happening to me?

It has to be of my own doing after all my time spent with Arlo having endless discussions regarding humans and their feelings. My internal questioning. The wondering. The 'what ifs'. And now, because of this, I'm been struck down, caused to feel what I was so curious to know.

Maybe this is an inflictive teaching from God who wants to show me what feelings are so that I stop defying what I know to be right.

Perhaps Arlo is also encountering these feelings. I could ask him. But wait, no, I cannot. I know this to be a doubled-edged sword. Because if he is feeling too, then he won't want to tell me for the very reason that I don't want to tell him. But, then again, knowing Arlo as well as I do - yes, he may sit with me discussing the complexities of humans, but never once would he consider how it would actually be to be one of them, how it would be to feel.

Unlike me.

Me, with my endless scrutinising thoughts, my inexplicable fascination for humans. I have, without realisation, stepped beyond the realms of mere fascination and into absolute curiosity. I have unknowingly crossed the line, something I know Arlo would never, ever, do.

I'm being changed irreversibly, and it's of my own doing.

And even with all of this new unwelcome knowledge, I still have no wish to leave James' side. I know I should, but I can't seem to. I'm willingly staying here as these feelings settle themselves erroneously into me.

James lifts the bottle to his lips and takes a long drink, draining it in the process. Then, unexpectedly, he leans forward and places it on the table, passing right through me as he does so. It happens so quickly, I have no time to react and the sensation it causes sends me reeling backwards. It's only in the briefest of moments but stuns me beyond belief. Words momentarily escape me. There are none to describe what just occurred within me, or none I have ever said before, or ever imagined I would.

I believe the correct thing for me to say is that there are no words to describe what I have just felt.

Felt. Feelings. Whatever they are, they should be beyond me.

It takes me a moment to steady myself before I can sit back down. But now it seems that all this strange occurrence has done to me is to pique my curiosity even further about James. I move closer to him.

He is very beautiful and he becomes more so with every moment I spend looking at him.

He's as beautiful as the Aurora Borealis, as beautiful as the reddened sky when the sun is journeying into the west.

No, truly, I'd say he is beyond even those things. James is singularly the most perfect thing I have ever seen in my entirety. Never before have I seen a human in this way. It's incredibly troublesome that I do so now.

What do I feel for James? Is it concern? Do I worry for him? I can see this being so with my link to Max. Or is it something else entirely?

What am I doing? Thinking? These thoughts are escaping me before

I even realise they exist. It's like I'm set to accept my fate. This cannot be.

Yes, over time I have wondered these things but never once did I envisage them being within me. And, yes, parts of it do seem very wonderful - miraculous in fact - but there is no way I can feel for James. Everything I am goes against it.

The inner turmoil is almost destroying me. It's like I'm fighting against myself and I'm sinking under the weight of it all. But walking away doesn't appear to be an option either because, as I sit here with James, it's like there is an invisible thread that has tied me to him.

What am I to do?

I think the only thing I can do is try and figure out why am I inexplicably tied to this particular human, why feelings chose to thrust themselves upon me in his presence. Because if I'm ever going to have a chance of freeing myself from this furore, I have to understand why.

James abruptly stands and I find myself following him into his kitchen. He yanks open the refrigerator door and grabs another bottle of drink.

All of a sudden I hear a shrill sound. I very quickly realise it's his telephone ringing. He sighs loudly, slams the refrigerator door shut, and trundles over to the telephone.

He reaches over and grabs it. "Hello?" he mutters, as he walks back into the living room, slumping himself down on the sofa. I, of course, have followed him back there and have regained my position on the table across from him.

"No, I'm fine," he says. His voice sounds dull, listless.

Without thinking, I begin to listen in on the conversation.

"You really shouldn't be on your own," says a female voice.

"Sara, really, I'm fine."

"You're obviously not. And I wouldn't expect you would be. Have you eaten anything?"

He sighs and takes a swig of drink.

"I'll take that as a no, then. I'm coming over and bringing food with me . . . and I'm not taking no for an answer." Her voice sounds very authoritative. I wonder who she is.

27

"Okay. Fine. See you soon." James clicks off the phone and throws it to the floor. Then he picks up the remote control and begins flicking through the channels. All the while I can't seem to move my eyes away from him.

It doesn't seem like much time has passed when I sense the approach of a human and hear a loud knock at the front door.

I follow James out of the living room and down the hallway. He opens the door to reveal a human woman. I'm assuming the woman he spoke to on the telephone - Sara.

She has golden hair, like honey, and her eyes are the colour of seaweed.

I watch them greet one another. Sara looks at James for a moment, and then pulls him into a tight embrace. I notice his reluctance at first, but then he hugs her back and his tears flow.

In an instant I'm struck by a veil of light. A new light. Something altogether different. It's dark green, flecked with sparkling blue, and much more forceful than the shimmering veil. In fact it's quite aggressive as it penetrates me, so edgy and poisoning that I actually flinch.

James and Sara are now no longer hugging but talking, and I can't absorb a word they're saying. I can't think straight. My mind is swimming.

Sara puts her arm around James' waist and leads him back to the living room. I don't follow. I just stare at Sara's departing back, wondering if it's her who has brought this new light to me, this new feeling. The jading light is like nothing before. What is it? And more importantly, if it is her, then why does she bring it with her?

I no longer want to be here.

Closing my eyes, I instantly return home, manifesting a meadow covered in lush green grass with a single willow tree standing tall.

I position myself under the tree, resting against its cracked bark, and gaze upwards to see the stars dancing between the parting leaves. For a moment the disquiet surrounds me, and it's almost as if something very big is drawing in a breath.

Then, with much urgency, I set on convincing myself that I'm not to go anywhere near James ever again. I have fulfilled my promise to Max. There is no other reason for me to see him, and I ignore the dull ache that that thought alone brings with it.

I know I feel for James, that without reason I am drawn to him. But, that aside, I have to see past it, rid myself of these feelings. The maelstrom surrounding me is repairable as long as I stay far, far away from him.

But even as I think it, doubt infects me.

No. I have to. It has to work, otherwise I'll no longer know where my place is or what I'll become with this change.

I'll not be ethereal, nor human. Something different.

Maybe, something wrong. Something, very, very, wrong.

Chapter 3

Rule Breaker

I managed one day without going to see James.

One pitiful day which I devoted entirely to thinking of him.

It's now been three weeks, two days and thirteen hours since the world as I knew it imploded and changed irreversibly. Because of him.

And for all this time, aside from when I'm tending to my duties, I have spent by his side. I guess you could say I'm keeping my promise to Max, and more so.

Every spare moment I have is spent with James, watching and learning all I can about him, about his life. But this is so very different from when I used to watch other humans. Aside from the feelings I now have, I'm interested in him. Not what I can learn from him, but just simply him.

I watch James work. That's what I enjoy most. He's a gardener. I have also learnt this is what he and Max did together. They have a landscaping business. Or I should say had. Now it's just James'.

I regard with fascination how James tends to flowers and plants seemingly with great care and attention. It gives me an internal glow. He is very adept at what he does. His creations are incredibly beautiful. But one thing I have noticed is that he works a lot, much more than humans normally do. He's out to work as soon as the sun begins to rise and doesn't return home until the night sky forces him to. But it appears to be the only time he relaxes, the only time he's at ease, when he's outside with the plants. It's as though he seeks solace in them. The rest of the time he just seems unhappy and restless.

I was by his side at Max's funeral. I was really lucky to not have any brings to attend to at that time. But, if I'm honest, nothing could have kept me away from James then anyway, not even God himself. I had to be there for him, no matter that he has no idea of my existence or how I feel for him.

It was a bad day for James and for me. I found it extremely difficult to see him in as much emotional pain as he was. Not to be able to do anything for him caused me immense discomfort.

James seemed to want to conceal his grief, but I knew it. It was emanating from him so strongly that I could practically feel it, and I was staggered by the intensity of those feelings. Then it only proceeded to get worse when I had to watch others provide comfort to him, something I very much wished to be able to do myself. Sara was the main comfort provider and the feelings I had to overcome from that were almost unbearable.

Straight after the funeral I was called away to tend to my duties. I didn't want to leave James and it was much later before I was able to return to him. I arrived to find him laid in bed, the room shrouded in darkness, his eyes open staring blankly up at the ceiling. He didn't sleep at all that night and I stayed with him, wishing his pain away.

And in all of this time spent with James, the only thing I have managed to figure out is that I'm in trouble. Big trouble.

I haven't found any way to rid myself of these feelings, and the emotional feelings I have for James seem to be growing with unbearable intensity. They are getting more and more out of control as time passes.

I'm finding the longer I have them, the more I'm not so sure I even want to rid myself of them. Frighteningly, I'm becoming accustomed to them, even though things are becoming increasingly difficult for me.

You see, I have all of these feelings but no way in which to express them, no way to release them. It's as if they're building up inside of me and I wonder what will happen when I reach boiling point.

It's not like I can talk to Arlo or any of the other Bringers about this. I talk to James, often, but obviously he doesn't hear me. A part of me wishes he could. A big part.

As time has gone on, I have also found myself feeling for other humans. Not in the same way, or with the same intensity as I have for James - I'm still yet to fully understand just exactly what type of feelings these are - but now, when I take a human to Heaven, it's become increasingly difficult for me to witness them struggling to come to terms with their deaths. I assume I'm feeling compassion and sorrow, but I could be wrong in this. Also, the pain from the humans they leave behind seems to reverberate all around, striking me from all angles, nearly knocking me senseless.

Everything as I knew it to be is gone. I'm so very confused. I want these feelings, and I don't. I want to be how I used to be, and I don't. My rational thoughts are being overtaken by emotions and I have no idea of what to do.

Also I seem to be careless of how much time I'm spending away from home. I'm sure the others will have begun to notice my distinct absence. I know Arlo, above all, will have noticed. I am being completely, and utterly reckless. I know the consequences of my actions but yet I still continue on as I am. So far Arlo has not yet sought me out to speak about this, but I know it's only a matter of time. What if he does whilst I'm with James? How would I explain that away? Honestly, I have no idea of what I am going to say to him when the time comes. What explanation I can provide? I don't wish to deceive Arlo, but neither can I tell him the truth.

Truly, I wonder how long I can continue in this way. James is consuming all of me and I'm losing the distinction of who I am or what is right any more.

I'm standing outside Heaven, having just guided the human - Summer Sophia Davies - through. I have another bring to attend to soon but have some spare time beforehand. I can feel myself being pulled to James, something I am fast becoming used too. But no, I have to stop and start thinking rationally about my situation.

Instead of immediately going to James as I usually do, I stay where I am and take a moment to clear my thoughts. I glance around my surroundings.

It's been so long since I just stood still and looked around the outskirts of Heaven. What a beautiful sight it is. The varying shades of pinks, blues, greens and purples, all blending genially into one another in sparkling enchantment. It makes me wonder whether, if the outside is as lovely as this, just how wonderful it is inside Heaven itself. I imagine it to be glorious. How lucky those humans are who are granted entrance to it.

For a tiny moment, I begin feel more like myself, how I used to be before all of this. Then my mind immediately slips back to my woe.

Okay, so what I need to do is divide my time more evenly. It won't solve my problem, but it will help not to arouse the suspicions of the others if I am at least around them more than I currently have been. I shall go now and see Arlo, spend some time with him. Then later I shall go to James. Easy.

I arrive to find Arlo with Rosamund. They are both standing amongst the throngs of humans at BC Place Stadium in Vancouver.

The realisation hits me like a dull thud.

It's the Winter Olympics. Arlo and I always watch together and it's been running for a few days now. I cannot believe I have forgotten this. I never forget anything.

Arlo will note my absence with curiosity.

"Lucyna," he practically smiles my name, "it's been some time since I saw you last."

And as I look at him, I instantly see him in a whole new light. Never before did I realise how truly beautiful a being he is. My vision was previously dulled by my lack of feelings, but now I'm equipped with them and this been the first time I've seen him since it happened.

"I know, Arlo. I have been busy. I have been venturing around the globe in search of new and wondrous sights."

I just lied.

Lied.

Where did that even come from? I didn't know I was capable of such a thing. I'm covered with shame. I daren't look at either of them for fear of giving myself away.

"I can understand that," Arlo says nodding. "Rosamund and I have just been watching the wondrous sports on display here." He casts his arm around.

"Hello, Lucyna," Rosamund says.

"Hello, Rosamund," I reply, in return.

Arlo turns to me. "I was beginning to think you weren't going to attend this year."

"I would never miss this," I answer a little too quickly. I force a smile onto my lips, hoping to be convincing enough. But then, why would Arlo ever have reason not to believe me? He wouldn't. That very thought sickens me.

Suddenly, the crowd of humans erupt into cheers as one of the competitors wins a race. The sound is practically thunderous. Oddly, it fills me with a warm glow. I quickly cast it aside, fearing Arlo and Rosamund will notice.

Rosamund shakes her head. "I shall never understand these humans. They are so competitive with one another."

"Rosamund, this is something humans appear to like very much," Arlo says, without taking his eyes off the ever-growing crowd which is gathering around the victor. "It appears to make them happy."

I'm suddenly bothered by Rosamund's words. If she thinks this way, then why is she even attending? She doesn't usually.

Then a terrifying thought strikes me. Does she know about me? About James? Is that why she is here?

No, that's ridiculous. Of course she doesn't know. She can't know . . . can she?

"Yes, that is an obvious fact," Rosamund replies, interrupting my inner conflict. "But they are such fickle creatures. I shall never understand them, and I do not wish too." She waves her hand dismissively.

I look away, pretending to be distracted by my surroundings, not wanting to be part of this conversation, knowing I no longer share her thought processes. Or did I really ever?

"So, Lucyna have you made any new discoveries on your travels?" Arlo asks.

"Unfortunately, no." The lies are slipping so easily from my mouth. I feel as though I'm coated in them.

"Well, I have been considering doing the same for some time myself. Next time I shall come with you. If you have no objection, of course?"

I fix my eyes ahead. "Of course not, Arlo. You are always welcome."

"Time for me to go," says Rosamund.

I'm relieved at the conversation break, but not welcoming Rosamund's imminent departure as it will leave Arlo and me alone and I fear I won't be able to keep my pretence up for much longer in that circumstance. Why did I not consider how hard this would be before coming?

Rosamund nods at us both respectively, then vanishes from sight. Momentarily, I find myself wondering where she is going to. Which human will she be taking to Heaven? Unexpectedly, I feel awash with sorrow and I very quickly quell it.

Arlo begins to walk through the arena and I follow along.

"I believe Rosamund is missing out on much learning there is to be done from humans. I find there to be distinctly much more to them than the categorisation she gives them. Do you agree, Lucyna?"

I can feel his eyes on me, a very surreal experience.

"Yes. I am inclined to agree with you, Arlo." *Much more than you realise*, I silently add.

"And that is why I spend my time with you, Lucyna. We think alike."

And you, Arlo, are my friend, my dear friend, I find myself wanting to say, but instead I simply answer, "Yes, we do."

My mind is swamped with guilt. I'm sure it is covering me in some obvious way. I glance sideways at Arlo as we walk on in silence, and feel an instant swell of affection for him. It throws me.

Instantly I find myself wanting to tell Arlo my troubles. They're practically bursting out of me. I want to unburden this guilt I have, rid myself of this internal conflict, seek his advice. Because, more than anything, I want help; I need help.

But my rash thoughts are quickly dampened as I know I never will, never can. I'm too ashamed and afraid to do so. I know I wouldn't be able to endure the consequences of my actions.

I'm all alone in this.

I wish things would go back to the way they were before I ever saw James. I wish I had never met him.

But do I really? Do I really want to go back to what now seems an empty existence since experiencing the phenomenon of feelings?

Do I truly want to walk away from James? Never again see him.

That thought alone fills me with consternation.

"When is your next bring, Lucyna?" asks Arlo, breaking me from my reverie.

"Very soon, Arlo. Minutes. You?"

"In twenty minutes. I'm going to Thailand. Such a beautiful place –" but I can't hear him any more, all I can hear is the name that's now echoing around my mind, the name of my next bring, the one that has pinned me to this stony floor.

James Maxwell Harrison.

I feel sheer and utter horror. Hysteria practically leaps up and grabs hold of me. It's so overwhelming, momentarily I don't know what to do with it.

Arlo, noticing my abrupt stop, turns back and looks at me with curiosity. "Lucyna?"

I can't move. I can't speak.

No. It can't be. Not him. Not James.

Arlo's eyebrow arches in confusion. "Lucyna?" he reiterates, taking a step toward me, awakening me.

"Time for me to go, Arlo." I desperately try to make my voice sound even. "I shall see you soon."

I don't wait for his response. I have no time.

My next actions are beyond me. My thoughts are erratic, scattered. The only thing I know for sure is that I have to save James. Nothing else matters. Just save him.

Instantly I'm there, looking at a burning car which is entangled with a tree, and trapped inside is James.

There's ninety seconds left before he's scheduled to die.

What do I do? Can I save him? Can I stop what God has set in motion? Surely not, I have no such power to override God's will.

But, James.

Eighty-five . . . eighty-four . . . eighty-three . . .

Without warning, an odd sensation suddenly ripples right through my very being and then something overtakes me. Before I know it I'm at the car, yanking the door open, pushing back the air bag and pulling at James's limp body. He's stuck. Frantically I search around to see what's trapping him. It's his seat belt. I tug hard but it doesn't give way. I follow its lead to the end, press a button and hear a click. It unravels in my hand. Taking hold of James, I put his arm around me and pull him from the car.

I half carry, half drag him down the gravelly road, his feet scraping along as I do so. Then once we're a safe distance from the car, I carefully lay him down on the ground and sit beside him.

Then it hits me.

I'm holding James. Physically touching him. I have carried him.

How?

I look down at myself and see a human body, skin covering every part of me. I'm wearing clothes. I look at my hands. I have fingernails. I'm solid matter. I look like a human.

What . . . how . . . how did this happen? How did I become this way? Questions are spilling from my mind.

Stop, Lucyna, there is no time for this.

I quickly gather myself together and look down at James. His skin is covered in black soot and he has some cuts on his face. A large one near his hairline has blood trickling from it, the blood clotting into his hair.

What should I do?

Reaching forward, I gently place my fingertip on the cut. Instantly a tingling sensation shoots up through my finger.

I jump back startled.

What on earth was that?

Curious, I again reach forward and place my finger on James' face, wondering whether it's his blood that causes this tingling sensation, or just him. But the moment my skin meets his, the same wondrous sensation once again presents itself, running up my finger into my arm.

Am I touching him? Is this what it's like? Can I now feel James?

Curiosity burns every part of me.

I keep my finger on him, marvelling at this wonderful experience, letting the sensation swill through me. Then, as if slapped around the face, I suddenly realise that James' precious time is still ticking away in my mind. It hasn't stopped. Why? I mean it should, shouldn't it? Have I not done enough to save him?

Forty-one . . . forty . . . thirty-nine . . .

Don't die, James. Please don't die. Don't leave me here all alone. If you do, then this was all for nothing.

I take hold of his body and shake him, vehemently ignoring the sensations it creates in my hands, and will him to wake.

He's not waking up.

Panic stricken, I shake him again - but nothing.

Twenty-eight . . . twenty-seven . . . twenty-six . . .

"James, please don't die," I beseech.

What do I do? I am completely and utterly out of my depth.

I lay my head on his chest in resignation and his warmth radiates through me. My face is ablaze. Wait, I can hear his heart beating. Yes, it's definitely beating. He's got a good, strong heartbeat. I feel a surge of relief. That's a positive sign – isn't it? But if he's going live, if I have managed to save him, then why is his time still counting down?

Sixteen . . . fifteen . . . fourteen . . .

Maybe I haven't saved him after all. I feel a sharp pain shoot right through me.

I trace my now-human fingers across his forehead, running them into his hair, something I have longed to do.

I can't lose him. I can't.

Making one last ditch attempt, I again take hold of his body and shake him with all my might. "James! Wake up, please!" I yell out.

Eight . . . seven . . . six . . .

His time is fast approaching its end. What if he dies here, what will happen? What will I do? I couldn't bear it if he was no longer here. How could I take him to Heaven and part with him? Never again see his beautiful face.

The thought terrifies me.

I don't know what else I can do, so now I'm literally willing him to live. "James," I whisper. "Please don't leave me."

Two . . . one . . . zero.

Disconsolately, I lie down beside him, look up at Heaven, and plead with the only one who has the power to save him. "Please, God, I beg you. Please don't take him from me."

Everything seems to stop. The wind stops blowing through the trees.

Animals stop scurrying around. There's not a sound in the air. It's so quiet. So serene.

Then I feel James stir and I scramble up to my knees.

His eyes flicker open and he looks up at me with his dark eyes.

"I . . . know . . . you," he mumbles. Then his eyes roll back into his head, and his lids come heavily to a close.

Chapter 4

Being Human

I know you.

I know you.

What on earth is that supposed to mean?

He knows me? How does he know me? He can't know me. Of course he can't, it's impossible. He was delirious. That's it. He didn't know what he was saying – did he? No, of course not.

I look over at James from my seat in the far corner of the dimly lit room. He's sleeping peacefully. He hasn't woken yet, not since he uttered those haunting words in any case.

We're at the hospital. As I very quickly discovered, I no longer have my abilities in this new form of mine. No extra sensory perception. No transporting in the blink of an eye. All my abilities are seemingly gone.

So I had to sit there on the roadside with an unconscious James and wait like any other human until a passing car found us. Luckily we weren't waiting too long.

The human rang for help from his mobile phone, told us an ambulance would be there soon, and waited with us until it arrived. And it did, very quickly, as did a whole host of other humans - policemen, firemen.

James was brought to the hospital in the ambulance. The police wanted to question me about what happened. I wanted to come to the hospital to be with James, so they drove me here in a car which, might I add, was a really strange experience, and they questioned me on the way.

I told the policeman who sat in the back of the car with me that I had been walking along the road when I saw James' car crash into the tree and instantly set itself on fire, that I pulled him from the burning car and carried him down the road, then waited there until we were found.

The policeman wrote down everything I said. He asked for my name and address. Panic ensued and I had to think fast. The only thing I could say was that I didn't have one, which is pretty much the truth now. He looked me over and asked if I was homeless, to which I promptly replied I was. He wrote something else down, and then his whole demeanour toward me changed. No longer was I the heroic human but someone he suddenly viewed with mild disdain. He asked if there was any way to contact me, and I knew I had to say something so I said that he could contact me through James. He regarded me with a raised eyebrow and said "but I thought you didn't know him". My immediate response was that I don't, but after saving his life I felt an obligation to stick around and make sure he was okay.

I could see the policewoman who was driving the car glancing at me in the rear-view mirror with a very sceptical look in her eyes. I don't know whether they believed me or not, but right now it's of no regard as I have far bigger concerns, like the fact that I have inadvertently taken on human form, that I now somehow look like a human not only to myself but they can see me too. I'm solid matter. Human but not actually a human. No functioning organs – well no heartbeat for starters. That is a pretty important thing for a fully-functioning human body, so I'm obviously not alive. But I'm here and still me, but not me. I can touch things, actually feel and touch them without my hand just passing through. No longer do I see a blaze of light that sparkles. Now when I look down all I see is a human body. So this does this mean I'm no longer a Bringer? But not human either.

What am I then?

I look down at my fully-clad body, wondering just where these clothes and shoes came from. Have I always worn them? And my hair, it's just hanging there, draping down my back, falling over my shoulder. And it's so very black, just like Arlo said. My skin, so creamy, so very human like. I poke myself in the arm. It's beyond strange. I can actually feel myself, poke myself in the arm. This is so unbelievably surreal, but so absolutely wonderful all at the same time, that it renders me speechless. There are no words to convey just how crazy this is. And I have never been more confused than I am right now.

I have so many questions spooling around my mind. Like for starters, how did this happen? How did I come to look like a human? I remember the odd sensation I felt go through me the instant before I saved James, and how I just did that on instinct. Okay, so the change obviously occurred then, but how? Did I somehow make this happen? I wonder if it's because I started having feelings like a human does. If so, can I take it back, can I change back? But then, do I want to? I glance over at James, my eyes lingering on his beautiful face, my feelings for him surging through me with such an overwhelming intensity that I grip hold of the chair.

I look down at my body, my new body that James will be able to see.

So I ask myself the question again. Do I want to change back?

No, I really and truly do not.

James' breathing deepens, pricking my attention. I stand from my seat and peer over at him. He looks like he's still sleeping and the monitors he's attached to seem to be functioning as they should. I quietly lower myself back into the chair.

I'm not supposed to be in here. I snuck in after everyone had left. I didn't want James to be alone. I'll always be here for him, no matter what form I take, or whether he knows it or not.

When I arrived at the hospital, the doctors and nurses were already tending to James. The nurse had asked if I was a relative, but when I said no, he said I couldn't be here. When I explained I was the one who had saved James, he was more forthcoming. He told me to sit in the waiting room until they were done with James and he would come back and let me know how James was doing, but after that I would most certainly have to leave.

I was waiting quite a while, all the time spent worrying about James. I could think of nothing else. But the nurse was as good as his word. He came back and told me James was going to be fine. He's got a broken leg - well it's broken in two places, his tibia and his kneecap - so they have potted it, and it will take up to three months to heal. He's suffering from the effects of mild smoke inhalation, and the cut on his head needed stitches. The nurse said James had been incredibly lucky. He's seen people come off a lot worse than that after a car collision with a tree - so have I, but I was reluctant to mention that. He went on to say that James owes me his life because if I hadn't have been there to pull him from that burning car, he would most certainly have died.

If only he knew.

I'm beyond relieved that I saved James. I wouldn't have been able to bear it if I'd lost him. Not that I've ever truly had him, or ever will. But to lose the joy of being able to see him every day would have been too much to bear. I know just how incredibly selfish of me that was, but I couldn't help it. At the time I didn't even think about my actions, or the consequences of them.

By saving James' life, I have changed the natural order of things. I have committed a cardinal sin and obviously have no regard for the consequences, as here I sit. There's no saving me now. I have crossed the line and strayed so far over it I know there's no return for me.

But I don't regret it. And I never will.

Because this is James and he makes nothing else matter. Everything else is inconsequential. He is, and will always be, the only thing that matters to me, and my only regret is that I hadn't been there sooner to save him from suffering these injuries.

I know, fully and completely, that I did the right thing, but I suppose the ultimate question is – right for whom?

Then I hear James' bed sheets rustle and see that he's waking up. I sit up in my seat, my back poker-straight. If I had a heart right now, I imagine it'd be beating out of my chest. James is going to see me. When he opens his eyes, he is actually going to see me for the very first time. A wave of nerves washes over me.

He groans a low moan as the pain from his injuries sets into his consciousness. He tries to get up.

"Don't get up," I say, moving swiftly toward him. "Just lay back and I'll call the nurse." I press the buzzer beside his bed and back away.

He slumps back, unable to do anything else. "Some water," he whispers, his hand rubbing his throat. His voice sounds raspy, from the smoke inhalation I guess.

I get the jug of water off the table and pour some into the waiting glass, and hand it to him. He struggles to drink, spilling some, so I help guide the glass to his lips. He sips slowly, his eyes blinking heavily. And I step back, leaning up against the wall, allowing myself to recover from the heightened sensation I feel every single time I touch him.

I cannot even begin to describe just how remarkable this moment truly is. I'm actually here with him.

He holds the glass on his chest, lies back onto the pillows, and turns his head, glancing at me in the dim light. He's looking right at me with his dark, impenetrable eyes, eyes that I never once dreamed would ever see me, eyes in which I'm waiting to see if there is any spark of recognition.

"Where am I? Who are you?"

Sweet relief. He doesn't know me.

"You're in the hospital. I'm —"

Confusion holds his face as he utters, "The hospital?" He reaches up and touches where the gauze sits on his forehead covering his cut.

"You have a cut there, it needed stitches." I glance down at his leg. His eyes follow mine. "And you've broken your lower leg and fractured your kneecap, so they've put a pot on it to help it heal." I look back up to his confused face. "And your throat hurts because of the smoke inhalation, I believe."

He brings his foggy eyes back to meet mine. "What happened?" He sounds more like he's addressing himself than me. "I mean, I was driving home from Joe's wedding and then nothing —" His eyes flicker. "Are you a doctor?"

I reach over and take the glass from him, placing it back on the table. "No, I'm not a doctor. I — well, you had an accident. You crashed your car. And I — I helped."

"That's pretty modest." I look up to see the nurse from earlier coming through the door. He leans over the bed and switches off the button that I'd pressed. "She more than helped. She saved your life. Pulled you from a burning car." He nods in my direction, smiling, giving a knowing look to James. "So how are you feeling?" he asks James, but James doesn't respond. He's just staring at me, wide eyes fixed on me. "You saved my life?" The surprise audible in his raspy voice.

"I —" I look down, away from his heavy stare. "— I — well —" My mouth's not functioning as it should. My lips feel heavy and clumsy.

"Yes. I saved you," I finally manage. I glance up at him, his eyes take hold of mine and that's it, I can't look away.

"I – I don't know what to say." His voice suddenly low, warm, caressing, our eyes still locked together. "I mean, what can I say?"

"Thank you is usually a good place to start," the nurse says with a laugh, and just like that the moment's broken. I look away.

"Right, you need to go," the nurse says, finger pointing at me. My eyes flick up.

"Go?" James and I both echo.

"Yes, go. You're not supposed to be in here, as you well know." He gives me a pointed look. "And he needs his rest."

Go, I can't go. I've barely spoken to James. I can't leave now. I need more time with him.

"But she can't go," James says urgently, his words practically repeating my thoughts, except mine sound more panicked and slightly unstable. I glance at him. His eyes are on me again and I feel a warm glow erupt deep inside me, lighting the whole of me. "I need to talk to you – about the accident, about what happened. About everything."

I open my mouth, but the nurse speaks before I have chance. "She can come back in the morning, at visiting time. It's not that far off now anyway." And I can tell by the firm look on his face he's not going to play ball.

James looks at me, a hint of shyness in his face, something I've never seen him wear before. It's captivating. "Will you come back in the morning?" he asks. "I know it's a lot to ask, but I really want to –"

"I'll come in the morning." I smile. He wants to see me again. I feel exhilarated, exuberant. It's hard to contain my happiness. He actually wants to see me again.

I look at the nurse. "What time is visiting time?" I ask.

"Nine-thirty."

I look back at James. "I'll come at nine-thirty."

James' lips curve into a faint smile. "Thanks."

The nurse signals to the door and I follow him.

"Will you be okay getting home? It's so dark out," James says, pulling me back, and I willingly return. The nurse is by the door, finger

45

on the light switch, his impatience radiating through the room. But I don't care. I'll eek this out for as long as I can.

"I'll be fine."

"You're sure?"

"I'm sure."

James' sleepy eyes gaze at me. "So, I'll see you in the morning."

"Yes." I smile. "You'll see me in the morning."

The nurse flicks the light off and closes the door behind us.

"I don't want to see you back here till visiting time," he says firmly, but with a warm smile on his lips.

"You won't see me until nine thirty." I return his smile, then turn to leave.

"That's quite a bond you guys have now," he says.

I turn back to him. "What do you mean?"

He glances up from looking at the papers in his hand. "Well when people share a life threatening incident, it ties them together in a way no one else can understand. I mean, how could you ever forget the person who saved your life, or the one whose life you saved?"

Utter happiness is filling me and I continue on down the hall, floating on an air of complete euphoria. I press the exit button and wait until the nurse buzzes me out. Now I'm stood in the lift lobby, unsure what to do.

The lift doors ping open and a man pushes out a wheelchair with a young woman in it. They both smile at me. I move out of the way, heading toward the staircase. A thought suddenly flashes through my mind as I take the steps down. There are lots of humans here, mostly ill or injured, but some also maybe dying. And a dying human brings only one thing. One of my kind. Oh no, what if one of them sees me here?

Panic shocks me into reality. I can't be wandering about like this.

I speed up, nearly running down the steps, and when I reach the bottom floor, I pause, quietly pull open the door and surreptitiously glance around. There are a few humans here, but I can't see any of my kind. But then, would I even be able to see one of my own kind in my current form?

I spot a sign for the ladies' toilets and head straight toward it, eyes

46

firmly fixed forward. There would be no reason for one of my kind to be here, well, unless someone is scheduled to die in the toilets, that is.

I push the door open and poke my head in. Empty. I lock the door firmly behind me.

Looking around the small room, I take in the white windowless walls, the sink, the mirror above it and the toilet.

Curiosity suddenly engulfs me and I slowly walk over to the mirror.

A woman with alabaster skin, long black hair, full pink lips and bright blue eyes stares back at me. I touch the cool glass with my fingertips, tracing the outline of my face. So this is me. Lucyna. My reflection. I draw closer to the mirror. After all this time, I can see what the others see. What Arlo sees. He was very accurate in his description of my eye colour. I think he caught it perfectly.

That's when I notice a few black marks on the sleeve and upper part of my clothes. It must be from James, the soot off his skin transferred onto me. I know humans keep their clothes clean, but it's not like there's anything I can currently do about it.

I look back up at myself, at my face, and begin examining myself closely. It's so strange, I really do look human. I look just exactly like one of them.

After a time of close scrutiny, and knowing I can't stay in the bathroom all night, I slip out of the door and, with my head down, walk quickly toward the exit.

The doors whoosh open on my approach and I find myself out on the pavement, the chilly air wrapped around me.

"Got any spare change, love?"

I look up to see an older man with long brown wiry hair standing before me. His clothes are old and dirty and I can smell a stale stench emanating from him.

"Spare change?"

He frowns at me and says impatiently, "Yeah, money, cash, readies, you know."

"Oh. No, I'm sorry." I spread my hands. "I don't have money."

He looks at me like I'm an oddity, shakes his head, then without another word saunters off into the night.

He's homeless, just like me. I instantly feel a pang of longing for home and gaze up at the sky, realising just how very alone I actually am, gravity weighing me down as the reality of my situation sinks in.

I sit down on the roadside.

I'm here on earth, alone. All alone. I have no home. Nowhere to go. I'm here with these humans, outwardly looking like one of them, pretending to be one of them, but I'm not. I don't have money like they do. And I have absolutely no idea how to be a human. I'm so very out of my depth. You'd think after all these many, many years I've spent observing them, I'd have some clue, but I don't.

But I guess I don't have much choice, because whilst I'm here I'm going to have to ensure I fit in. I can't arouse suspicion to myself, and I know the police have already figured out there is something different about me, so I'm going to have to learn quickly.

Right, so all I have to do is act human. I'll spend tonight thinking over all of the things I've seen, their behaviour, their mannerisms, how they converse with one another. Then I'll know how to be one of them. Being human. Lucyna the human.

Well, that is until the Elders find me, which I'm sure will not be long. Then again, I wonder if they'll be able to trace my essence now I'm no longer one of them. Either way, I know they will look for me and one day, in the not too distant future, I will be taken away from here, taken away from James. The panic hits me like a tidal wave. I wrap my arms around my legs. I don't want to leave James. Not ever.

I'm so confused. I made a decision, the right decision, every instinct telling me I had to save James. But ironically, I saved him because I couldn't bear to be without him and now as a result of my decision, I will one day, very soon, never again be allowed to see him.

The reality is there pinching at me, like the cold night is pinching my skin, but I'm just not ready to face the thought of leaving him, not yet anyway.

Why did James have to be scheduled to die now, only mere weeks after I find him? Then a plaguing thought hits me. Was this not a coincidence? Was God taking him now because of me? Is this punishment for my behaviour, because I feel for him, that I feel because of him?

I mentally shake myself. Of course not. How can I even think such a thing? What am I turning into too?

An ambulance comes wailing past, knocking me out of my black thoughts. I can't think about all this now. I have to think about the here and now, have to figure how to act human in the next few hours and also what exactly I'm going to say to James as to why I was there, on that road in the middle of nowhere, late at night.

I stand up, wrap my arms around myself, the cold biting at my skin, and wonder just what exactly to do for the next five hours before I can see James again.

Chapter 5

Visiting Hour

I'm standing outside the door to James' room.

It's nine-thirty and I'm finally allowed to see him, but for some reason I can't seem to make myself go through the door. I mean this is it, what I've always wanted. After all this waiting I'm finally going to speak to James alone.

I try to move my feet again, but they won't respond. I'm nervous about going in. Really nervous. It's just going to be me and James, alone. What if he doesn't like me?

I hear a door bang shut to my right and turn to see a man wearing a dressing gown standing outside the room next to James'. He's looking at me. I guess I must look pretty strange, just stood here staring at the door.

I smile a bright smile, trying to come over as human as possible. "Good morning," I say.

He returns my smile and says, "Good morning", then turns and walks down the hall away from me.

Right, I can't stand out here all day, and every second I do is a second wasted that could be spent with James. I place my hand on the green door, compress my fears down, and slowly push it open.

And there he is, laid in bed, watching television, looking as beautiful as always.

He turns his head, his dark eyes warm and inviting, smiling at me. "Hey," he says, his voice still croaky. He switches the television off with the remote control and sits himself up.

My skin is practically rippling with nerves, my theoretical heart singing with joy at the sight of him. "Hello."

"Come in."

I let the door close behind me with a gentle thud and tentatively walk into the room, all the time very aware of the fact that James' eyes have not once left me.

"Take a seat." He gestures to the chair by his bed.

I sit down but my whole body is jittery. I know I should speak, say something, but truth be told I have no idea what to say. After all this time imagining how our conversations would be, I now can't seem to form words. It's almost as if they've been stolen from me.

"I'm so glad you came." His voice breaks, so he pauses and takes a sip of water, clearing his throat. "I was worried you might not. I mean I knew it was a lot to ask after what you've already done for me, but I really wanted to talk to you."

"I was always coming," I smile. "I never break my word."

His renewed smile reaches all the way up to his eyes. "I realised after you'd gone that I didn't even get your name?" He holds his hands out apologetically.

"Lucyna."

"Lucyna," he echoes, and I love the way my name sounds on his lips. It infuses me with warmth. "Pretty name. I'm James."

"I know."

He lifts his brows and gazes at me. "The nurse told me your name last night," I say quickly, covering up my slip. I'm in his presence less than a minute and I mess up already. Great start.

He runs his fingertip around the rim of his water glass. "Lucyna, I don't even know where to begin, and I know it sounds so lame in comparison but thank you so much for saving my life. I know that doesn't even begin to repay you for what you did but, really, thank you."

I look at him, the daylight glowing cordially on his face. And I wish I could tell him that he doesn't need to thank me, that I would have saved his life a thousand times over, that I would never, ever, have let him die as there is nothing I wouldn't do for him, but all I can say is, "Thank you is plenty enough."

He reaches up and touches his head where the gauze covers his cut. "No, it's not." He shakes his head. "It doesn't even scratch the surface. The police were here at breakfast time and they told me the full extent of what you did, how you risked your own life to save mine, how you pulled me from my burning car. I just can't believe you did that." He leans forward and grabs my hand. For a moment everything goes still. His eyes spark something, recognition maybe, but no sooner is it there, it's gone. "I just wish I could –" He pauses, urgent eyes boring into mine, and I feel exposed, like he can see into the very soul of me, my skin blazing under his touch, and oddly, I notice just how rough and calloused the skin on his hand is. "– come up with something better to say than thank you." He shakes his head again and laughs.

But I can't join in. My throat is clogged up with all the words I wish I could say to him, the things, I more than anything want to tell him.

"There's no need," I finally say, slipping my hand out from under his.

He glances down at his empty hand and leans back against his pillows. Then I see his eyes run over me, down to my feet and back up again.

"So, you got home okay?" he asks.

"Yes." Well, if home was wandering around the park in the hospital grounds for a few hours trying to teach myself how to behave like a human and also worrying whether one of my kind would see me and then, when I could no longer bear the cold, clandestinely sneaking back into the hospital and heading straight for the cafeteria after deciding one of my own shouldn't be in there unless someone was scheduled to die - which fortunately they weren't – then yes, I got home just fine.

He continues to stare at me with an unreadable expression on his face and then he promptly rubs it away with his hand. "Good, I'm glad. I was worried about you getting home okay at such a late hour. I felt really bad. After all, you were only here because of me, and then I drag you back here again a few hours later. I've caused you so much trouble."

But all I hear is 'worried'. James was worried about me. No one has ever worried about me before. Well, okay, no one's ever had reason to worry about me before and everyone I know can't worry, but, still, it's a wonderful feeling.

"You haven't caused me any trouble. I wanted to come back to see you." I smile. "I mean, after all we've been through –," *more than you'll ever know*, "– with the accident, and me saving you, I suppose – I feel – sort of –" I lower my eyes and my voice. "– connected to you in a way."

I don't know where these words are coming from. It's like one minute, I can't speak and now I can't seem to stop.

His eyes brighten and he sits forward, his voice eager as he says, "I know what you mean. I mean, of course I wanted to see you again to talk about the accident, but I also wanted to see you because – well it seemed so final last night, you know – I just couldn't leave it there –" I nod, in agreement until he goes on to say, " – because I just feel so incredibly indebted to you, Lucyna. I had to see you again so I can find out some way in which to repay you."

I stop nodding as my whole body sinks. And I can't stop my face from falling. He feels indebted to me. Indebted. I inwardly cringe at my moment of stupidity. Of course he does. How could I have been so stupid to think for one moment that he may have wanted to see me for any other reason?

I see the look of confusion swilling around his eyes and I quickly erase any trace of woe from my face, forcing a smile onto my lips. It feels awkward and loose, but I hold firm as I say, "You don't have to do anything, James. You don't owe me anything."

"No, I do," he nods vigorously, "and I will find some way to repay you." He sighs and rubs the back of his neck with his hand. "What did happen last night? I mean what did you see? It's all a bit of a blank for me. Last thing I remember, I was driving through Surrey heading home from Joe's wedding and my sat nav was playing up, fucking thing." He shakes his head. "It decided to detour me down some back roads and I was trying to find my way to the motorway, then nothing, just a big fat blank, until I woke up here, that is."

"Well, I was walking down the road and you drove past me in your car."

He frowns. "I drove past you?"

"Yes."

He rubs his head, his eyes narrowing onto me. "I don't remember seeing you, but, then again, I don't remember much of anything," he says, his gaze relaxing. "Sorry, carry on."

"Well about twenty or so seconds later after you'd passed me, I heard tyres screeching and then a sort of crashing, explosive noise. So I ran toward the noise and saw the front of your car mangled up with a tree, and it was on fire – your car that is. I managed to get the door open and saw you were unconscious, so I released your seatbelt and pulled you from the car. Then I carried you down the road away from it as far as I could manage."

He's looking at me with what can only be described as awe, shaking his head. "I just – can't believe – you did that."

I shrug, feeling abashed.

"Well I think you're amazing," he says, and I can feel my face heating. "It's a huge thing you did for me, Lucyna. Most people would have run in the opposite direction from a burning car." He reaches over again, taking hold of my arm, squeezing it, sending a jolt searing up my arm.

I glance up at him and he's staring intently at me. He doesn't look away and neither do I. Our eyes are locked together.

"I don't understand that," I murmur. "How another hu - person - could leave someone to die like that."

He shrugs. "I wouldn't, but there's plenty out there who would."

"I could never have left you." I can feel myself been pulled to him, almost like there's a magnetic force drawing me closer

James smiles a crooked smile and relaxes his gaze, instantly bringing me to my senses. I shift back in my seat and avert my eyes, looking out of the window.

"There has to be something I can do for you, some way I can repay you."

His words instantly remind me of his reason for asking me here, that he views me as nothing more than his saviour, as he should. I forget that he's only known me for a few hours, unlike the weeks I've known him. Those few intense weeks. Obviously he doesn't feel for me as I do for him. I need to rein myself in and behave like any other normal human being would in this type of situation. I shake my head. "There's nothing I need, James."

"Nothing?" He echoes disbelievingly, eyes amused, leaning toward me.

"Nothing." I smile.

He laughs, shaking his head and resting back onto his bed.

"So how long do you have to stay here?" I ask, opting for a subject change.

He stretches his arms above his head, crooking his head from side to side. "They're letting me out today." He smiles, but it doesn't quite reach his eyes. "The doctor came round first thing and said I was okay to be released home. I'm just waiting for them to let me know when. Surprising really, usually takes ages to see a doctor. They're probably short on beds." He laughs, but it sounds forced.

"That's good news for you." But that's not what I'm really thinking. All I can think, is when will I be able to see him again? The realisation hits me with a dull thud. It's not like it used to be, I can't just choose to see him whenever I wish. When he leaves here, I can't just drop into his house at any given moment. At least whilst he's in the hospital I can use the visiting aspect as a reason for seeing him, but when he's at home I can't do that. Things are changing so quickly and I can't decipher whether it's for the best or not.

"Yeah," he says quietly, his voice suddenly dull. "I can't wait to get home." I hear his words, but know he doesn't really mean it. I can see the traces of sadness shadowing his face which most people might have missed. I wish I knew exactly what it is he's thinking. But I'm guessing it's the thought of going home alone that makes him sad, knowing he'll be thinking of Max, that he's missing Max. It makes me want to hold him, comfort him, tell him Max is fine, that he's in a wonderful place, a place where James should be right now, where he would be with Max. Maybe that's what he would have wanted; no doubt he would have been happy there. I know how unhappy he's been since Max died. I can openly see it now in his face. Maybe he would have preferred it if I had let him die so he could again be with his family. But now I have gone and interfered, changing his destiny for my own selfish reasons.

All my arrogance, my assurance that I had done the right thing for him was really that I was doing the right thing for me. What a self-serving being I have truly become.

Guilt shrouds me, prickling at my skin, the truth sinking its sentient teeth into me, wounding me. I wrap my arms around myself and avert my eyes to the floor, desperately trying to contain my feelings.

"Lucyna?" The tone in his voice instantly draws my eyes up to his. I can see the affliction in them as he says, "I wanted to ask you −"

But he never finishes the sentence because the door bursts open. I nearly jump out of my seat. For a moment, I think it's the Elders coming for me. It's not, obviously. It's Sara, James' friend.

"James! Thank God you're okay! Why didn't you call me! I mean I had to bloody hear it from Neil of all people, whom you rang, might I add, and then he rings me to see if I'm going to see you in the hospital, and I'm like *what are you on about*? Jesus Christ, I've been so worried! I tried to call your phone but −" she stops abruptly as she registers my presence. Her eyes flick from me, to James, then back to me.

"Sara, this is Lucyna." He gestures to me, then he points in Sara's direction. "Lucyna, this is my friend, Sara."

She openly runs her eyes over me, appraising me.

"Nice to meet you, Sara," I say.

"Yeah. Same." She walks around to the other side of the bed, dragging the other chair up beside James. I see the narrowed look he gives her, but she's too busy eyeballing me to notice.

"Lucyna saved my life," James says with that reverent tone in his voice he's seemingly taken to using whilst on the subject. My face once again grows hot with embarrassment at his erroneous opinion of me. "She pulled me from my car whilst it was on fire."

"Your car was on fire!" she says aghast.

He sighs, running his fingers through his hair. "Yeah, I'm not sure what happened but on the way back from that wedding I told you I was going to, I somehow managed to crash my car into a tree, and it set on fire. Lucyna pulled me out of it. If it wasn't for her I'd be dead right now."

She scoots her chair closer to him. "My God, James. I can't believe it − Jesus Christ. I just −" She pauses and shakes her head. "But you're okay now, though?"

"Yeah, I'm fine. Just a broken leg and a few stitches." He points to his head. "I'm lucky. It would have been much, much, worse, if it wasn't for Lucyna."

She nods her head slowly, gazing at him, then pulls her eyes away from him to look at me. "Thank you for what you did, for saving James," she says with real sincerity before placing a protective hand on his arm. "I don't know what I'd do without him." She shakes her head. "Well it doesn't even bear thinking about." She gazes back at him and I suddenly feel like I've intruded on a moment I don't really belong in.

But James's eyes aren't on her. He's staring straight ahead. He picks up his glass of water and begins to sip it. Sara looks down at her hands. For a few seconds there's a really awkward, prickly silence in the room, making those seconds feel like hours.

Sara looks up at me and forces a smile onto her lips, her eyes drifting to the door behind me. I'm getting the distinct impression that she doesn't require my presence here any more.

Maybe I should go, give them time alone to talk. But I'm torn as I really don't want to leave James. Selfish, I know.

Fortunately the reasonable, selfless side of me wins, even though parting from him for even just a short space of time fills me with dread. But I have to redeem myself in some way, show myself I'm not totally self-serving.

I stand up. James' surprised eyes instantly follow me up. "I should go." I point toward the door.

"Go?" His brow furrows. "Oh, right, I just, I – er, I haven't had a chance to thank you – I mean properly. I really need to do something to repay you –" The hesitancy in his voice is audible and I somehow manage to keep the smile from my face at his reaction to my impending departure while ensuring I avoid acknowledging the scowl on Sara's.

"I can come back later if you still need to talk to me about the accident," I say.

His face relaxes and his eyes crinkle up at the corners. "Would you? I'm not –"

"James?" He's interrupted by a female voice, and I glance at the door to see a large portly woman in nurse's attire, with glasses perched on the tip of her nose, standing partway into the room, her hand holding the door open. She pauses momentarily, peering over her glasses at us all, then continues on to say, "Your discharge papers will be ready for you sometime this afternoon."

57

"Thanks," he says.

"Are you okay getting home or do you need transport arranging?" she asks.

"I'll be fine. I'll take a taxi."

"I can arrange that for you."

"You sure?"

The nurse nods.

"That'd be great then, thanks." He smiles.

"You don't need a taxi," Sara says. "I'll take you home."

"You'll be at work. You should be there now," James says, glancing up at the clock on the wall.

"It'll be fine. I'll just take a flyer -"

"No." He has a smile on his lips, but a stern tone in his voice. "I don't know exactly what time it'll be when they release me and I don't want you getting into trouble at work. I'll take a taxi."

I can hear the nurse tapping her fingernails on the door and her intermittent sighs of impatience as James and Sara continue on with their fruitless disagreement, and I stand there wondering if I should just make my exit now or not.

"But how will you manage?" Sara says.

"I've only got a broken leg," he laughs. "I'm not an invalid. I can manage."

"But you'll need help and —"

"I can help," I interject wanting to relieve us all from this going-nowhere conversation, and two pairs of eyes instantly flick to me. I focus on James. "If you need help, I can help you get home. I can't drive but I can ride in the taxi with you and help you into your house, help with whatever you need," thus meaning I can spend that little bit more time with him. Admittedly, my motives are not completely selfless in this instance, but who can blame me?

For a split second I can actually hear a pin drop in this room, I can feel Sara's sharp green eyes on me, but I just keep looking at James' warm, dark brown ones. I'm sufficiently up with reading human behaviour to know that, for some reason, Sara has taken an instant dislike to me.

58

"I'll be okay," he says to me warmly, his tone instantly changed from a moment ago.

"It's not a problem, James, really."

He shifts his upper body turning toward me. "I'm sure you must have better things to do than help me home."

I stand behind the plastic chair, gripping hold of it with my fingers. I smile, suppressing a laugh. "Not really. I'd be happy to help you."

"You sure?"

"I'm sure."

"Well, I'll take you up on the offer, then." A smile plays on his lips. "I guess that's two things which I have to thank you for."

"So we're sorted, then?" the nurse says to James with a sigh.

"Yeah, we're sorted," he says, his eyes drifting back to me.

"Good. I'll book that taxi and be back this afternoon with your discharge papers."

"Cheers," he says, but she's already gone, the door swinging shut in the wake of her departure.

He turns back to Sara who is currently looking pretty vexed, at me, I assume.

"You should be getting yourself to work," he says to her, seemingly oblivious to her annoyance. "You don't wanna piss your boss off by taking too much time off."

She holds her hand up in protest, but then seems to change her mind, dropping it back in her lap. "Yeah, you're right. I'll get off, but I'll see you soon. okay?"

"Okay," he nods. "Thanks for coming though." He leans over to hug her.

I feel a sharp pain at their embrace. It stabs me hard, right in the centre of my chest.

"Of course I was gonna come, you idiot." She smiles bashfully, then kisses his cheek and straightens herself up, brushing her hands down her skirt. "Oh." She reaches down and retrieves her bag from the floor. "I swung by your house on the way here and picked you up some clean clothes. Thought you might need them."

"What would I do without you, eh?" He looks at her gratefully,

59

taking the clothes from her. "You're a real mate, Sara."

I see her eyes cloud over and she quickly forces a smile onto her lips. "You're very welcome," she chirps. "Okay, so I'll see you later, then." She turns to me. "Goodbye, Lucyna. it was nice to meet you," and I can tell from her tone that's far from what she really thinks.

"Nice to meet you too, Sara."

The door closes behind her and the room falls silent.

I take my seat back beside James. "So I guess I'm staying, then."

"I guess you are."

"Can I do anything for you? Get you anything?"

"I could murder a coffee, if it's not too much trouble?"

"Of course not. Where do I get one?"

"Just turn left out the door, the machine's a bit further down the corridor on your right."

I leave the room, feeling James' eyes on my back, and happily go off in search of this coffee machine. I find it fairly easily, but have no idea how to work it. It's got so many buttons and no visible instructions. In the end I have to get a passing nurse to help me.

I'm gone a while before I return back with his coffee.

"Thanks," he says, as I hand the steaming cup to him.

I pull the over-bed table up for him to rest it on. "Sorry it took me a while." I shake my head shyly. "I couldn't work the machine."

"Yeah they're not easy, are they?" He laughs, but it sounds different, uncomfortable, almost forced.

I sit down and there's silence between us. That's when I notice the charge in the air, almost as if something's changed whilst I've been gone.

James blows on his coffee, takes a sip and puts it down. He's staring at the coffee with a thoughtful look on his face and begins drumming his fingers on the side of the cup. I can tell there's something he wants to say, and at that thought he clears his throat and says, "So you managed to get home okay last night?"

Didn't he ask me this already? "Yes. I got home fine, thanks."

He runs his fingertip around the rim of the cup. "Whereabouts is it you live, Lucyna?"

I look down at my hands and start examining my new human nails. Come on, you decided this earlier on, you were just going to stick with the same story you told the police and tell him you're homeless if he asks. Just say it, it's not difficult. "I'm —" I start but for some reason I can't seem to bring myself to finish the sentence and, before I know it, I hear myself saying, "You probably wouldn't know it." I can feel his stare but I can't bring myself to look at him. I don't know what's wrong with me, why can't I just tell him?

"Right." He pauses but I can tell he's not finished. "But it's in Surrey?"

"What is?" I lift my eyes, meeting his inquisitive stare.

"Where you live?"

"Oh, yes."

"Right . . . well I know Surrey really well so I'm sure I'll know it." The persistence is clearly there in his voice, telling me he's not going to let it go, and I struggle to contain the panic rising up inside me as James' expectant eyes wait for an answer.

Chapter 6

Home Sweet Home

I stare past him, my body riddled with discomfort.

Do I know any places in Surrey? I must do. Think, Lucyna, think. But for some reason my brain won't work properly. "It's — it's just this little place in —" *Stop this stupidity Lucyna. What's wrong with you? Just tell him the truth. Well, the partial truth, anyway.* So I meet his dark curious eyes and shake my head as I say, "I don't have a home. I did. But I don't any more."

And he doesn't react. He doesn't say anything, almost as if he was expecting it. He just continues to stare at me with those big deep brown eyes, and I feel like I have to bridge the gap.

"It's fine, though," I say brightly. I try to add a light-hearted laugh at the end but it comes out sounding cringe-worthy, bouncing off all four walls and straight back at me.

His eyes focus in on me with determination and, for a moment, he looks exactly like Max did when he was trying to talk me into caring for James. "No, it's not okay," he says resolutely. "How could it be? Someone like you shouldn't be homeless. Well, no one should be homeless — but not you — no." He shakes his head. "I did wonder when you came back this morning wearing the same clothes you had on last night and when you said you'd been out walking at such a late hour when I had my crash. I did think — well it doesn't matter what I thought — where did you sleep last night, after you left here?"

I press my lips together and shuffle uncomfortably in my seat.

"You don't have to tell me if you don't want to."

"Here." I twist my lips nervously. "Well, I didn't actually sleep, I just spent a bit of time in the park in the grounds, and then I stayed in the canteen as it was a bit cold outside. I wanted to be close by so I could come back to see you."

He sort of grunts an angry sound. "Bloody hell," he mutters, shaking his head. "It's dangerous out there, Lucyna. All sorts of freaks about. If

I'd of known, I'd have done something last night. I'd have sorted you out a place to stay, a hotel or something." He sounds angry and I'm not sure if it's with me or himself.

"I'm not your responsibility, James," I say quietly. "My situation's not for you to fix." But how I wish he could. Little does he know that we're thinking on two very different wave lengths here, and having two very different conversations.

He looks at me, dark eyes wide, flaming. "I know, but I can help you. God, Lucyna, after what you've done for me, it's the very least I can do." His voice fills with conviction as he emphatically states, "You're coming to stay with me at my house, until you get yourself sorted."

"Oh," I say, a little more than surprised. That I wasn't expecting. Then a lovely warm glow erupts in me, like hot molten lava coating my insides.

"I mean obviously I can't force you to, but I'd really like it if you did. I'd certainly sleep a lot better at night knowing you were safe under my roof. And you do want me to get some sleep, don't you?" His lips twist into a grin. "Because I look pretty shocking when I've had no sleep – hair all over the place." He twists a lock of his hair around his finger. "Dark circles under my eyes. it's not pretty sight, I can tell you –" And I hold off telling him I already know just exactly how he looks when he doesn't sleep, because he hardly ever does, and still always manages to look beautiful. "– and I get really moody when I'm tired." He nods with certainty. "Then I'll be cranky at work and I'll take it out on Neil who works for me and probably the customers as well. Then Neil will quit, and my customers will go elsewhere, and I'll be out of business and lose everything, and then I'll end up on the streets too, and –"

"Okay." I cut him off laughing, feeling exasperated just listening to him. "I get the point."

He looks at me earnestly. "Look, Lucyna, I know you barely know me, but honestly I'm not a serial killer, sexual predator, drug addict, or raging alcoholic – yet." A mischievous grin etches onto his lips. "Oh, and I don't smoke – any more - scouts honour." He does a two-fingered salute, and I laugh at him. "Ask anyone - I'm a pretty normal guy, well, except for a fairly serious caffeine addiction." He taps his cup. "Seriously though, I have two other bedrooms just sitting there empty. And I live in Chelsea. It's a nice place – so what do you say?" he asks, hopeful eyes gazing at me.

I look at him for a moment. I know why he's doing this and I also know what I have done by saving him. But what is done is done, and I can't change anything now, and if I'm being honest, probably wouldn't if I had the time again. Then knowing there would never be an instance in which I would say no, as this will mean I get to spend more time with him before I'm taken back home, I say with absolute delight, "Yes, that would be wonderful," and struggle to control the beaming smile that's etching itself across my face. "Thank you so much. It's really kind of you."

He beams widely. "Great. That's settled, then." He shakes his head. "And don't thank me. Like I said, it's the least I can do for you after what you've done for me."

"It was nothing."

"No, Lucyna, it was something. It was huge. I'd be dead right now if it wasn't for you."

How very true that is, and he doesn't even know the full extent of it.

* * *

We spend the rest of the morning through to the afternoon talking, well mainly me asking James question after question, wanting to learn all I can about him. There's nothing I don't want to know. And obviously I can't tell James very much about myself, so every time he asks me a question or tries to steer the conversation in my direction, I do a great job of side stepping and pointing it right back at him.

The nurse comes back mid-afternoon with his discharge papers. I leave the room whilst she helps him dress, then I follow behind carrying his crutches whilst the nurse pushes him in a wheelchair into the lift and outside to the waiting taxi.

It takes about an hour to get to James' house from the hospital. We don't really talk much in the car, so I spend most of the time looking out of the window, watching the outside world whiz past before my eyes.

64

When we arrive at James' house, he pays the driver, and I help him out of the car and hand him his crutches. He hobbles up the path, struggling to use them for the first time, and I follow behind, gazing up at my new home. Funnily, considering how many times I've been here, I've never seen the outside of James' house, but then I guess I've never had reason to come out here before. It's an old three storey red brick town house, a big bay window downstairs and a bright white front door with frosted glass panels. It's homely.

James unlocks the door and I step inside the wide hallway, my shoes tapping loudly against the oak floor amid the immediate quiet. And the warmth and safety of James's home radiates over me, wrapping comfortingly all around me.

I cannot begin to describe how happy I feel, hardly able to believe that I'm actually going to be living here at James' request. I have been here so many times, but obviously he is unaware of this. Now, I'm here because he wants me to be.

James slumps down awkwardly onto the sofa in the living room. He leans his crutches up beside him, reaches over and pulls the footstool before him and lifts his potted leg to rest on it.

And I'm just stood here gazing at him, remembering how he was sitting there the very first night I came to visit him, remembering the countless times I've sat next to him in that very spot back when I existed only for the dead.

He sighs and rakes his fingers through his hair. "Okay," he says sounding slightly breathless, "my bedroom is the one at the front." He points his finger upwards at the ceiling. "So feel free to take any of the other two on that floor. I'll show you upstairs in a bit if that's okay? Journey home's just done me in." He lays his head back onto the sofa and glances up at me.

I take a seat on the chair across from him. "Don't worry. I'll find my way round just fine." Of course I will. I'd know my way round this house blindfolded.

"There is a bedroom up on the top floor with its own living area and bathroom. I'd offer you it but that was, erm . . . " He pauses and rubs his eye with the palm of his hand. "Well it was my dad's and he, erm —

well he passed away recently and it's still full of his stuff so. . . " He looks down and shrugs.

"I'm really sorry, James, about your – dad." I have to stop myself from almost saying Max's name.

"Thanks." He nods.

And it suddenly occurs to me – how would James feel if he knew the truth, if he knew I was the one who took Max to Heaven, that I was the one who took his father away from him? A sick feeling washes over me.

"James." He looks up at me and I can see the sadness he tries to hide, buried deep in his eyes I have to restrain myself from getting up and going over to him and wrapping my arms tightly around him. Once again knowing I'm partly to blame for his sorrow, I grip my fingers into the plush chair, momentarily distracted by the soft feeling. He lifts his questioning brows and now, forgetting what it was I was initially going to say, I say instead, "Just to have a place to stay is wonderful. Thank you again. It really is kind of you –"

He dismisses my words with his hand. "Like I said, I owe you, big time."

James picks up the remote control and switches the television on. My eyes drift to it and I watch as he flicks through the channels. He finally settles on one. There's a music video playing. As I listen, I hear the band's singing about not going somewhere, or something – I'm not sure.

I glance at James to find his eyes on me. And that's it, I'm hooked right into his gaze. And for those few seconds I can feel a charge buzzing off me, infusing me with such warmth, and feelings so intense, I can barely control them.

I force a blink, and when I open my eyes again, James's is looking at the television. "I like this song," I say, wanting to say something, anything, to cover the awkwardness I've probably just created.

"Yeah, Oasis are awesome," he says, turning the volume up slightly. "Especially this song, 'Don't Go Away'. It's one of their best. Well, it is in my opinion anyway." He smiles.

"Oasis?"

His brows knit together. "Yeah – Oasis – the band that's playing on the TV now." He points to it with the remote control. "You never heard of them?"

I shake my head. Oasis? I thought that was an isolated area of vegetation in a desert which surrounds a spring, not a music band.

He looks surprised. "I thought everyone had heard of them." A sceptical expression plays on his lips, and I worry that maybe I should have just said I had heard of them. But then music's never really been of interest to me. I never got it before, never understood why humans love it so much, well not until I started feeling that is. And as I've recently discovered, music's all about feeling. You have to feel the music, to understand it.

"I saw them in concert a couple of years ago, not long before they split," he enthuses. "They were amazing live."

I nod. "Yes they seem – great. This song is – great –" I trail off.

He glances at me and laughs, then turns the volume lower as the song comes to an end, and asks, "Lucyna, do you have anything – I mean any clothes or belongings that you need to pick up from somewhere?"

I shake my head.

"You don't have anything?" He sounds astonished, and not in a good way.

"No." I wrap my arms around myself. "When I left – well – home – I kind of left in a hurry." Which is pretty much the truth. "So, I only have these." I trail my hand down my clothes.

He rubs his forehead. "Well you're gonna need some stuff. Do you have any money?"

I shake my head.

"No worries. I'll lend you some till you get sorted so you can get some new clothes and things."

"Thank you," I say, feeling abashed and not really understanding why I feel this way. "I will return the money as soon as I can," knowing how essential money is to humans.

"No rush," he reassures me. "And you can't stay in those, they need washing." He points at the dirty marks on my clothes, forcing me to look down at the clothes that I somehow came to be wearing when I

67

turned into this human-ish being. "You'll have to borrow some of mine while you wash them. They'll be too big for you, but they'll have to do you for now. I'll go get you some." He reaches for his crutches.

"Don't get up. I'll get them." I shift forward in my seat. "Just tell me where your clothes are?"

He rests his crutches back down and says, "There's some clean stuff in the dryer." He points toward the hall. "Help yourself. Stick your clothes onto wash as well if you want whilst your there."

I get up, and even though I know where the utility room is as I've seen James wash his clothes there many times, I still ask, "Whereabouts is it?"

"Straight down the hall, through the kitchen, first door on your left."

I end up wearing some black jogging trousers. I go for those as they have a drawstring on the waist which means I can tighten them to fit me, but the legs are trailing on the floor. And I pick out a black t-shirt with a motif on the front, which is also pretty big on me. I put my own clothes onto wash, recalling how I've seen James do it before, and then return to the living room.

He looks up as I enter. "Rolling Stones," he says nodding at the t-shirt I'm wearing. "Good choice." Then his eyes move down to my legs and he laughs. "Bit long for you. They need turning up."

I look down at my hidden feet unsure as to what he means.

I glance up and catch the questioning in his stare, but all he says is, "Here." He motions for me to go sit on the footstool beside his leg. He reaches down and cups my leg with his hand, lifting it to rest beside him, then begins turning up the hem of the trousers. And I'm frozen. I am literally afraid to move in case I do something stupid, something not in keeping with normal human behaviour, because currently my whole body feels like it's going to explode from the touch of his hands on my skin.

He rests my leg down and motions for the other one. I lift it up without saying a word, curling my fingers around the edge of the stool for support, because now adjoining the explosive feeling, I've also got these little tiny bursts of energy that keep shooting up my leg each time his skin grazes against mine. I can feel my face growing hot.

"All done." His eyes meet mine. I hold his gaze for a moment then look away. I lower my leg back to the floor. "Thanks."

He stretches his hands above his head, yawning, and rubs his eyes roughly.

"You're tired?"

"Hmm. I am," he says, sounding suddenly sleepy. "Sorry, I know it's only early."

"Don't be sorry. You've had quite a day. I'll help you up to bed."

It takes us a while, but we finally make it up the stairs and I see him to his room.

"Thanks," he says, leaning up against the door frame.

"It's no problem. I'm happy to help you." I take a step back. "So I think I'll go to my room and sleep too."

"Goodnight, Lucyna."

"Goodnight, James."

I walk along the landing, heading toward the back of the house, knowing exactly which room I'm going to stay in. The one that provides the perfect view of his beautiful garden.

I shut the door behind me and go over to the window. The night's drawing in, preparing to coat everything in its blackness. I look around the room, taking in just where I actually am.

I am in James' house. He's just down the hall from me. And he knows me, he actually knows me.

And I finally release the euphoria that this knowledge brings, the one I've been working so hard all day to contain, and I let it run through me with all its heavenly urgency, releasing the smile that wants to own my lips forever. I lie back onto the bed, and begin to replay my day with James over and over again in my mind.

Chapter 7

Cross Your Heart

I've been downstairs for hours as I've discovered I don't sleep.

I haven't slept since I became this – well – version of a human I've become. And I've already gathered that my new body doesn't require other humanly functions to survive, as I've had absolutely no desire for food or drink. But I wasn't sure about sleep. I didn't know if my body would need to rest or not. As it turned out, it doesn't. I did try. I laid on the bed and closed my eyes for quite some time, but nothing happened. And I haven't had any signs of fatigue, as human's do – no yawning or desire to stretch my body of any sort, and considering how long I've been awake, I surely would be tired by now if I was ever going to be.

So I just stayed in my room and wiled the hours away thinking about James, distracted by just how close he was to me. Then I read a book I found in my room. It was a new and joyous experience, and one I most certainly want to repeat. Some humans really do have a way with the written word. And finally I watched the sun rise.

Then, when it seemed like a reasonable hour for a human to arise after sleeping, I came downstairs.

I've being trying to think of ways I can help James today as he is partially incapacitated. The first thing I came up with was breakfast. Humans need to eat, and James doesn't eat nearly enough, as I've seen, so I decided to make it for him.

I searched through the kitchen cupboards and found some cereal. Then I located bread, browned it in the toaster and, when it was ready, buttered it. Finally I prepared James' coffee in his coffee machine, just as I've watched him do nearly every morning for the past three weeks.

I survey the kitchen table. It's all set up with the food and drink I've created, and I feel a sense of achievement. Toast, cereal and coffee. It looks enticing – I think.

"Morning." I hear James's warm, husky voice come from behind me

70

and turn to see him in the doorway surveying the table. "You didn't have to do this." He motions to the food. "Well, assuming some of it is for me." He grins, standing there one arm resting on his crutch, the other raking his fingers through his dishevelled hair.

But I can't answer. I can't form words. And it's not just because he looks glorious with his hair all messy and rumpled from sleep, his jogging bottoms that he's cut up the leg to accommodate his pot hanging so loosely around his navel – no, that's not what has clamped my mouth tightly shut and sent every particle of me into frenzy. No, it's the fact that I can see from his navel all the way up to his broad expansive chest, his bare skin perfectly smooth, exposed here before me. I can't take my eyes off him. I've never seen James, well – naked, before. I was always very respectful whilst I was here watching him, always departing when he would be about to undress.

He raises his brows in a question mark, forcing me to finally say, "Yes, of course it's for you." But my voice breaks, betraying me. I turn away, face flaming, and move over to the sink. I look up to see James watching my face in the reflection of the window. I look away.

He chuckles softly, then I register the sound of a chair scraping against the wooden floor as he pulls it out. "Thanks for this. You really didn't have to."

I turn back, lean up against the sink and desperately try not to stare at his chest – it's harder than you'd think. "I wanted to."

He smiles. "Well thanks. I really appreciate it." He pours himself a coffee, takes a sip, and then tips the cup in my direction. "Coffee's spot on. Cheers."

I smile, glowing, happy I've pleased him. "You're welcome." I take a seat across from him at the table, noticing for the first time that the gauze on his forehead has gone. "You removed your gauze." I touch my forehead in the equivalent spot to where his gauze used to be.

"Yeah, they said to take it off when I got home. Let the air get to it."

I gaze at the cut that sits cleanly under his hairline, tiny stitches holding it together, as his fingertip touches just shy of it. "Another scar to add to the collection." He sighs dramatically, rolling his eyes with obvious amusement, his finger drifting to the older scar on his brow.

"How'd you sleep?" he asks, picking up a slice of toast.

"Oh. On the bed. It was really comfortable. For eight hours. How did you sleep?" I worry because I know just how little he actually does.

He raises his eyebrow, lips curving and puts down the untouched piece of toast. "Oh yeah, I slept on my bed as well, for about ten hours." He nods grinning.

I smile, pleased he's slept for so much longer than normal. "That's really good."

He laughs, then says, "Hmm, yeah, I was expecting to be up all night with this thing on." He taps his potted leg. "Must be the painkillers the hospital has got me on that knocked me out." He picks up his toast and takes a bite.

"You not hungry?" he asks, words muffled by his mouthful of toast.

"I ate before you came down. I hope that's okay."

Another lie and it concerns me how adept I've become at this lying business. And honestly, I wish I could eat the toast and drink the coffee because the smells wafting up from the table are wonderful.

He laughs. "'Course it is. This is your home now, Lucyna. You do as you please. You don't have to fit around me." He leans back in his chair, cup in hand. "So what are your plans for today?"

"Oh – I don't know." I rest my arms on the table, linking my fingers together. "I hadn't really thought past breakfast."

He takes a sip of coffee, then puts it down. "I need to do a few things work-wise this morning, well mainly I have to get on the phone and sort a temp to help Neil and the lads out with the workload whilst I'm out of action. And then I really need to go to the supermarket, as you'll have noticed –" He gestures to the kitchen cupboards. "– there's not much in, and I thought it would be an idea for you to come with me . . . obviously I need the help –" He scrunches his face up, squinting at me cheekily. "– but I also thought we could get you some clothes and stuff while we're out."

"Sounds like a wonderful idea."

"Good. We'll have to take a taxi, though, as obviously I don't have a car any more. I've got the work van but it's not like I can exactly drive with this thing on – unless you drive." He looks at me hopefully.

I shake my head. "No, sorry." *I used to be able to travel at the speed of light, but now I have to walk to get where I want to go.*

"No worries, we'll take a taxi." He smiles.

After happily watching James eat nearly all the breakfast I've made, I go upstairs and take a shower for the very first time, knowing this to be a normal humanly thing to do. And it's the most amazing experience I've had so far – well except for every time James looks at, or touches, me, that is.

I stand under the hot water, exhilarated by the feel of it as it cascades down onto this body of mine. After a while, I reluctantly get out, wrap a towel around myself and stand in front of the mirror, not really knowing what I should do with my now wet hair. I know human women generally put a lot of effort into the appearance of their hair, but I haven't got a clue where to start. So I just wring the water out with a towel, leave it to hang down my back, and put my original clothes back on now they're clean.

We take a taxi to Kings Road. James steers me into a clothes shop first. It's probably one of the most challenging things I've done since I landed here in my new attire, well aside from saving James' life. Wonderful but daunting. I'm wandering around this shop with absolutely no idea of what I'm supposed to buy, trying to act like I do. But part of me, well a big part, can barely believe that I'm actually here amongst these humans, looking like one of them, pretending to be one of them. It's truly beyond imagining.

There are so many different clothes to choose from. I do the best I can, mainly by watching what other women in the shop are picking out, which mostly consists of t-shirts, skirts, jumpers and jeans.

"What about this?" James is standing before me holding up the prettiest dress I've ever seen. It's the colour of the sky, with these little jewels embellished along the neck line.

"It's really lovely," I say fingering the silky fabric.

He smiles. "I thought it'd suit you. We'll take it, then." He peers at the tag inside the dress. "I think I got the right size – you're about an eight, aren't you?" his cheeks colour, "not that I know much about women's dress sizes, but you are – well, you are tiny."

73

What size am I? I've just been picking up what I thought looked like it would fit me. I nod. "Yes a size eight is perfect." Then I surreptitiously begin flicking through the clothes I've got, checking the labels for sizes. Mainly eights and some tens. They'll do.

"You got everything you need, then?"

I look down at my arms laden with clothes and nod. I follow him over to the counter where he proceeds to pay, which oddly makes me feel extremely uncomfortable.

"So you're gonna need some shoes to go with all these clothes you've just got," James says once were outside the shop.

I look down at the many bags in my hands. He's spent what seems like a lot of money on me already. I don't want James to spend all of his money on me because he feels like he owes me for saving his life, which I only did under fraudulent circumstances.

I shake my head. "No, I'm fine with what I already have."

He looks at me, brows raised, and says with absolute certainty, "I'm buying you some shoes, Lucyna, and I'm not taking no for an answer." Then he moves off before I can attempt a shot at resisting and, for a man currently on crutches, he's moving pretty swiftly, might I add. So I just dutifully follow along behind him.

I manage to get him down to two pairs of shoes. Then, as we're leaving the shoe shop, James clears his throat and says, somewhat awkwardly, "Er – Lucyna, do you erm – well you're gonna need some – underwear, aren't you? You know, like – bras and stuff."

Underwear, of course, humans always wear this beneath their clothes. I regard his flushed face, his uncomfortable demeanour, not seeing the source of his embarrassment and without, even bothering to contest over the money, knowing it to be a fruitless exercise, I say, "Yes, I will need some."

It's odd to see James like this. He's usually so self-assured, so sure. It's incredibly endearing. It makes me want to reach out and run my fingertips across his glowing cheek.

"Right, well La Senza's just there," he says, voice somewhat gruff. I follow his gaze to a shop across the other side of the busy road which has women's underwear artfully displayed in its window. "Here's my card." He pushes his credit card into my hand. "Get whatever you need. My pin number's –" He moves closer to me, his body almost pressed against mine, only the thin layers of our clothes and a sliver of air separate us, as he whispers in my ear, "One, three, three, seven." His breath blows over my neck, setting my body on high alert. He moves back, looking down at me with opaque eyes which instantly clear. "I'm just gonna go in here." He points to a shop advertising DVDs and computer games in its window. "I'll meet you outside La Senza in fifteen, okay?"

And he's gone, leaving me standing in the middle of the busy street, my body buzzing, kindling, practically spitting off flames. I mentally shake myself into the now, and, with his credit card in hand, slowly walk toward La Senza.

The woman in the shop is really helpful. She asks if I know my sizes, to which I obviously reply no. So she takes me into the changing area and measures me with a tape measure, and then brings bras for me to try on. I just buy the ones she brought me and the pants to match, and also some sleepwear – well if I'm acting like I sleep I may as well go the whole hog and dress the part too. And after paying, recalling just how James had done it, I go outside to find him leant up against the shop window, crutches resting under his arms, a bag in his hand, waiting for me.

"All done?" He smiles, back to his usual, certain self.

"Yes, thank you," I say handing his credit card back to him.

Lastly we go to the supermarket. It's packed full of humans. I steer the trolley around whilst James walks alongside, filling it with food and toiletries he says I'll need. I just agree, nodding in what I hope are the right places, praying I get it right and come across as just like any other normal human being would.

We take a taxi back to James' house, well my home now too. I put the food away in the kitchen whilst James rests on the sofa. The shopping trip really tired him out. Then I put my new clothes away in the wardrobe in my bedroom.

I'm on my way down the stairs when I hear James on the telephone in the living room. His voice terse, strained, as he says, "It's my house. I

75

can do as I please and after what she did for me – well it doesn't even fucking measure up. I'm not gonna argue with you about it, she's staying here, end of . . . I know you are but – . . . Jesus Christ, Sara! What the fuck! You don't even know her to make those kinds of assumptions! . . . No. Seriously, I don't wanna hear it. I'll speak to you later."

I hear the television go on and wait a few minutes before going in the living room. I don't want him to think I was listening in on his conversation - which I obviously was.

He looks up when I enter, eyes dark, a frown etched deep into his forehead. I take a seat on the sofa beside him. He starts tapping the phone loudly against his pot.

"Are you okay, James?"

"Yep." There's an edge to his voice.

I link my fingers together. "You don't seem okay, you seem –"

"I'm fine," he says curtly, cutting me dead, his tone surprising me.

"I'll leave you alone." I get up to leave.

He puts a hand on my arm, stopping me. "I'm sorry." He shakes his head, and sighs. "I didn't mean to snap at you, I'm just – really pissed off." He tosses the phone onto the sofa beside him. "You remember my friend Sara – the one you met at hospital?" I nod. "Well she's just kinda –" he half smiles, " – pissing me off at the moment, which is weird really 'cause we never row." He rubs his brow thoughtfully. "To be honest, I can't think of a time we have in all the years I've known her."

"How long have been friends?" I ask.

He looks at me, his face less tense now. "Since we were kids. Our dads were best friends. We grew up together. She's kinda like a sister to me. Our families always went on holidays together, days out – you know that sort of stuff." He pushes his fingers through his hair. "But she's just . . . overstepped the mark a bit. She thinks that –" He looks at me with weary eyes, then shakes his head and smiles. "It doesn't matter – so anyway, did you have a good time shopping today?" And just like that he changes the subject.

"Yes, it was great, and thanks again for all the clothes and shoes . . . and other stuff."

"Don't thank me, it's the –"

" – least you can do after what I did for you," I say, finishing his current aphorism with a smile.

He laughs, a real laugh, reaching all the way up to his eyes. "Touché," he grins, "touché."

* * *

At five o'clock James' employee, Neil, comes by the house to go through some work things with him. After the obligatory introductions, with me pretending like it's the first time I've ever seen Neil - it's not; I've seen him many times before when I used to watch James - I make myself scarce, leaving them in the living room to get on with their work.

I go in the kitchen, fill a glass with water and take it into the garden with me. I have no intention of attempting to drink it but I need it to appear to James that I do actually drink every now and then, and it doesn't hurt to dirty up a few glasses here and there as proof.

I sit down on one of the chairs on the paved area overlooking the big garden, resting the glass on the table, and let the afternoon sun drift over me, savouring the absolute tranquillity of this garden, the calmness it offers, as the heady scents emitting from the blossoms whirl gently around me.

I could spend forever sitting here.

After about an hour, Neil pops his head out of the back door.

"I'm off now. It was really nice to meet you, Lucyna," he says, smiling.

I return his smile. "It was nice to meet you too, Neil."

"See you, then." He waves and disappears off.

Five minutes later James comes out with a coat in his hand.

"I brought you this in case you were getting cold." He hands me the coat and sits down in the chair beside me.

"Thank you." I slide my arms into the sleeves, pulling it around me. It smells of him, all musky and intoxicating. "Your garden is really beautiful, James."

"Thanks – well I suppose it should be with what I do for a living." He laughs. "Wouldn't be a good advert if it was a mess."

I get up and begin wandering around, my eyes grazing over the colourful creations. "What do you call these?" I point to a cluster of bright purple flowers.

"Purple Asters."

"They're really pretty," I say, bending down to get a better look at them - bright purple petals centred with yellow nectar. I press my nose to one, inhaling its sweet scent.

"They're pretty hard to get. Usually the colour comes out violet but this season I got some true purple ones." He smiles proudly. "They're a symbol of love and patience, you know" he adds knowingly. "In olden times, it was believed that if you burnt their leaves, the perfume would ward off evil spirits. They're one of my favourites." He laughs again. "I know, not very manly to have a favourite flower but, hey, I am gardener after all."

"They look like stars," I say, fingering the soft petals.

"Yeah, I suppose they do," he replies, voice suddenly sounding uninterested. I can hear his fingers tapping on the wooden arm rest of the chair and after a moment he says, "Lucyna, can I ask you something?"

I stand up. "Of course."

"Well I've been wondering . . . how did you come to be homeless?"

I look down at my feet. Stupidly I hadn't thought this far, overlooking the glaringly obvious fact he would naturally be curious about my past.

"You don't have to tell me, if you don't want," he adds, voice soft. "It makes no odds to me."

I look up at the very reason why I left my home, my one and only reason for existing as I now do - James, with his infinite pools for eyes; his curious brow creased, tilting his scar; his full lips pressed together, as he waits for my response. And it just kind of hits me smack bang in the centre of my chest, straight into my theoretical heart.

I love him.

And then it all just seems so very simple.

"I fell in love," I hear myself saying, "and for me to be able to be with him meant that I had to leave my home." I know just how close to the truth I'm skirting but at this moment I have neither the wish nor the care to stop.

James's gaze drifts out over the garden. "And . . . it didn't it work out with this guy?"

"Not in the way I had hoped."

"Do you still love him?" he asks, eyes fixed on mine.

I hold his gaze, willing him to hear me, to really hear me when I say, "I will always love him, whether we're together or not."

He breaks from our gaze, looking down at the shoe he's begun scuffing against a paving stone. "So why didn't you go back home after you'd broken up."

"I couldn't. I'd broken the rules."

He looks back up at me with what can only be described as incredulity. "Rules? Jesus Christ, Lucyna, what rules?"

I turn away from him.

And for a moment neither of us speaks.

After what seems an infinite amount of time, I hear his warm voice come from behind me. "I'm sure your family would want you back. How could they not?"

"Maybe they would," I wrap his coat tightly around me, pressing my nose into the collar, inhaling his scent, "but I'm not so sure I want to go back. Ever."

I hear him sigh deeply. "Lucyna, look, you don't have to answer this if you don't want, but I'm gonna ask anyway." He takes a deep breath, then says, "Did you use to live in a cult?"

I turn round to face him. "A cult?"

"Yeah you know, a cult, where there's loads of you all living together, like rurally, and you believe in a certain religion – and other stuff."

I stare at him troubled. "I know what a cult is James. I'm just wondering why you think I'm from one?"

He rubs his hand over his face. "Because you're just so different, Lucyna – so completely different to anyone I've ever met. You talk different, act different and everything's like –" He leans forward in his seat, arms resting on his legs, "– I don't know how to describe it. It just seems like everything's brand new to you, like the world's a new place to you, almost as if you've never really ventured out into it before, and I was trying to figure out why you'd be like that, and the only thing I could come up with was that you'd maybe – lived in a cult of some sort." He shakes his head, embarrassment creeping over his face. "It doesn't matter anyway, obviously I'm wrong, so I'm just gonna stop talking – now."

I sit down on the chair beside him and glance at his mortified face. Then I laugh. I can't help it. He thinks I'm from a cult and I'm fully aware of what that word's been denoted to mean since, well, the latter part of the twentieth century, what those places are, the very polar opposite of the good and righteous place I truly come from.

He glances at me and a smile quickly creeps onto his lips. "Okay! I know it was a stupid thing to say but you didn't have to laugh!"

"Sorry." I curl my legs up onto the seat, turning to face him. "James, I know I'm different from what you're used to but it's not because I'm from a cult."

He keeps his eyes on me. "It wouldn't have mattered to me if you had been – you know."

"I know."

He starts tapping his fingers on the chair again, opens his mouth to speak and closes it, seemingly changing his mind.

"What do you want to ask me?"

He smiles. "I'm asking too many questions, I know, but I'm just so bloody curious. I mean I know nothing about you but at the same time feel like I've know you for ages, which is weird because I've known you for exactly two days. Do you know what I mean?" He looks at me, wanting reassurance, and I nod. Of course I know what he means, well except I've known him for exactly three weeks and nearly five days – a bit longer than his two.

"Maybe I'm so intrigued because of the whole 'you saved my life' thing," he adds. "Well that and the fact that you're so bloody cryptic all the time." He laughs, nudging me with his elbow, then murmurs, "You're such a mystery, Lucyna."

"Is that a good or bad thing?" I ask.

He regards me for a moment, his eyes opaque, his expression unreadable. "Both." He smiles then sets his gaze out over the garden.

I can feel his unasked question still hanging in the air around him.

"What was it you wanted to ask me before, James?"

He laughs. "See, you know me so well already and I know – well not very much about you." He grins. "Okay, well you said you're different from everyone else and I wondered – what did you mean by that?"

I look down at my bare feet. "I just meant that I'm well . . . my family, they have different ways, old ways. I guess you could say . . . I was shown the world from a different view. I was raised differently from everyone else. So this is all . . . new to me. How you are, is new to me."

"How do you do that?"

I look at his amused eyes. "What?"

"Answer a question without actually answering it."

"Years of practice," I smile.

He shifts his position, stretching his good leg out before him. "So what do you think you'll do?"

"What do mean?"

"Well, I just wondered what your plans are. How long you'll be here for?"

Does he want me to leave? Has he tired of my company already? "Oh – I don't know – I hadn't thought. I just –"

"I'm not asking you because I want you to go, because I don't," he says with certainty. "You can stay for as long as you want. Well forever, if you like – but only if you keep making as good a cup of coffee as you did this morning. That stops and you're out," he quips, thumbing over his shoulder toward the door. "But no, seriously, I just meant what will you do? Will you get a job?"

A job? I pull my knees up to my chest, wrapping my arms around them. "I don't think I'll be able to get a job. I have no . . . skills."

"I'm sure you have." He leans toward me enthusiastically. "I mean I could probably hook you up with something. I have a few contacts. What did you used to do, before you were erm – homeless?"

Take humans to Heaven. I somehow don't think that's going to aid me here on earth in attempt to get a human job. "I used to deliver."

"What like packages?"

I nod. "Yes – packages."

"Well there you go, then," he says resting back on his chair, smiling. "You have got a skill. You could get another job doing that. I'll ask around a few people I know, see if there's anything going. But in the meantime you could sign on at the job centre and get some benefits. I know they don't give you much but it'll be some money of your own till you get a job."

"Yes." I begin playing with my fingers. Benefits? What are they?

"I don't mind giving you money, it's not that, it's just I imagine you'll want some of your own. But don't worry, though," he pats me on the arm, my skin prickling at his touch, "you've got plenty of time and I'll just lend you what you need till then. Just have a think about it and go from there. There's no rush. I'll help you – you know I will."

"Thank –"

He waves his hand cutting me off. "New house rule. I'll stop with my annoying adage if you stop thanking me for everything. What do you say – is it a deal?"

"It's a deal."

"You promise."

"I promise."

"Cross your heart and hope to die." He laughs, it petering off at my foggy expression. "You know – cross your heart and hope to die, stick a needle in your eye – you never heard it before?"

I shake my head.

A grin plays on his lips. "God, we always used to say that when we were kids. You sure you haven't been off living on the moon or something?" He regards me with amusement. "Don't know who Oasis are – now this." He chuckles, shaking his head as he gets up from his chair tucking a crutch under his arm. "You want a coffee – I'm making?"

"No, thanks." I shake my head at his retreating back. "I'm fine with my water."

'Cross your heart and hope to die'. His words ring around my mind like warning bells. The irony of a saying that could never in a thousand years, ever apply to me but I take heed because I know when I do have to leave him, which with every dawning day comes ever closer, then it really will be like dying. Because to think of spending a day, let alone an eternity, without ever again seeing his beautiful face or hearing his voice is unbearable.

I know then I will unequivocally wish for the day to come when I can truly cross my heart and die.

Chapter 8

Hunger

Turning my gaze from the beige coloured walls up to the white ceiling above, I watch as beams from the morning sun dance across it in perfect symmetry, a mosaic of colours glistening all above as I lay here on my bed.

Which I've done for the last eight hours.

I haven't read a book, or watched the sun rise, or done anything of substance. I've done nothing but watch the dark through to light and think of James, wondering how I didn't see it sooner that I'm in love with him, how I didn't realise that what I felt for him was love?

Everything is making such sense now - the strength of the feelings that initially confounded me, my constant desire to be by his side, the things I have done to be with him, all pointing to that one emotion. At least I now know it was love that fuelled my desire to save him, that my selfishness was sanctioned by my level of feelings.

Love – the ultimate emotion, the crux of all others.

But how can such a euphoric feeling as love, ignite me with happiness and dull me with misery at the same time? To love him is so extraordinarily wonderful but to have him so close and for him to never be mine tortures me beyond belief. More than anything I want to feel the complete ecstasy that love creates but I can't because the darker side of it resides within me too - a yo-yo of emotions - my happiness tarnished the instant reality strikes like a cacophonous peal of thunder, yanking me back to the now.

So instead of fighting against them, I relinquished control to the medley of conflicting emotions and just let myself imagine how it would be if James and I were together, if I weren't a Bringer, if I were human, if James felt for me as I do him. If he loved me.

And what a dream it is.

Once again closing my eyes, I imagine his voice whispering the words I long to hear. He holds me in his strong arms, wrapping them around me, pulling me close to him. I can almost feel the heat of his skin on mine. I tilt my head up, eyes meeting his, and then he leans down and kisses me, a wondrous, tortuous vision of a reality that will never be mine.

I open up my eyes after the closing scene, knowing I can't spend all day in my fool's paradise, that soon enough these thoughts will be all I'm left with for eternity.

Forcing myself into reality, I sit up, swing my legs over the edge of the bed and, seeing straight out the window, I'm surprised to see James sitting in the garden by the large barrel pot examining the plants in it.

An overwhelming rush of exhilaration charges through me at the sight of him. It's like now I have this knowledge, now I'm fully aware the extent of my feelings for him, they've ramped their velocity up to the maximum. And I can barely contain the excitement at the thought of just being near him.

I'm changed out of my bed clothes and into a pair of jeans and t-shirt in under a minute, and on my way downstairs.

James is sat with his back to me and doesn't register my presence, so I just stand here for a moment, leant up against the door frame, watching him, giving myself a little time to lock in my overzealous feelings, to stop myself from just blurting out the truth of how much I'm truly in love with him.

When I finally feel I'm safe to speak, I say, "Good morning."

He turns at the sound of my voice, eyes squinting in the glare of the morning sun. "Hey," he says, voice gruff. "How you doing?"

"I'm well. How are you?"

"Mmm . . . couldn't sleep." He stares down at the ground. "Came out here for a bit and saw how shabby this was looking." He gestures to the barrel with the tool he's holding. "Thought I'd tidy it up a bit."

"Why couldn't you sleep?" I ask, concern noticeable in my voice that I don't bother to hide. "Is everything okay?"

"Oh yeah, fine, just . . . have a few things on my mind is all." His eyes fleetingly meet mine as he runs his fingers through his dark hair.

"Is it anything I can help with?"

He presses his lips together and shakes his head. "Nah, but thanks.

It's nothing major – just work stuff."

I know he's not telling me the truth but I don't push the subject.

"So can I help you with this instead, then?" I gesture towards the barrel.

He glances back. "Sure. If you go in the shed there's a new pair of gardening gloves just in the top drawer and the secateurs are hanging up on the wall," my puzzled expression prompting him to add, "You're looking for one of these." He holds up the scissor-like tool in his hand.

"Right." I nod.

I venture into the shed, easily finding the gloves and secateurs, and take them back out with me. I kneel on the hard floor beside the barrel near James. "So what do I do?" I ask, pulling the gloves onto my hands.

He runs his gloveless fingers over the bushy green plants. "You're looking for any browning leaves, anything that looks dead basically, then cut it off."

I begin looking through the plants, moving my fingers through the leaves, as James is, and our fingers bump together. I glance up at him and he smiles, and even though my hands are covered with these clumpy gloves, I still get a surge of warmth from his touch. I get back to the task and it happens again, this time he laughs. "How about you do that side and I'll stick to this one."

With a nod and a touch of disappointment, I retract my hand and stick to my assigned side. I find a browning leave and snip it off and place it on the floor beside me. Then I find another, and another. And before I know it, I've clipped quite a few dead leaves off. I can see a noticeable difference in the plant already; it's starting to look far healthier than it did a few minutes ago.

"This is quite enjoyable," I say. "I can see why you like doing this as your job."

"Yeah, I used to love it," he murmurs.

I stop what I'm doing and look up at him, shading my eyes from the sun with my hand. "Used to?" I ask.

"Well I just –" He shrugs. "– I spent all of my working life with my dad, and when he passed away – well it's just been tough not having him around." His leans forward, arms on legs, shoulders hunched over, hands tightly clasping the secateurs. I reach over and touch his arm with my gloved hand.

He glances at my hand, then up at my face. He takes a deep a breath. "I'm enjoying this, though, working here with you." He holds my gaze for a long moment until finally I look away and awkwardly withdraw my hand, aware that all my intense feelings for him are quickly bubbling up to the surface, knowing if I'd have kept his gaze or touched him for a second longer I wouldn't have been able to keep my feelings in check.

"I imagine you and your dad must have been close, living and working together," I say, attempting to fill my mind with other thoughts than my need for him as I get back to my pruning.

"Yeah, we were. We drove each other mad most of the time," he laughs lightly whilst turning the secateurs over in his hands, "but it was always just us two. He was more like my best mate than my dad. And I guess we kinda relied on each other – me on him more than I'd realised."

"You miss him a lot?"

"Yeah," he says avoiding my eyes, voice suddenly low, thick.

I resist the urge to touch him again. "I'm sorry. I didn't mean to pry."

"No. It's fine. It's just – well – I find it hard to talk about him." He looks at me. "But it's not like I haven't done enough prying of my own with you . . . even if it has been fruitless." There is a hint of frustration in his expression.

I move back, sitting on my behind, and watch him as he starts snipping off the dead leaves again. My eyes travel the expanse of his perfect face, studying him as he presses his lips together in seeming concentration, but I know otherwise. I know he does this when he's concealing his grief, causing me to want to offer words of comfort to him.

"You giving up?" he challenges me playfully.

I shake my head. "No, I was just thinking – well I think your dad will be looking down at you from Heaven –"

He cuts me off with a laugh, a genuine laugh, as he shakes his head. "My dad and the word Heaven don't really go together – purgatory more likely."

"You'd be surprised," I utter quietly to myself as I get back up to my knees, quashing my temptation to tell him just how very wrong he is. "Well, wherever he is," I add. "I think he'll be feeling incredibly proud of you."

He glances at me, eyebrow raised. "What makes you say that?"

"Well just look at what you're doing, keeping his business going whilst recovering from a car accident and, in addition to that, taking a stray into your home and helping her out." I use the word 'stray' to try to lighten the effect of what I am saying.

"You're hardly a stray," he says, voice suddenly intense. And the way he's looking at me, so warm, so caring, sky rockets my emotions out into the stratosphere. I want to reach out and touch his face with my fingertips. I can feel them itching to move. It's like I crave his touch, hunger for him. I clasp my hand tightly around the secateurs to control the urge.

"How long have you had the business?" I ask, needing a distraction to stop myself from doing something stupid.

"My dad started it when I was about six," he says reaching down and picking up the coffee cup that's sitting on the floor beside his chair. "He'd always been a gardener and he just got sick of working for everyone else, so he started his own business – small at first, just local contracts, and it grew from there, and now we're doing pretty well." He takes a sip of his drink and puts it back on the floor.

"And you've always done this? Worked for your dad's business, I mean."

He nods. "Yeah, well after I finished uni. I'd wanted to come and work for him as soon as I left school but he wouldn't have it. I had to do my A-levels." He smiles. "Then I had to go to uni. But I just wanted to work for him, it was all I ever wanted to do – you know be a gardener like him, but he wouldn't have it, he wanted me to do all the things he'd never had the chance to, and if you'd of had the pleasure of knowing my dad, then you'd have known he had a very persuasive manner. You just couldn't win an argument with the man, it was literally impossible!" He laughs shaking his head, and I join in, knowing just how very true that statement is. "So before I knew it I'd agreed to go to uni," he continues, "but I told him if I was going I was doing a degree in Landscape Design. So I did my degree, came back home and have worked for him ever since – well except for now, obviously – I mean it became my business when he died." His eyes instantly cloud.

"And is it just Neil that works for you?" I ask to keep him talking, to stop him dwelling on his grief, even though I already know otherwise.

"Nah, there's six lads altogether. Neil's worked for the business as long as I have. He's kinda my right hand man – I just promoted him last week to team leader. He deserved it. He's good at what he does and he helped keep the business going when dad died. I wasn't in a great place, obviously, and he just took hold of the reins and got on with it. We'd have probably lost a few contracts if it wasn't for him. He's helped me a lot. And now I'm out for a few months because of this." He taps his finger on his pot and looks directly at me. "But I'm not a lazy boss, you know." He grins, a slow languid grin. "That's why I had to get a temp in to cover me. I don't just sit back and give orders. I'm very hands-on." His voice suddenly sounds husky and he's looking at me in a new way, in a way he's never looked at me before. It's almost as if his eyes are daring me, tempting me. I'm frozen to the spot, unable to tear my eyes from his.

His mobile phone starts ringing and his eyes instantly flicker back to life. He glances down at his pocket, brushes the dirt off his hands onto the shorts he's wearing, and digs the phone out of his pocket.

"Speak of the devil," he utters looking at the caller display. "I wondered who'd be ringing this early." He clicks the phone on. "All right, mate, I was just talking about you . . . Nah just telling Lucyna how crap you are at your job . . . yeah, yeah, whatever! . . . oh right you are, okay, hang on a minute." He moves the phone away from his ear. "Its Neil," he says to me. "Work stuff. You okay if I leave you doing this for a min?"

I nod. "Yes, I'll be fine."

He presses the phone back to his ear. "Neil, I'll just have to get the drawing's out so I can see what –" The sound of his voice disperses as he disappears off into the house.

I sit back in shock, little tremors of hope rippling through me. Was James just . . . flirting with me? I mean the seemingly suggestive manner in which he said 'I'm very hands-on', and the way he was looking at me. Maybe he likes me in the way I like him . . . or maybe it's just my wishful thinking. Come on, Lucyna, these are your own desires that you're projecting onto him making you think this way.

I shake the thoughts from my mind and carry on trimming off the dead leaves, desperately trying to ignore the little shots of stupid hope that keep trying to force their way in.

James is gone a good while and, when he comes back outside, he's carrying a tray containing food and drink.

"Sorry about that. There was a bit of confusion over the plans for the job that the lads are going to do down in Hove. All sorted now, though." He is seemingly back to normal, confirming that whatever I may have thought occurred between the two of us obviously didn't. "Anyway, I thought I'd get us some breakfast whilst I was inside."

He sets the tray on the table. I glance over at it seeing coffee, croissants, butter and a jar of jam. He places one of the cups of coffee and a plate with a croissant on it across the table from him where I assume I'm to be sitting.

I go and take my seat, pull my gloves off and lay them on the table, all the while wondering how on earth I'm going to get out of this. So far I have managed to avoid eating with him, telling him I'm not hungry or that I've already eaten. But now I'm stuck here, faced with food and drink that he's made, with no easy way out. I can't say I'm not hungry as he knows I haven't eaten this morning. Maybe I should just try and eat it, but then I don't know what would happen if I did and I really don't think it's a risk I should take.

I look down at the flaky pastry before me, assessing it.

"Do you not like croissants?" he asks. "I can get you something else, if you want?"

"No, I like them just fine." I pick the croissant up and tear a small piece off, looking at it sitting there stodgily between my fingertips. It really does smell heavenly, if only I could eat it. I glance up to find James' eyes on me. He smiles. I smile back, and I know it comes off as an awkward smile.

I really need a distraction of some kind.

I begin pulling bits of the croissant off, attempting to project that I'm doing so in an absent-minded manner, placing them casually around my plate as I say, "I know I'm not allowed to thank you anymore," I smile warmly, praying this will lead his thoughts away from the fact I'm not eating, "but I want you know that I really do appreciate all of this, James, everything you're doing for me."

He laughs, pausing to swallow the food in his mouth. "Well I know I'm not supposed to say, 'but you saved my life, Lucyna, it's the least I can do' – but you did and it is."

"I know but I've just come in here and invaded your life." I rest my foot up on the edge of my chair, dropping the remaining part of the croissant back onto the plate.

"Invade away." He looks directly at me, eyes on mine. The air suddenly becomes thick between us. And there it is again, that possibility, the possibility that he maybe just might . . . "I was just rattling around in this big house on my own anyway," he adds, cutting right into my thoughts, removing his eyes from mine.

"Why don't you have a girlfriend?" I ask, keeping my eyes on his face.

He looks back to me and shrugs. "Haven't met the right girl, I guess. I mean I've had a few relationships in my time but none of them ever stuck."

Ignoring the stab of pain I feel at the thought of James and other women, I say, "She'll be out there somewhere, you know, the right girl, probably just waiting for you to notice her." Hinting, wanting to shout out that it's me, Lucyna, the one sitting right in front of you, the one who loves you above all else. Well, okay, maybe I'm not exactly the right girl, but I want to be, so that has to count for something, doesn't it?

"Maybe." He picks his coffee up and takes a long drink, and puts it down, his fingers tapping the handle, eyes firmly fixed on it. "Well, I did think maybe . . ." he trails off, leaving his words hanging in the air.

"You thought what?" I prompt, linking my fingers together around my knee.

His face breaks into a sheepish smile. "Well there was this one girl – from ages ago, who . . . well she was amazing, really great. Different to all the others. And – well for a brief time I thought maybe . . ." He shrugs, fingers now fiddling with the half-eaten croissant in front of him. "But it just wasn't meant to be." His face lifts, a positive smile now firmly adhered to his lips as he adds, "So I've been meaning to tell you that it's my birthday this Friday and I'm having a bit of a party." And once again, just like that, the subject slips away, and this time I'm thankful because the last thing I need to hear about is the one-time almost love of his life. I'm not even sure why I started this conversation off to begin with anyway.

"How old will you be?" I ask.

"Thirty-two."

"Thirty-two," I echo. It's funny I've never even thought before about how old James is. Or should I say how young he is.

"Yeah, I know I'm getting old." He laughs, adding, before putting the remainder of the croissant in his mouth, "How old are you, Lucyna, if you don't mind me asking?"

His question throws me. It's not like I can say well I'm roughly about . . . okay well I don't know exactly how old I am because when you've been around as long as I have you don't really tend to keep count but, put it this way, if you think thirty-two's old then I'm . . . archaic. But seriously, how do I even answer his question? I'm not entirely sure how old I look for a human. So with quick thinking I say the only thing I can think to say, "I'm thirty-two, same as you." I paste a smile on hoping to come across as genuine.

He looks surprised. "You don't look it," he says. "I had you pegged at about twenty-five, twenty-six."

Maybe I should have said that but I guess it's too late now. "Well you look really good," he adds. "Unlike me. Too many days spent out in the sun." He rubs his hand over his face.

"I think you look . . . well – just fine." I keep my opinion brief, withholding my true thoughts that I think he's beautiful beyond belief.

He grins. "Thanks – I think. So what do you think to the party, then?"

"Well . . . I think parties are nice," I nod, not really sure what he's looking for from me.

He does that eyebrow raising grin I've noticed he does a lot around me. "Good, so you'll be here for it, then?"

"I'm invited?"

"Of course you are!" He laughs loudly, eyes amused, and nudges my bare foot under the table with his, skin on skin, sending a thrill running up my leg. "As if I'd have a party and say, right well off you go, then, make yourself scarce for the night. God, you crack me up, Lucyna!" He shakes his head, still laughing.

I can feel my face prickling with embarrassment. I will it not to go red but there's no stopping it, so I look down and set to task shredding the final part of my croissant.

He nudges my foot again, forcing my eyes up to his. "I know you won't know anyone there, but Sara and Neil are coming so there are two friendly faces, and of course there's me."

Well I wouldn't put 'Sara' and 'friendly' in the same sentence. And I don't know why but I instantly felt irked the moment he mentioned her name.

"So are you and Sara getting on okay now, after yesterday?" I ask, trying not to sound as brittle as I feel.

He shrugs. "Well, I haven't spoken to her since then but, yeah, we'll be fine."

"That's good." I stand. "Have you finished?" I waggle my outstretched fingers toward his empty plate.

He looks up at me. "Oh, er, yeah, thanks." He puts the plate in my hand, his fingers grazing against mine. I ignore the sensation it creates and put his and my plate and cup onto the tray.

"Not hungry?" He nods toward my plate that's neatly arranged with shredded croissant.

"Sorry, no." And I ignore the inquiring look he gives as I hasten to make my exit back into the house before he can question me further.

93

Chapter 9

Teardrops

"James?"

He looks up from the bowl he's filling with crisps. His eyes instantly widen in his gaze. "Wow. Look at you. I mean you look . . ." He shakes his head, seemingly lost for words. "You look great – really great."

A feeling of utter bliss trickles through me, setting my skin aglow. I glance down at the dress I'm wearing, the beautiful blue dress that James picked out that day he took me shopping.

"I knew it'd suit you," he adds nodding. "The colour really brings out your eyes." He shakes his head and laughs. "And I also know how incredibly lame that just sounded."

I smooth my hand over the silky fabric. "Not lame – nice. Thanks."

I run my eyes over him, taking in the black v-neck jumper he's wearing down to the dark blue jeans cut up the leg to accommodate his pot, us both dressed in our best clothes ready for his birthday party. "You look – well . . . great too," I add, as my eyes travel back up to his face to find his still on mine and, when they meet, he grins and we both laugh.

But although we're laughing, I know it's forced, manufactured in some way, because if truth be told things have been – well strange between us for the last few days, and I'm not really sure just when, or why, it started – I simply all of a sudden realised.

I can't even put my finger on exactly what it is that's changed because, on the surface, we talk as normal and spend time together as normal. Everything as normal. But underneath all the normality there's an obvious layer of tension. The air between us is so thick and dense, I'm sure if I just reached out and poked at it with my finger, I'd make a dent. I have no idea where it's come from or how to make it go away.

I've wanted to say something to him, wanted to ask him if he feels it too, but every time I've attempted to do so, something's stopped me, held me back.

"Is there anything else that needs doing?" I ask, knowing there probably isn't as I helped him prepare earlier - well I mainly did the shopping for the food and alcohol.

He shakes his head as he rips open a bag of peanuts with his teeth and pours them into a waiting bowl. "Nope, all sorted." He picks some peanuts out of the bowl and pops them in his mouth.

I lean against the edge of the kitchen cupboard, arm resting on the cool marble surface. Our eyes meet. I look away, suddenly feeling jittery, and the only sound in the room is the crunch, crunch of the nuts as he chews them.

Like I said, things are – strange.

At that moment, thankfully, the doorbell rings.

He looks past me toward the hallway. "I'll get that." He throws the empty peanut wrapper into the bin on his way and brushes past me heading through the door, his arm stroking mine, setting off such a combustible amount of heat and energy surging through me that it nearly knocks me off my feet. I curl my fingers around the edge of the work surface to steady myself and glance down at my bare arm, feeling sure for a moment there that my skin was actually on fire.

James introduces me to his friends – Jack, Lewis and Anna. As I discover, James plays Sunday football with Jack and Lewis, and Anna is Lewis's girlfriend – or a football widow as she puts it. We all make our way out into the garden as it's such a warm summers evening, and it's not long before more people arrive and the garden is buzzing with the sound of music and chatter.

I'm stood lingering near the rosebushes, holding a half empty glass of wine pretending to drink it, when Neil comes through the back door with a bottle of beer in his hand. I had been talking with Anna but she went off to use the bathroom.

He smiles widely when he sees me. "Hey, Lucyna, nice to see you again. So how's our lifesaver doing?" He walks over to me, covering the gap in a few strides.

"I'm really well, thanks. How are you?"

"Yeah, I'm good, ta." He takes a swig of beer. "How you finding it living here with James? He as much a slave driver at home as he is at work?" He grins, brushing his blonde hair out of his eyes.

I shake my head and smile up at him. "No, James is really great to live with."

We fall silent. I glance down at my wine glass. Neil takes another drink of his beer. "So whereabouts is it you're originally from then, Lucyna?" he asks, and puts the bottle back to his lips, this time taking a long drink, all the while keeping his friendly blue eyes on mine.

I smile, pressing my lips together, attempting to conceal the dismay I feel when the dulcet tones of James' voice come from behind me, blanketing me with their warmth. "Ignore everything he says, 'cause whatever he's telling you, it's probably a lie." He laughs, resting his arm loosely around my shoulders. My whole body stiffens. I glance up at him to see him smiling, eyes moving between me and Neil. "You're not trying your crap one liners out on her are you, mate?" he says dryly, eyes now on Neil.

"Only the ones you taught me," Neil banters back, eyebrow raised, pushing his tongue between his teeth.

"You got me there, mate. I've got no come back," James raises his hand in mock surrender and takes a drink from the bottle of beer in his other hand.

"Hey, do you remember that one you used on that girl when you, me and Sonny were in Ibiza," he says to Neil, as his hand rests back on my shoulder, fingers lightly trailing over my bare skin. My whole body instantly responds to his touch. I tighten my grip around the glass. "It was hilarious," he says to me. "Casanova here went up to this girl in the bar we were in and said 'We're not gonna be able to have sex if you're sober', handed her over the half full bottle of tequila we'd been drinking and said 'You're gonna have to catch me up – drink this, then call me when you're ready.' James laughs, louder this time. "It was fucking hilarious! And the worse thing was it bloody worked as well!"

Neil shrugs, lips pursed, eyes twinkling. "What can I say, I'm a charmer. The ladies just can't say no." He grins, eyes fixed on me. James' hand grips my shoulder harder.

"James?" We all turn at the sound of Sara's voice. I can see her eyes resting on James' arm, the one sitting around my shoulder.

"Hey," he smiles at her, removing his arm from around me. And I know the disappointment is obvious on my face, so I look away hoping no-one noticed.

A smile appears on her face as she quickly moves toward him. "Happy birthday," she says, kissing his cheek. And I stand there beside Neil feeling like I've just been hit.

"I brought you this." She pushes a small gift into his hand.

He looks down at it. "You didn't have to."

"As if I wouldn't." She smiles, tapping him lightly on the arm.

And I inwardly cringe at the realisation. A gift, of course it's customary for humans to give one another gifts on their birthdays and what did I get him? Absolutely nothing.

"Hi Neil," she says sweetly. "Lucyna." Her tone hardens on my name.

Both Neil and I say our hellos but Sara's already turned her attention back to James. "So you gonna get me a drink, or what?" she says, hand on hip. "Some host you are." She laughs but I can hear the edge to it.

"Oh, yeah, 'course." He turns to me and Neil. "Either of you need a top up?"

I glance down at my half full glass of wine and shake my head.

"Don't worry about me mate," Neil says swilling the remaining liquid around the bottle. "I'll get myself a cold one out the fridge in a min."

Sara links her arm through his and starts to walk away but James doesn't move. I see out of the corner of my eye that his eyes are on me.

She pulls on his arm and rolls her eyes dramatically. "Come on, I'm gonna die of thirst here." She laughs again, trying to sound light-hearted but now there's too clear an edge for it to go unnoticed.

"I'll catch you both later, then." He turns and lets himself be led off by Sara toward the table where all the bottles of wine and spirits are.

"It always surprises me them two have never got together." Neil's voice comes from beside me, suddenly sounding closer.

"Who?" I ask, even though I know full well who he means.

"James and Sara," he says in an obvious tone. "I think they'd make a good couple."

"Hmm, yes," I say, non-committal, unable to say anything else because now all I feel is edgy. I look over at the two of them and, at that same moment, James looks in my direction and catches me staring at him. I look away.

Neil leans closer to me, his arm pressing against mine. "I think Sara would like it that way as well," he says in a conspiratorial tone.

I look up at him to find him considerably closer than I'd realised. "Has she said this to you?" I ensure my voice comes out lighter than I currently feel.

His blue eyes pierce mine. He shakes his head. "Nah, I can just tell. She dotes on him."

I glance at them again from the corner of my eye. James has just said something to Sara and she's laughing loudly, head thrown back, her hand on his chest. My skin is prickling with discomfort. "Do you think James feels the same?" I ask, maintaining the same light tone.

He drains his bottle and shrugs. "Dunno. He says they're just mates, but who knows. To be honest I don't know why he wouldn't. She's a real nice girl and pretty to boot – but I suppose they have been mates forever, so maybe he doesn't want to spoil it. And it's not like he's ever been able to stick with one girl for too long." He smirks. "He gets itchy feet, does our James."

Then it's almost like I see what Neil sees and the world closes off, and all I'm aware of is this insistent buzzing in my head. Almost as if all my thoughts have just come to life at one.

"Can you excuse me," I say, barely managing the words. "I just need to use the ladies' room."

"Yeah, no worries, was gonna go grab myself a bottle anyway."

Neil follows me into the house and I just concentrate on putting one foot in front of the other, then we split off in different directions, him to the kitchen, me to the downstairs bathroom.

I lock the door behind me, rest my forehead against the cool glass, close my eyes and try to line up my thoughts into an orderly manner.

What am I doing here? Hoping against hope that James might one day love me whilst I carry on pretending to be human, when all I really am is a fraud, a walking, talking lie? And now, as I've just discovered, my only reason for being here is quite possibly a philanderer – and one very likely to end up with Sara which, if I'm being truthful with myself, is the way it should be.

The absurdity of it all actually makes me laugh out loud. But it's a laugh tinged with sadness. For all I really feel is hurt and confused. Because to want something so badly as I want James, and to know I'll never have him, is causing an actual physical ache inside me, and I truly wonder what I've done to deserve this kind of torture.

My head is throbbing with the pain. I grip my fingers tight around the basin.

I want to go home, go back to where it was simpler, back to when I didn't have to feel any of this - where I was happy. Okay, well I wasn't happy because I didn't know what happiness was but I must have been content in some way.

It's funny, all this time I've spent worrying about how long it will be before the Elders find me and praying they won't, and now I just wish they would. Because no matter how I may feel, no matter how much it hurts, I know I'll never be able to leave him of my own accord. The only time I'll ever go is when they take me, or James definitively tells me to.

I hear the handle try on the door, then a knock. "You gonna be long in there?" comes a woman's voice from the other side of the door

I open my eyes and move my head back. "No, I'm all done," I say to the mirror.

I unlock the door and open it to reveal a woman with red hair who I met earlier but whose name I've now forgotten. "Thanks, hon," she says, bouncing on the spot. "I'm absolutely busting." She rushes past me into the toilet, closing the door behind her.

Putting a smile on my face, I venture back into the party even though I feel like I'm dying inside.

I spend the rest of the night avoiding James and desperately trying, albeit not successfully, to not look at him or anywhere in his vicinity, which is not such an easy feet, especially in such a small space. But then he hasn't come to talk to me either, or looked in my direction that I've seen. I'm trying to ignore the fact, knowing that his time has been mainly consumed by Sara and his other guests. Well, Sara mainly. So I've spent most of the night talking to Neil who seemed happy enough to keep me company.

Finally finding myself alone, I go into the kitchen to rid myself of this hours-old wine. I watch as it paints the running water with its golden honey like colour. I put the glass down on the drainer and turn around to find Sara stood in the doorway eyeing me closely.

"Hi," I say in the most pleasant voice I can muster when I feel anything but.

Without speaking, she closes the door behind her and moves into the room, leaning forward onto the free-standing island. She begins tapping her long pink nails on the marble counter. "Look, Lucyna, I won't beat about the bush here. We're both intelligent women and I think you'd appreciate my honesty, as I would yours."

This time I'm the one who doesn't speak. Her prickly tone is sitting distinctly uncomfortable. I wrap my arms around myself.

"Okay so you've probably guessed I don't like you," she continues when she sees I have no intention of responding. "I think you know why. And I don't know what your game is with James, but he's been through a lot recently and doesn't need someone like you messing with him."

"I don't know what you mean," I say, my voice oddly coming out sounding hoarse.

She sneers. "Yes, you do. You're after something and I want you to tell me what it is."

"I'm not after anything." Well aside from James' love – but I omit that from my sentence, knowing that wouldn't go down well.

She stands upright, hands on her hips. "I know you are. I can tell. I've met your type before. Its money, isn't it?" she says with bite. "That's what you're after. I mean, come on, you and I both know that James is pretty well off."

I open my mouth to speak but no sound comes out.

"I mean, yeah, you saved his life and we're all grateful, really. But then apparently you have nowhere to live and James being James offers you a place to stay because he feels obliged to, then you just rock on up here and walk about like you own the place." She runs her fingers through her smooth blonde hair. "I certainly can't imagine anyone like you being homeless for starters and, yeah, I think you probably do fancy

James because, well, you'd have to be blind not to. But there's something more here, something not right about you, something that doesn't sit right about this whole situation. I don't know what, but I'm gonna find out."

There's this strange feeling stirring deep inside me that's quickly bubbling to the surface, rushing up fast. My face is tingling, my throat constricting and my lips are trembling.

"Did you find out that he'd come into a lot of money after the death of his dad. I mean the business alone is worth quite a bit and this house –" she gestures around, "-well it's not exactly a two up two down in Brixton, is it?" Her eyes narrow onto me. "Did you think you'd target a rich, unhappy guy who'd just lost his dad, seeing him as an easy target and get all you could from him?"

Really she couldn't be further from the truth. If only she did know.

"I don't want James' money." My voice sounds thick and wobbly.

She laughs caustically. "Well for someone who doesn't want his money, you've done a pretty good job of spending it so far." She points a long nail at my dress, trailing the length of it.

I glance down at it. Then my eyes blur and I feel water trickling down my cheek. I touch my fingertips to my face. There's water coming from my eyes.

I'm crying.

"Oh god, don't start the waterworks," she says callously. "I'm not James. Tears won't work on me."

I look down at my hand to see the tears running carelessly down my fingers.

So this is how it feels to cry. Funny, really, that Sara's the one who manages to make me cry for the first time, the one whom I vie with for James' affections. Quite poetic really.

She's glaring at me with utter impatience, her foot tapping against the wooden floor. I find my voice and, even though it's weak, I manage to get out, "No, Sara. You've got it all wrong. Really I don't -"

"Come on, I'm not stupid," she chides, sweeping her blonde hair off her face, in that one motion managing to make me feel like I imagine a child might, even though I'm years - far beyond her imagination – older than she is. "If it's money you're after, I'll give you some and you can be on your merry way and leave James the fuck alone. How much will it take to get rid of –"

"What the fuck are you doing?" I jump at the sound of his James' fury and my eyes snap up to see him stood in the doorway.

Sara spins around at the sound of his voice. He looks angry, really angry, and Neil is stood behind him looking really uncomfortable.

"Jesus Christ, Sara, what is with you," James says, frustrated. "It's all I hear from you at the moment. Just what the fuck have you got against her?"

My eyes dart between James and Sara who has now sidled around the island putting a bit of distance between her and James. I really don't want to here, to be part of this. I want to move, get away but I can't, I'm rooted to the spot.

"She's just using you James, can't you see that?" she says, face red, voice slightly unhinged.

"She's not using me, you idiot. She's just living in my house and, really, what the fuck has any of this got to do with you?"

"What has this got to do with me?" Her eyes widen and she grips her head in frustration. "It's got everything to do with me! You're my best friend, you're like my family and I won't stand by and watch this little bitch bleed you dry because you're blinded by a pretty face!"

"What the fuck!" He shakes his head with disbelief. "I just don't fucking believe you! She. Saved. My. Life." He enunciates every word, singly and distinctly. "What is it that you don't get about that? I owe her everything! I'd be dead if it wasn't for her! She pulled me from a burning car, risked her own life to save me! I'd give her a fucking million quid if I could! So trust me, giving her a roof to live under until she gets back on her feet doesn't seem that big a deal!"

"But you don't know anything about her –"

"I know enough." His voice comes out as sharp as a knife.

I see the tears welling in her eyes that she's furiously blinking back. That's also when I notice a few people standing behind Neil, obviously hearing the commotion, come to watch the show, a show I do not want to be a part of.

My legs finally obey the commands my brain is giving them. I take a side step edging toward the door. "I'll go."

"No, Lucyna. Stay where you are." James points me to the spot. And yet again I freeze. "You're not the one who should be leaving," he says forcibly, eyes narrowed and fixed on Sara.

"I don't believe this!" she cries. "You're choosing her over me."

"There was never a choice," he says coolly.

I see her flinch as his words hit her, and honestly the level of hostility in his voice takes me by surprise too.

Neil sidles past James heading straight for Sara. "Come on, Sara, I'll take you home." He puts his arm around her shoulder and steers her away. "We've all had a bit too much to drink. Talk about it tomorrow when you're sober."

As they both move past where I still stand, Sara's eyes dart over at me, giving me a parting look of such anger, such resentment, it blankets my skin with a chill.

James comes over to me now everyone's left the kitchen and places his hands on my shoulders, his fingers gently gripping me. My skin burns under his touch. "I'm so sorry. I don't know what's got into her. She shouldn't have spoke to you like that."

"It's fine." My voice comes out a shaky whisper.

"No, it's not. You don't deserve this." He wipes away the teardrops that have once again started to cascade down my cheek with his thumb, his hand encompassing my face. His thumb traces down my jaw, lightly brushing over my lips. I glance up at him. His eyes are on my lips, lips that want the feel of his on mine. His eyes move up to mine, dark pools that are now flickering and flaming, and I couldn't move even if I wanted to. There's something in the way he's looking at me that makes my legs feel wobbly, that look eliciting all those feelings for him I've hidden, all quickly bubbling up to the surface.

My skin is prickling with desire. He holds my face in both his hands, his fingers tenderly invading my hair, eyes set on mine, unwavering, as he leans closer to me, my eyes closing in anticipation . . .

"Oh, sorry, mate."

James instantly steps away from me, turning to the sound of the voice. My body wilts with disappointment. I look past him to see Joe, one of the men that works for him, stood in the doorway.

Joe looks uncomfortable, about as uncomfortable as I feel when I notice the three other people hovering behind him, my cheeks instantly colouring as to the size of our audience.

"Sorry to interrupt, just –" Joe thumbs over his shoulder at the others, "-well we're – er – well we're gonna head off."

"Oh right, yeah, no problem, mate. I'll see you out," James says. He glances back at me, his look unfathomable. Then he's turns and leads his friends out the door.

And I'm left there feeling alone, and very, very confused.

Chapter 10

Starry Eyed

James hasn't said anything about the almost-kiss and neither have I. Well truthfully we've barely spoken to each other since.

Not long after Joe and the others left, the other party guests pretty much followed suit and the party soon dwindled to a close.

Now it's just me and James left cleaning up the debris in complete and utter silence.

And the tense atmosphere is back, with a vengeance, almost as if whatever's been brewing in the air for the last few days has now hit boiling point.

James drops a bag of rubbish into the bin with a clang and then, taking some time to do so struggling with his leg, awkwardly sits himself down on the blanket that's laid out on the grass. He rests back on his hands, legs stretched out in front of him and looks over at me.

"So, did you have a good night?" he asks, voice normal, as though nothing nearly happened between us just under an hour ago, making me momentarily wonder if I imagined it. "Well apart from when Sara flipped out on you, that is," he adds.

I refrain from thanking him for the reminder, and skipping over the addition, I say, "Yes. I had a really lovely time. Your friends are all very nice."

"Apart from Sara."

I look down and shuffle on my feet.

He laughs. "It's okay, you don't have to like her. I wouldn't if I was you."

I take a moment to process my feelings. "I don't dislike her. I think I'm just confused by her."

He laughs again. "That's a nice way to put it. A hell of a lot nicer than I would have." He rubs his forehead and pushes his fingers into his hair. "I just don't know what's with her at the moment? Why she's got it in for you?"

I drop my bag in the bin and go sit beside him, crossing my legs in front of me, and rest back on my hands. "Does it make you sad?"

He turns his head to me, gaze fixed on mine. "It only makes me sad because she's hurting you."

"I'm fine."

"I wouldn't be if someone said those things to me."

I shrug because right now all I can think about is how close my hand is to his. Really close. I could literally just reach out my finger and touch him. And with all these intense feelings floating around me, it's very hard to resist the urge to do so.

James shuffles his position and his fingers lightly stroke against my hand. My skin prickles. He doesn't move them away.

"And just for the record," he says, voice deep and sure, "I don't think a word of those things she said is the truth. I don't believe you're after my money." He nudges my arm with his. I look at him to see he's now grinning. "Not that I have as much as she seems to think I do. It's not like I'm a millionaire or anything."

"It wouldn't matter to me if you were."

He rests his chin on his shoulder, regarding me closely, eyes curious. And my whole body shivers, though I'm not cold. "I've never met anyone like you, Lucyna. You don't seem to care about money or material things. You just seem so . . . relaxed with who you are. "

"Is that wrong?"

He shakes his head, smiling. "No, it's refreshing."

He rests his head back and gazes up at the night sky and I follow his gaze. The stars are out in force tonight, twinkling down on us, leaving me feeling very starry-eyed, or maybe that's just from the effect his touch is having on me.

James's quietly shuffles closer to me and lays his fingers over mine, gently gripping them with his. He's practically holding my hand and all my thoughts have gone fuzzy.

In attempt to clear my mind I say, "James, I wanted to say I'm sorry I didn't get you a gift for your birthday —"

He waves me away with his free hand. "Don't be stupid. I know you're not in a position to be buying me stuff – and I don't need anything anyway."

"I know but still . . ." My voice peters off.

We lapse into silence.

"I'm sorry we didn't get to talk much at the party," he says. "I didn't seem to get a minute to myself. But I saw that Neil kept you company."

"Yeah, he's nice," I say struggling to concentrate as he now traces his fingertip in concentric circles across my hand.

"Yeah, Neil's a good bloke . . . so what did you guys talk about?" he asks, his voice suddenly quieter.

And Neil's words come flooding back to me. I press my lips together, suddenly feeling nervous, anxious, tempted . . .

"James, why aren't you and Sara together like a couple?" I blurt out. I honestly have no idea where I'm going with this line of questioning.

He sits up, his hand moving from mine. "What makes you ask that?"

Keeping my eyes straight ahead, I say, "Just when I was talking to Neil earlier he said that he thought you two, I mean you and Sara, should be together as a couple, and I thought well . . . maybe he was right."

He shakes his head. "Sara's my friend – well she's skirting on pretty thin ice at the moment, but still, I'd never see her as anything more."

"But she's very beautiful and –"

"I'm not interested in Sara," he cuts me off, his insistent tone forcing me to turn to him. His serious eyes roam my face and he leans closer to me. He's so close I can feel his hot breath on my skin. And for a moment I'm transcendent. Then his voice, the only sound in this still night, says, "I'll never be interested in Sara because I'm only interested in you."

Then he leans forward and kisses me and nothing else matters.

His lips touch mine, so gently at first, but then very quickly the kiss intensifies. His stubble grazes against my face sending shivers rippling through me, the heady scent of his aftershave intoxicating me. This is beyond amazing, so beyond anything I could have ever dreamt up. All I feel is complete and utter euphoria. Then like a bolt out of the blue, I suddenly get a sense of familiarity. Like I've done this before. With him. Which is obviously impossible. It must be all my dreaming and wishing that's caused a sense of déjà vu.

Then, without warning, James breaks away leaving me cold. He moves back from me breathing heavily. My lips are throbbing and I'm so charged, so heated, I can't form words.

"I'm sorry, I shouldn't have done that," he says, breathing hard.

And just like that the atmosphere has disintegrated, the happiness of the moment snatched away from me.

"You're sorry you kissed me?" My voice sounds unnaturally high.

"No! Well yes – I mean no. I mean – I don't know what I mean." He shakes his head, and glances up at me through his lashes. "I wasn't sure if you would want me to . . . I thought maybe you might but –"

"Did my reaction not tell you I did?"

"Yeah I guess so . . . I just –"

"You just?"

He brings his knee up to his chest, wrapping his arms around his leg and rests his chin on it. "Look, Lucyna, I know you said the other day that you still love your ex, and I also know I was the one who just kissed you – but I really don't want to come in the middle of something, because when we spoke it sounded like you had unfinished business with – your ex, and well if we started something and then you decided to get back with him then –" He shrugs, eyes away from me.

Oh no.

I didn't even consider how he would interpret my words. How could I be so stupid? How on earth am I going to get around this?

Of course I want to tell him the truth. I want to tell him he is the guy, that he is the only reason I feel love, the only guy that I ever have – and ever will love. But how do I manage that without telling him the rest, without telling him I've lied about everything.

I look down at my hands as though they can somehow help me, whilst desperately trying to search for the right words. "James, I –"

But he cuts me off before I can even make an attempt. "No, it's fine, Lucyna. You don't need to say anything." He tries to get up but struggles, so in the end I help him to his feet.

He stands before me, affliction in his dark, brooding eyes. "Seriously, I get it. It's fine. And it doesn't change anything about you living here, honestly. Look, I'm tired, I'm gonna go to bed," he adds, before walking away. "Don't worry about the rest of the mess. I'll sort it in the morning."

I stare after him, watching as the light at the end of the tunnel dims, flickers, then goes out completely, wondering just exactly how I went from complete euphoria to complete misery in the space of five minutes.

Chapter 11

All The Time In The World

Two minutes later, and I'm still stood here in the garden on the same spot where James left me, still feeling the wake of his departure, still trying to fathom what just actually happened.

It's at times like these when I see why we Bringers aren't supposed to feel. There would be no way we would cope with death in the manner we have to when feelings are so complex, so intense, so imperious . . . so raw.

Everything insistent. Everything urgent.

Emotions discharge like rockets, change course and then change again within a matter of seconds and, honestly, I struggle to keep up. My head feels like it's spinning on my shoulders.

The only thing I can register right now, which thankfully is the most important thing, is that James has feelings for me. And these are not just feelings of friendship or because I saved his life, but they are *those* kinds of feelings, the feelings I have for him.

Actual, real, one hundred percent feelings. For me.

My whole body is tingling in the knowledge and I would be jumping up and down on the spot with elation if it wasn't for the fact that things aren't exactly turning out as I would like.

Because James thinks I love someone else, this being purely down to my idiotic way of trying to subtly tell him that I'm in love him.

It would be funny if it wasn't so tragically ironic for me.

'He gets it,' he said. I wanted tell him that he really doesn't get it, that he's so far from getting it he may as well be on a different continent. I wanted to tell him that I have spent the last four weeks dreaming that he would feel this way about me, dreaming that he would kiss me.

But I didn't because I can't.

I put fingers to my lips to the place where I can still feel his kiss.

I have to correct my mistake in some way. I don't know exactly how or what I'm going to say to him, but I'm sure the right words will come when I need them to. I'm so adept at lying now and, really, what's another one to add to my ever-growing collection.

Before I know it I'm stood outside his bedroom door. The lights are out in his room and all is quiet. Nerves ripple through me.

I lift my hand to knock on his door. Nerves withdraw my hand. Maybe he doesn't want to talk to me. I take a step back.

No, I've come too far, given up to much, to just chicken out, especially when I'm so close to having my dream, so close to having him.

I lift my hand and quickly knock on the door before I can change my mind.

"Come in," James's deep voice comes from the other side.

I push the door open. He's sat up in bed, duvet covering his legs, his chest bare, back resting against the headboard, the room now aglow with the light emitting from the lamp on his bedside table.

"Hi," I say quietly.

He pushes his fingers through his hair. "Hey."

I close the door behind me, and linger there. I never felt so nervous since, well . . . since I started feeling. I clasp my hands together and stare at the wooden floor that sits cold beneath my bare feet.

It's so silent in the room, neither of us speaking, and I know I should be the one to speak, but I can't find my voice. Then, oddly, I realise this is the first time I've been in his bedroom since I changed form.

"Are you okay?" His warm voice caresses me.

I shake my head and glance up meeting his dark eyes. "No, not really." I wrap my arms around myself. "Are you?"

"Nope." His lips curve ever so slightly. "Come here." He pats the space on the bed beside him.

Nervously I go and sit down.

"I'm sorry if I've complicated things between us," he says regretfully.

My eyes flick up at him. "You haven't complicated things. If anything, I have."

He shakes his head ruefully. "No, you haven't. I knew how things stood with you and your ex and I shouldn't have kissed you. But I just

111

couldn't help myself – and, honestly, I've been really trying not to act on how I feel – but it's just tonight you looked so . . ." He sighs and rests his head back against the headboard. "And then when you were talking to Neil, I guess I . . ." He glances over at me, his expression forlorn. "Look, Lucyna, I like you –" He rubs his hand over his face. "– a lot."

He likes me. A lot. Maybe it's not exactly the three words I want him to say but it's a start. A very good start.

"But –" he adds, and my theoretical heart sinks. He's looking anywhere now, but at me.

I take hold of his hand. He glances at me, eyes a mosaic of emotions and I hold his gaze.

"You've got it all wrong, James. I don't love my ex in that way. I love him purely platonically because he meant something to me once, but I don't feel about him anymore – in the way I feel for you." Where is this stuff coming from? Well honestly I don't care as long as it works. "James, I like–" *love* "– you too. A lot. And I'm never going to get back with my ex. I'm only interested in you. I want to be with you."

His fingers curl around my hand and for a moment we just sit eyes locked together, neither of us speaking.

"Okay," he finally says. "So what now?"

And that's when I know my words have worked. I twist my lips together suppressing the enormous smile I feel. "Well I was kind of hoping you'd kiss me again."

He grins, reaches over and plunges his fingers deep into my hair, pulling my face to his. He kisses me, so intensely, so passionately, that my whole body trembles.

When he finally releases me, I feel light, like I'm floating on air.

He smiles at me and I smile back. Then he runs his fingers between mine, gripping hold of my hand again, bringing it to his mouth, pressing it to his lips, resting our entwined hands against his bare chest.

I glance down at our hands, my eyes lingering on his chest. When I drag my eyes back up to his face, his are still on mine.

"Do you wanna stay in here with me tonight?" he suggests, and I'm assuming it's the look on my face that prompts him to add, "No funny business, I promise. I'll keep my hands to myself." He looks at me seriously but he's unable to hide the twinkle in his eye.

I quickly consider my options. A night alone in my room wiling away the hours, or a night in here with James?

Hmm, let me think . . .

"Sure," I say.

He grins sheepishly, his face suddenly colouring. "Er . . . I'm kinda naked under here. You mind passing me those boxers?" He points to a pair of black boxer shorts hanging over the edge of his laundry basket.

My face instantly flames. "Of course."

I retrieve them for him and look away, giving him some privacy whilst he struggles to get them on under the duvet; assumedly his pot is causing him problems. I'd offer to help but it really doesn't seem appropriate.

"All done," he says after what seems a long time, sounding somewhat breathless.

I turn to see he's moved over to make room for me and is holding the duvet back.

I climb in beside him. His body is so warm. He lays the cover over me, and reaches over and switches the lamp off, plunging us into darkness.

I turn onto my side, facing him. James stays on his back but turns his head towards me.

"How many women have you had?" What is wrong with me? Why do I keep blurting these clumsy questions out at him?

A snort of laughter comes from him. "What makes you ask that?" he says, still laughing, but I can hear the surprise in his voice.

And I'm truly thankful it's dark in here, so he can't see just how red my face has gone.

"Nothing. It doesn't matter," I mumble, embarrassed. I turn my head burying it into the pillow, realising where that question's come from. Neil's words have been playing on a constant loop in my mind ever since he uttered them to me earlier.

He strokes my arm with his finger. "You wouldn't have asked if it didn't."

I lift my face up and push my hair back. Then, feeling like a broken

113

record, I say, "It's just Neil said, well kind of implied, that you'd had a lot of women – that you were a womaniser – I think."

"The little shit." He laughs. "He'll be lucky if he still has a job on Monday." He cups my chin and brings his face closer to mine. His eyes are glowing at me in the dark. "He was having you on, Luce." His voice sounds more intense, more serious. "I'm guessing to lead you away from me and straight to him. Trust me, I'm not a womaniser. I've had a fair few women in my time, don't get me wrong, but I'm certainly no womaniser."

"Luce?" I say with surprise, suddenly distracted.

He runs his hand down my neck and over my shoulder. "You don't mind if I call you that, do you?" He leans over and presses his lips to mine.

"No," I murmur, our lips touching.

He takes a deep breath. "I know I should have said this earlier but you looked – look incredibly beautiful tonight."

Beautiful. James thinks I'm beautiful.

"You think I look beautiful?"

"I always think you look beautiful." He kisses my forehead, my cheek, my jaw. "I've wanted you from the very first moment I saw you," he groans, voice low as he kisses my neck.

I don't say anything, mainly because I can't. I'm so overawed by what's happening right here, right now. Things only my dreams were made of.

His lips find mine again. At first he kisses me slowly, then more passionately. My body is heating, responding to his touch. His hands go around my waist and he pulls me on top of him. A bolt of desire shoots through me. Our bodies are pressed together, his pot coarse against the bare skin on my leg, but I don't care. His hands are on my back, slowly moving lower, as he devours me with his lips. I put my hands on his bare chest. I can feel his fingers inching my dress up.

Then suddenly he brings his hands up to my face, cupping it and gently pushes me back, away from him.

He closes his eyes and takes a few deep breaths, whilst I look on at him in confusion, my lips throbbing, my body aching.

He blows out a final breath, opens his eyes, a serious expression now on his face. "Getting a bit carried away there. But I promised you no funny business and I meant it." He tips the end of my nose with his finger. "We've got all the time in the world for that."

I lay down beside him, disappointed, but knowing he's right, even if his reasoning is far different from mine.

Because no matter how badly I may want him, I know it's not right. Not when he doesn't really know me.

He slides his arm under my shoulder and pulls me closer. I rest my head on his warm chest and listen to his heart beating.

But even the warmth of his body and the comforting thump of his heart can't take away the chilling effect his words have left on me.

'We've got all the time in the world.'

If only we did.

Chapter 12

Guardian Angel

"Are you happy?"

James regards me with his intense brown eyes, his lips curving into a heartbreaking smile. "Of course I am," he says. "How could I not be when I'm with you?" The smile suddenly drops from his face. "You're happy aren't you – with me?"

"Of course," I beam. "I've never been so happy."

It's early Sunday morning, a few days since we first kissed. We're laid in his bed. And no, it's not how it sounds. We haven't done that. All we've done is talk – in-between all the kissing, that is.

James hasn't attempted to move things any further which I'm pretty relieved about. I'm fairly sure he would like to but I know he's been respectful. And it's not like I don't want to have sex with him because if it's anything like the kissing, well . . . let's just say if it is then I most definitely want to.

But I also know it wouldn't be right. How could we make love when he doesn't even know who I truly am.

It's bad enough how much I deceive him already, but really, that would be just taking it to the extreme.

I know I'm running out of time. He is going to want to have sex soon. It's only natural. And I have absolutely no idea what I'm going to do or say when the time does finally arrive.

"I love this, you know," he says trailing his fingers across the exposed skin on my back where my vest has ridden up, "waking up beside you every day."

"Me too." I smile warmly.

"Here's a thought," he says moving closer to me. "Let's just stay in bed forever, never get up, just the two of us cocooned here in our own little world. We could get takeaway delivered three times a day . . . obviously you'd have to get out of bed to go get it from the front door." He grins.

If only he knew how much I wish that could be true. But instead of saying the truth, I just laugh and say, "You'd go stir crazy stuck inside."

"Not if I had you to keep me company." He kisses the bare skin on my shoulder, his two day old stubble scratching against me.

"Okay then, I'd go stir-crazy," I smirk.

"Nice," he mock chides. "Looks like I'm gonna have to hold you hostage in here with me, then." He laughs and lays back, arms folded behind his head, eyes on the ceiling. "I'm not letting you get away, Luce."

And I say nothing.

Because I know one day soon I will have to go and there will be nothing either of us can do about it.

I prop myself up on my elbow and put my hand on his face, our skin so different in contrast. His dark, mine light. He glances at me and closes his eyes. I run my finger over the scar on his eyebrow. "How did you get this?" I ask

He opens his eyes. "The scar?"

I nod.

"I did it when I was seven. I was going through my superman phase and I told my mate Carl that I could fly just like the man himself. He said I was a liar – which obviously I was." He smirks. "And, well, Carl said he'd only believe me if I showed him. He dared me." He glances at me, eyes amused, and shrugs. "Well, it wasn't like I could back down even if I was totally shitting myself."

I touch the scar again. "I take it it didn't go so well."

"You could say that." He laughs, his expression soft. "I went for it, though, put my superman cape on and everything. You'd have been impressed. I got up on our extension roof, nearly puked a few times when I saw the drop," he laughs, "somehow managed to contain myself, and after a few deep breaths, I just closed my eyes and went for it."

I sit up aghast. "I can't believe you tried to fly."

He stares up at the ceiling and laughs.

"So . . . what happened?" I ask tentatively, lying back down on my front propping myself up on my elbows.

117

He grins sideways at me. "Well, I didn't fly, obviously. I just kinda dropped and landed right on Carl's bike which was sitting directly below. I was lucky it was there 'cause it broke my fall. Carl wasn't so chuffed – I broke his bike." He lifts his right arm up. "Broke my arm in a couple of places and cut my head open. Hence the scar."

"You could have died."

He widens his eyes in mock-seriousness and chuckles. "You look so cute when you're concerned." He runs his fingertip down my nose.

I bat his arm away. "It's not funny."

He catches hold of my hand and lifts it to his lips and kisses my fingertips.

"Sorry." He tries to say it soberly but I can still hear the snigger in his voice. "That's what my dad said – not sorry, that I could have died – well amongst many other things." He presses his lips together, stifling a grin, knowing I'm not in the mood. "The doctor said I'd been incredibly lucky, said I must have a guardian angel watching over me."

I look down at the bed sheet as though it's suddenly the most interesting thing I've ever seen.

"Maybe the quack was right," he says emphatically. "I mean think about it, Luce, that's two pretty serious scrapes I've survived now. Shame you hadn't been there to save me back then, though, inside of Carl's bike."

I don't say anything.

"Hey, what's wrong?" he asks, seeing my expression. He chucks my chin with his finger but I don't look up.

"Have I upset you?" he asks, voice soft.

I lift my head up and find myself gazing straight into the depths of eyes. "I just don't want anything bad to happen to you."

He wraps his arms around me, pulling me closer. I rest my head on his chest. "It won't," he says earnestly, kissing the top of my head, "especially not whilst I've got my very own guardian angel around keeping me safe."

I close my eyes, concealing the truth in them.

"God, I'm starving." He stretches his long, lean body out obviously done with the conversation. "You want some breakfast?"

"No, I'm okay thanks."

He shuffles down the bed, forcing me off him so we're laid face to face. "You're not hungry, eh?" He raises an eyebrow. "No surprise there, then."

"What's that supposed to mean?"

"It means you never eat."

Okay so now I wish I'd never asked. "Yes, I do."

"No, you don't."

I sit up. "Yes. I. Do."

"No. You. Don't."

"I DO!" I yell, wide eyed with exasperation, even though he's right, I don't.

He shuffles up the bed, resting up against the headboard and rubs his hand over his face.

We both sit in a stony silence.

Then finally he says in calm voice, "Luce, you can talk to me, you know. About anything. I won't judge."

"I know."

He looks at me expectantly.

"What?" I say.

"So go on, then." He gestures with his hand. "Talk."

"There's nothing I need to talk about."

He sighs loudly, eyes fixed on me and shakes his head. "Do you have an eating disorder?" he asks bluntly.

"What?" A burst of laughter explodes from me. It quickly dies out when I realise from the look on his face that he's not joking. And now he looks kind of annoyed.

"I don't have an eating disorder, James."

"But you never eat."

"I do."

"You don't.

I shake my head and look away, refusing to get dragged into this again.

"Look it doesn't matter to me if you do," he says voice softer. "I just want to help."

And for a moment I actually consider just saying I have, at least it's a way to explain why I don't eat, but then, knowing James, he'd watch me even more hawk-like than he obviously already is, trying to ensure I eat. And when I don't, because I can't, the questions I'd have to face would be far worse.

I look directly at him, face as serious as I can muster. "James, I don't have an eating disorder."

He frowns, eyeing me suspiciously then his gaze suddenly softens. He takes my hand in his, interlocking our fingers. "Look, Luce, I know you said you left home because of a guy, but, well, you never talk about your past at all and I was thinking – well I thought that maybe the truth was that you'd been in a clinic for treatment because, you know, you were ill – with like anorexia or something, and that you'd run away and didn't want to tell me because, well – because you didn't want me to know the truth, so you made up the story about the guy and –"

"I left because of a guy," I say shortly, which for once is the absolute truth. He just doesn't know that he is the guy. "And I don't have anorexia," I add.

I'm starting to get really uncomfortable at his line of questioning and I know it's only because he's skirting kind of close to the truth.

He sighs and let's go of my hand and pushes his fingers through his hair. "But I've never seen you eat, Luce. Honestly, I've really thought about it and I can't think of one single time."

"Well . . . I just don't like to eat in front of people."

He raises an eyebrow.

"And I'm not a big eater," I add for extra effect.

He shakes his head, disbelievingly.

I really don't want to have this conversation anymore. I get up off the bed to leave but he grabs my arm and pulls me back down.

"I don't want to fight with you, babe. I'm just worried about you." His face so sincere, so caring.

The guilt washes over me like a wave and I still it.

"You don't need to be. I'm fine. If I had an eating disorder I would tell you. I promise. Scouts honour." I do a two finger salute and add a smile. It feels awkward and clumsy but I hold it there, unable to do anything else.

He twists his lips. "So that's it, you're telling me you're just not a big eater and that you don't like to eat in front of people?"

"That's it." I nod.

I hate this. I hate having to lie to him, again, but what other choice do I have other than to tell him the truth, that is?

He looks down, examining his nails. "Okay," he says slowly and shrugs. "You say you don't have a problem, then I believe you."

I know he doesn't believe me. He knows he doesn't believe me, but thankfully he doesn't push it any further. And honestly it makes me love him even more, if that's at all possible.

He reaches over and grabs one of his crutches from beside the bed and stands, tucking it under his arm. "I'm gonna go down. You coming?"

"I'll be there in a minute."

After he's gone I flop back onto the pillows and stare up at the ceiling. I turn my head and press my face into the pillow. It smells of him, his scent setting off an ache deep inside me.

This is too hard, harder than I ever imagined it could be. I hate deceiving him all the time. And, as I've just discovered, he's starting to notice things are different about me. But I guess it was only a matter time; he's not stupid.

And for how long do I think I can keep up the pretence? I mean, really, how long it will be before he also realises I never sleep, or that I don't breathe, or have a heartbeat, or do any of the things that define being a human.

And, really, does he not deserve the truth before he figures it out for himself.

But is that a risk I should take, exposing myself to him like that? And if I did, would he even believe me? Humans are nothing if not sceptical, generally refuting what they don't know or understand – it's in their nature to do so.

But what about when the Elders finally find me? Do I really just want to up and disappear without a word, leaving him to think that I just left him without him ever knowing the truth? Knowing how much I love him. Knowing what I sacrificed to be with him.

And part of me wants him to know me. The real me.

I feel a sudden burst of urgency.

I have to tell him. I want to tell him. He'll understand, I know he will. This is James. He's wonderful and caring. Once I explain everything, he'll be fine, I'm sure of it. And if he isn't, then I'll cross that bridge when I get to it.

All I do know is that I have to tell him – now.

Shoving all my misgivings aside, I jump out of bed and practically run out of his room and across the landing toward the stairs.

I'm just going to go downstairs, sit down and calmly tell him everything, reveal the whole truth about myself and then deal with the consequences.

I suddenly feel very liberated at the thought.

As my foot hits the bottom step I become aware of voices talking in the kitchen.

Someone's in there with James. But who would be here this early in the morning?

A few worrying scenarios skip through my mind as I walk down the hall toward the closed door, sending a chill shuddering through me.

I prepare myself for the worst and very slowly push open the kitchen door.

Chapter 13

Disruptions

It's Sara.

I don't really know who I was expecting, to be honest. It's not like it would have been one of the Elders turning up to collect me, stopping off to have a chat with James first.

I am surprised to see her here, though. James hasn't spoken to her since the party, since the argument.

He's ignored her calls and deleted the many text messages she's sent him. And I've just stayed neutral saying nothing. I haven't encouraged him to speak to her. And maybe that's wrong of me but I really didn't want her to come here and launch another attack on me. And selfishly I've just been too revelling in our togetherness to even bother to think about anything else.

"Hello, Lucyna." She glances up at me, nervously fiddling with her fingers.

"Hi," I say. My skin feels like it's got bugs crawling all over it.

I straighten up preparing myself for another battle and then I notice how dark the skin around her eyes is. Also her eyes themselves look red and puffy and her face is looking much paler than I remember. Actually she doesn't look like her usual radiant self at all. She looks unhappy. Miserable in fact.

And I instantly feel responsible for her unhappiness.

Her and James are only having problems because of me. They were close friends before I arrived, I know this because I saw it for myself and they have been for a long time. And now faced here with it, it's impossible to ignore. The guilt practically drenches me, soaking into my skin

How would I feel if someone came between Arlo and me in that way?

Arlo.

I feel a sudden pang of longing for him.

I hadn't realised how much I have missed him until just now. I've been so wrapped up in James I haven't even thought about him since my change. I'm sure he will be concerned in his own unfeeling way over my disappearance. I wish I could see him.

I take the seat opposite Sara. All the determination I'd built up to tell James the truth has disintegrated. My urgency has gone.

James carries over three cups of coffee, hands one to Sara then puts one down purposefully in front of me. He takes the seat between us.

Sara picks her coffee up, blows on it a couple of times, then takes a sip and places it back down on the table. I can see her hands are shaking ever so slightly and she grips hold of the cup again, wrapping her hands around it. James doesn't seem to notice.

She clears her throat and glances at me. "Lucyna, I want to apologise for my behaviour on Friday night. I'd had a lot to drink, although that's no excuse, I know that." She takes a deep breath. I can see how hard this is for her. "I shouldn't have said the things I did. I don't know what came over me and I hope you can accept my apology."

I glance at James out of the corner of my eye, seeing the hopeful look on his face.

"Of course. Just think of it as if it never happened." I run my fingertip around the rim of the cup. The hot steam billows up, caressing my fingers.

She smiles and visibly relaxes, sits back in her chair and sips her coffee.

James gently squeezes my leg under the table, his dark eyes smiling gratefully at me. I smile at him, but don't really feel good.

I'm not naive enough to think Sara meant a single word of what she has just said. I know she's only done this because she loves James and wants him to forgive her, not me. But for that to happen she had to apologise to me. I'm fine with that really. I can't fault her for wanting to make James happy, because ultimately that's what I want for him. And I know by accepting her apology that it will make things okay between them.

He's happy; so am I.

But that still doesn't mean I'm going to feel elated about the situation as a whole.

"So what you been up too?" Sara says, focussing all her attention onto James, and they launch into conversation.

I stay for a short while, smiling and nodding in all the right places. Making an excuse about needing to have a shower, I take my coffee upstairs with me so I can dispose of it down the bathroom sink.

I have a lovely hot steaming shower. I would never, ever tire of these if I was human. I'll really miss them when I'm gone. Home. I shudder at the thought of leaving James, so I lean my head back, letting the water wash over my face, rinsing away all the tainting thoughts down the plughole.

After a while, and very reluctantly, I get out of the shower, dry myself off with a towel and put on a skirt and vest top.

Assuming Sara will probably have gone by now, I head back downstairs to see what James is up to, taking my empty cup with me.

I reach the bottom of the stairs and turn the corner seeing straight into the kitchen and that's when everything starts to feel like it's moving in slow motion as I see something that freezes me cold.

James is kissing Sara. Or Sara is kissing James.

I'm not sure which. But what I do know is he's backed up against the kitchen cupboards, her in front of him with her hands on his face and their lips are pressed together.

I feel like I've been physically hit.

I stumble backwards, tripping over a pair of James' shoes and drop the cup. It hits the wooden floor with a loud bang, as do I.

"Oh no, Luce!" James' distressed voice comes loudly from the kitchen.

I desperately scramble up to my feet.

He's advancing toward me, moving pretty quickly considering he isn't using his crutches. "It's not what you think! She just grabbed me and kissed me! I swear I didn't —"

"Yes, he did," Sara callous voice addresses me. A smirk stretching right across her pallid face, it makes her look almost haunting as she casually walks down the hall behind James. He's almost reached me by this point, his face taut with worry.

"He wanted to kiss me," she continues. "You see James loves me. He wants to be with me."

He turns on her. "Are you seven shades of crazy? I don't even fucking know you anymore, let alone love you!"

For a moment she looks as though he's just slapped her but she quickly regains composure. "James, I know you love me. You just can't admit it to yourself."

He glares at her, eyes hard, and shakes his head. "No, Sara, I don't love you."

Her composure instantly disintegrates. "But, James, I love you." There's a low desperation in her voice, it's uncomfortable to hear. She reaches for him, but he moves away closer to me, leaving her grabbing at air.

Anger covers her face. "You should be with me!" she spits. "Not her! It's what your dad would have wanted!"

James' face freezes at the mention of Max. "You need to go." He sounds oddly composed, his tone not matching his face at all.

"No." She stands firm. "You know he would. He'd be disappointed that you've got this bit of trash living in his house." She jabs a finger at me. I recoil backwards, feeling stung.

"Sara. Go. Now." His composure has gone, his face a mask of anger, his voice detached, cold. I can see he's struggling to control his rage.

She shakes her head, balling her fists at her sides. "No."

"Get the fuck out of my house!" he roars, tone savage, and I nearly jump out of my skin

He grabs her by the arm and, opening the front door, roughly shoves her out of it, ignoring her protests, then slams it loudly in her face.

He leans back against the door, chest heaving up and down, his eyes flashing anger.

I hear the sounds of Sara's defeated heels as they click slowly away against the pavement outside.

My legs give out on me and I crumple down onto the bottom step. Leaning forward I put my head in my hands. My whole body is trembling. I don't know what to do? What I'm supposed to do in a situation like this? I'm completely out of my depth here. I have no idea

126

what to do with these raw emotions which are coursing through my body like a poison.

I never once imagined something could hurt as much as this.

And just like that, I'm hit again with that feeling of familiarity, that sense of déjà vu, as if I've felt it before in some other time, some other place. Just the same as when James first kissed me. It doesn't make any sense.

James comes over and struggles to sit at my feet. I don't look at him, and I don't help him.

In the end he just kind of drops himself down to the floor with a thud.

"I didn't kiss her back," he says earnestly. "I swear."

I say nothing. I just stay as I am, leant forward, head in my hands as silent tears roll down my cheeks.

"Lucyna, please."

I look up at his imploring tone. He looks anxious and saddened. I move my eyes past him and look at the door. I'm half-expecting Sara to burst back through it at any minute.

"I know how it looked," he says frankly, palms spread out, "but honestly it wasn't that way at all. It just all happened so fast."

I glance at him and he holds my gaze. "We were talking like fine and then I made the mistake of telling her that me and you are together." He shakes his head and sighs. "And then I don't know — it was like a switch flipped in her and she went fucking mental, started saying that she loves me, that she always has, that we were meant to be together. And then the next thing I know she was just on me, trying to bloody kiss me —"

"It looked like she succeeded to me." Tears are dripping off my face onto my clothes.

"I didn't kiss her." He looks as determined as he sounds. "Christ, Lucyna, I wouldn't do anything to risk losing you. You mean too much to me. I'm crazy about you." He lifts his hand up to my face but I move away from him.

I see the hurt plainly in his eyes which only makes me feel worse. And, honestly, I don't even know why I just reacted like that.

He lets his hand fall into his lap and looks down. "If I was gonna cheat on you, would I really do it whilst you were only upstairs?"

I see the logic in his words and I already know he's telling me the truth – I knew the instant I looked into his sincere eyes.

But I just feel so confused, nothing's tying together properly. The pain is still here, not easing one iota.

He sighs disconsolately and rakes his fingers through his dark hair. "I don't know what more I can say to make you –"

"I believe you."

He looks up at me, the relief on his face palpable. He reaches for me and taking hold of my hand, gently pulls me onto his lap.

"I'm so, so sorry." He takes my face in hands, his callous skin is rough against mine. "I just don't know what's gotten into her. She's never done anything like this before. It's just not her. She's like a different person."

"She's only behaving this way because she loves you," I say, sounding oddly rational when it's the last thing I feel at the moment. "Just give her some time and I'm sure things will be okay."

He regards me questioningly. "How can you be like that?"

"Like what?"

"So understanding? Sara's done nothing but treat you like shit since the first day you met her, and all you've ever done is be nice about her."

I just shrug because I'm unable to say the real reason why I'm like I am is that I've spent many years studying human behaviour to better understand why they behave as they do. But mainly it's because I know first hand how love can make you do crazy things, things you never thought yourself capable of. And really I'm no better than Sara is – in some ways I'm worse. Far worse. At least she's honest, which is lot more than can be said for me.

I'm the worst kind of coward.

"You're so great," he says, pulling me close, burying his face into my hair, "and I'm so lucky to have you."

His words do not make me feel better.

"This thing with Sara," he murmurs into my hair, "I don't want it to come between us."

"It won't." I discreetly brush the tear from my face, knowing this to be the least of my problems. Sara won't be the one to come between us, I will.

He pulls back and brushes his lips against mine, my woe momentarily disappearing, only for it to return the instant our lips part.

"How do you fancy going out for the day?" he says brightening up. "We could go into town? Do something touristy like go on the London Eye? I know I'm not fully mobile but we could do with getting out of the house, especially after that." He nods toward the door.

I force a smile. "Sounds like a great idea."

"Good." He presses another kiss to my lips and I lean into him, prolonging the kiss for as long as I can, not wanting the unhappiness to return to me. I slide my arms around his neck, pulling him close, not ready to let him go just yet.

He pulls away breathless, chuckling. "We won't be going anywhere if you kiss me like that again." His eyes glisten.

I get up off his lap and offer my hand to him, ignoring the disappointment in his eyes. He takes my hand and I attempt to pull him up but I'm a lot smaller than he is and I nearly end up toppling onto him instead.

"I'll take it from here," he laughs and shuffles himself up onto the bottom step, lifts himself up to the next one and I help him up from there.

"Right, I'll just go have a shower and shave." He rubs his rough chin. "Then we can get off."

I help him up the stairs and leave him by the bathroom. I turn to go back downstairs.

"Luce?" he calls, pulling me back. "You fancy getting a takeaway tonight? We could get a film, a bottle of wine and curl up on the sofa together. What do you think?"

"Sounds great," I smile.

He smiles warmly at me, then taps his hand on the door with an air of finality and disappears into the bathroom.

I lean my back up against the wall and let the smile drop from my face.

I can't let this go on for much longer. I have to tell him the truth. It's the very least I owe him.

We'll spend the day together as planned, and tonight I'll tell him everything. I just pray that he'll understand.

At least one upside is I don't have to worry about how to dodge eating in front of him tonight, as he'll soon know the real reason as to why I don't.

But the thought doesn't make me feel any better.

I push off the wall and head downstairs to wait for him, ignoring the tiny voice in my mind that's nagging to be heard, desperately trying to tell me that it's not a good idea to tell him, that no good can come of telling James that I'm not the human he believes me to be.

Chapter 14

Candour

I'm sat on the chair in living room, trying not to think about the wonderful day I've just spent with James, but now instead focussing on what I have to tell him.

My hands start to shake. I clasp them together.

I'm absolutely terrified but I can't back out. I have to do this.

He might accept what I am about to tell him, accept who I am. I know it's a long shot but it could be a possibility – a small one, but still.

Of course I'm not naive enough to think he won't be surprised at my revelation, to say the least. But he cares for me. That has to count for something – doesn't it?

"You ready to order this food?" I look up to see James coming into the living room with a takeaway menu in his hand. "And no fobbing me off with you're not hungry. I know you've eaten nothing all day, so . . ." He lifts his shoulders, his lips curving upwards.

He looks so incredibly beautiful with an expression of such happiness on his face, and he has such trust in me, trust I'll shatter if I tell him truth.

This is too hard. I can't do it. I'll tell him tomorrow.

"What do you fancy having, then?" he asks whilst perusing the menu. "I was thinking we could get some starters and a couple of mains to share –"

"We need to talk." The words are out of my mouth before I realise I'm speaking.

He glances up from the menu. "What's up, babe?"

Oh God, I can't do it. I can't.

"Nothing." I smile. "It doesn't matter."

He looks at me for a moment, then back to the menu. "So, I was thinking maybe some spring rolls, and chicken satay –"

"Actually," I say cutting him off, this unknown strength suddenly spurring me on. "It does matter. I have to talk to you."

"Okay . . ." He comes and takes a seat on the sofa opposite me.

I press my trembling hands together, palm to palm. I can't bring myself to look at him, so I keep my eyes on the floor but I can feel his gaze burning into me.

"The thing is . . . I have to tell you that . . ." And now the words won't come. My throat is so clogged up with them I'm practically choking.

"Lucyna," his voice comes softly, "whatever it is, you can tell me. I'm here for you."

I know what he's thinking. He thinks I'm about to confess that I have an eating disorder. If only it was that.

I look up, staring directly into his warm, trusting eyes. "There's something about me that you need to know – have a right to know." I instantly correct myself.

He smiles tenderly. "Babe, don't worry, it's okay, I know what you're going to say. I know you have a problem – with food." He lingers over the word. "I'd have to be blind not to. But don't worry, I'll get you all the help you need, I promise, and I'll be right by your side all the way."

And that's when I realise just how much he truly cares for me. Making this so much harder for me to say.

"Come here," he says, beckoning to me.

I shake my head, briefly closing my eyes. "No, it's not that. That's not what I'm trying to tell you."

His brow furrows. "What is it, then?"

"I – I'm . . ." my voice trails off into oblivion. A tear rolls down my cheek.

"Luce – what is it?"

I stare at him with helpless eyes.

"Do I have to fucking guess?"

"No – I –"

"Are you married?"

I look at him with complete surprise. "No."

"Have you got kids?"

"No."

"Were you born a man?"

"No! Just stop, James!" I hold my hand up. "Give me a minute, please."

He goes silent and begins rolling the menu up in his hands. I can see just how frustrated he is.

I bring my knees to my chest hugging them. "This is a really hard thing for me to say and it's going to be even harder for you to hear." My voice is barely above a whisper.

"Just say it." His tone is harsh, impatient, taking me by surprise

I quickly recover and, finding my backbone, I put my feet down to the floor, look him in the eye and say, "I'm not human." Then I prepare myself for the worst.

"Funny," he says, without a trace of humour, "you're really starting to piss me off now. Will you just say whatever the fuck it is and get it over and done with!"

I look at him feeling wrong-footed. "I just have – I'm not human," I repeat calmly even though I feel anything but.

He sighs and starts to get up off the sofa. "If this is your way of getting out of eating then –"

"I'm serious, James"

I think it must be the tone of my voice that stops him because he hesitates. So I seize the moment.

"I'm a Bringer – well I was – I'm not really sure what I am now," I ramble. "But I – well, we Bringers take human souls to Heaven when they've died. It's what we exist for. My home is a place called Pure Land. It lies on the Astral plane between Heaven and earth . . ." And now I'm actually saying these words, I can hear just how very unreal they sound, and just exactly how they must sound to him.

He probably thinks I'm crazy.

"I know it's hard to believe," I add with emphasis. "But I am telling you the truth."

I can see his mind working, quickly, trying to processes what I've just told him. His face obtuse, uncomprehending. Then he laughs, awkwardly. "You're seriously expecting me to believe that you're - what - an angel?"

"Yes. Well, no." I shake my head. "I'm not an angel. But I am sort of

133

the conception that you have of them. Angels do exist, but well I'm what is called a Bringer."

He taps the rolled up menu against his knee. "Right. Okay." He pauses pushing his tongue between his teeth, making a kind of hissing noise. "Seriously, Luce, this really isn't funny. I know you have an odd way but honestly –"

"I'm not trying to be funny. I'm trying to be honest with you."

He leans forward, forearms resting on his legs and crushes the menu between his large hands. "Okay, and let's just say for a minute that I believe you – which right now I'm having a really fucking hard time doing, then what are you doing here with me? Why aren't you off in Heaven – erm – doing whatever it is you Bringers do?"

"Because I can't go back – well I mean I could – I think, but I don't want to," I say, feeling discomfited. "James, the night of your accident, I was there to take you to – well I mean – you were supposed to die that night." I glance over at him to see his eyes flicker and I know there's some tiny part of him that maybe kind of believes me, even though his common sense is strongly telling him otherwise. I press on, "I was there to take you to Heaven. But I couldn't. I couldn't let you die, I had to save you and somehow I changed – to this human form, and I could touch you and you could actually see me, and I didn't want to let go of that and lose you and –" I peter off.

He rubs his head. "Hang on, so what you're saying is I was supposed to die and you were there to take me to Heaven but you changed into a human and decided to save me instead?" he says this with a really patronising tone to his voice and a smile creeping onto his lips.

"Yes – well there's a lot more to it than that, but essentially – yes."

"Right." He nods his head disbelievingly.

"I am telling you the truth," I reiterate.

He sits back in his chair. "Yeah, sure you are."

"I knew Max."

His eyes flick up at me.

"Max, your dad," I reaffirm.

"I know what my dad's name is," he says coldly. "How do you –" He swallows loudly, "– how did know my dad?"

And that's when I know he's finally listening to me, that I've finally got his attention.

"I was his Bringer. I took him to Heaven. That's how I first met you."

"I don't —" He shakes his head and rakes his fingers through his hair. "What the fuck are you talking about?"

"The day Max died — July second, at three fourteen pm. I was there in the hospital room with him, well his soul — and you."

His eyes narrow to confusion but I keep mine fixed on his.

"I was talking to Max, trying to help him come to terms with his death when you came in the room and something happened to me that had never happened before —"

He suddenly sits forward, angrily. "I don't want to listen to this."

"No, James, you need to hear this and I need to say it," I continue on, not giving him a chance to respond. "I didn't have feelings — emotionally or physically. It's just the way we are. But from the very moment I saw you, I started to have them, feelings, I mean, and I was so confused and curious . . . about the feelings — about you. And then Max asked me to watch over you and —"

"He what?"

"He asked me to watch over you. He was worried about leaving you alone, he said you wouldn't take care of yourself properly and he asked me to look in on you to make sure you were okay, so I visited you to fulfil my promise to him. And also I wanted to understand them — the feelings, understand what was happening to me and then I discovered that mainly the feelings I was having, well they were for you, and then I couldn't seem to stay away. And on the night of your accident, fortunately out of all of us it was me that was called to be your Bringer and —" My throat closes and tears suddenly spill from my eyes. The enormity of it all dawning on me. "I just couldn't let you die." I shake my head. "I couldn't bear the thought of never seeing you again —"

He rubs roughly at his face, and laughs discordantly. "I just can't fucking believe I'm hearing this!"

"I know it's a lot to take," I say through my tears.

"No you don't." He looks at me sharply. "You have no fucking idea how I'm feeling right now." He gets up. "This is just — fucking ridiculous!

It's too much . . . I can't listen to this shit – I have to get out of here."

He hobbles quickly out of the room.

"Where are you going?" I scamper after him, the panic audible in my voice but I don't care.

He doesn't answer and I get in the hall to find him already at the door.

The panic grips a tighter hold of me. "James?" I cry. I know how frantic I sound but I can't seem to control it. It's like the fear's taken over and I no longer have control.

He turns abruptly. "Why are you doing this? Everything was going so great and –"

"Because it's the truth and because you have a right to know." I wipe the tears off my face. "And I knew I couldn't hide it for much longer. You were already starting to notice things, like how I don't eat –"

"And there was me thinking you had fucking anorexia!" he yells fiercely.

His tone hits me like a slap across the face.

"And I – I wanted you to know me," I say in a quieter voice. "The real me. Before anything happened between us, I mean before we were intimate – I didn't think it was right –"

He laughs hollowly. "Haven't we been intimate enough already?" His voice is like ice, coating me with its horrifying chill and I just want to shrink down and be invisible.

"I know, I meant – I'm so sorry." I wrap my arms around myself.

I'm too afraid to look at him, afraid of what I'll see on his face, afraid that he's repulsed by me now he knows who I really am.

I could hear the disdain in his voice. I don't want to see it in his eyes.

"This is just too – too fucking weird," he says uncomprehending, clutching his head. "I have to go." He presses down on the handle.

I grab hold of his arm. "James, please don't go!" I say, my tone desperate. "I love you."

He spins around. His face is livid. "Love me – fuck!" He shakes his head. "Do you even know the meaning of the fucking word?"

"I – I – please if you'd just listen to me, let me explain –"

"No!" his voice like thunder, eyes blazing. "I can't listen to you anymore!"

I start at level of his rage. "I'm so sorry," I sob still desperately clinging to his arm. "But I'm still me. The me you said you were crazy about. The me you said you wanted to be with."

He stares at me eyes, filled with contempt. And then for a split second I see a glimmer of warmth there before it dies, fracturing into a million pieces, a kaleidoscope of darkness that may never again be fixed.

"Still you!" he says incredulously. "I don't even know who the fuck you are!"

Then he pulls his arm free from my hand and walks out the door.

Chapter 15

Don't Go Away

James hasn't come home.

He's been gone hours. Well, three hours and thirty five minutes, to be exact.

And I just sat there on the sofa for all of those three hours and thirty five minutes, waiting, torturing myself, crying my eyes dry.

And now, finally out of tears, I'm stood here in the garden, contemplating what I know I have to do.

It's time for me to go home. I have to go to the one place I know Arlo will visit, so he can take me back.

I can't continue on like this. I'm not human. I'm just residing in the shell of what represents one, and no matter how much I may want to be human. I never will be.

It was a really nice dream to have whilst it lasted, but now it's time to let go – let him go.

The pain tightens around me, confining me to it, and I know this is how I will always feel from now on, so I had better get used to it.

The night sky is casting its shadows across James' beautiful creations.

I usually love the night, the glowing moon, the twinkling stars, but now it just seems so black, so bleak – so utterly, compellingly depressing, and I fit right in to it like the missing piece of a puzzle.

I gaze at the spot where James first kissed me.

I close my eyes and let the memory blanket me, remembering exactly how his lips felt on mine, how his touch warmed and fired inside me, how one smile on his lips sent every particle of me into a complete frenzy and how, when I was with him, when he was near, he was all I knew, was all that mattered.

From the very first moment I saw James, he changed me irreversibly, turned me from an empty shell, into something more. He made me someone, someone that mattered – for a time.

Nothing will ever be the same again and I don't regret one second of it.

I can't even begin to think about how much I'm going to miss him, and no matter how much this is crushing me, I know it's time for me to go.

I force my feet to move, and turn to see James lent up in the doorway, watching me.

I falter at the sight of him. "I – I thought you weren't coming back," I stammer. My voice sounds hoarse like it hasn't been used for days.

"Well I do live here," he shrugs. "I had to come back sometime."

I say nothing, feeling foolish.

We stand in silence just looking at one another. He looks exhausted. I debate with myself whether I should just leave but now, faced with him, I cannot bring myself to move.

"Where have you been?" I finally ask, even though I know have no right to.

"Sat in the work van across the road." He laughs self-mockingly, tapping the pot on his leg. "Couldn't get very far with this thing on."

Across the road in his van. Why didn't I even consider that he hadn't gone far, that he couldn't? I feel like kicking myself.

"James, I want to say I'm so sorry – for everything –"

"Is this the truth," he cuts me off. "Are you absolutely one hundred percent telling me the fucking truth?"

I nod. "Yes."

He regards me for a moment, eyes intense on mine.

"I never meant to hurt you," I say, knowing my words are as feeble as my voice sounds.

He rubs his hands over this face, and sighs. "I've been going over, and over this in my mind and I just can't get my head round it. It's just – I don't know – really fucking surreal."

"I know how hard it must be for you."

His eyes snap up at me. "Do you? Do you really? Because honestly, I don't think you even comprehend just how big a fucking bombshell this is to drop on me, especially after everything we talked about, after everything we've said to one another." He closes his eyes, pinches the bridge of his nose and takes a deep breath.

My eyes start to sting.

"I have some questions," he states calmly.

"Okay," I say nervously, unsure as just what to expect.

He crosses his arms over his chest. "You said you were with my dad after he died?"

"Yes."

"Was he – is he okay?"

"Yes, he's fine." I wipe away a stray tear. "He loves you a lot, you're the most important thing in the world to him, and he just wants you to be happy. He stayed there with you, James, in the hospital room, for as long as he could, until it was time for him to go."

He takes a deep breath and closes his eyes. It's a long moment before he speaks again. "And the night of the crash, what happened?"

"I wasn't there when you actually crashed, I arrived just afterwards. I mean I didn't know it was you until it had already happened, that's how it works – we don't receive the name of the hu–person we're to go to until a few minutes before they're, well – before they're supposed to die. But I had to save you. I couldn't just leave you to die. And, like I said earlier, I somehow took on this human like form and pulled you from your car, and I have remained the same ever since, not returning to how I was before. And . . . the rest you know."

"When you say 'human like form' what exactly do you mean?" His questioning stare is staid fixed on me.

I look down, feeling unnerved. "I mean I'm here, I'm me, I look just like I did to others of my kind – I think. But whilst my body looks human, essentially I'm not. I don't – can't sleep, or breathe, or eat. I don't have a – heartbeat." I cringe as I say those words. "I'm not mortal like you are. I don't need those things to sustain myself." I glance up at him. His eyes are still on me, unmoving.

"But all those things aside," I add quietly, "I feel human. I mean I have feelings like you do. I can touch things, and be touched, and feel all the sensations that brings –" I tail off.

He says nothing. Just continues to stare at me, an unfathomable expression on his face.

140

I feel awkward, unsure what to do. And even though we're only a few feet apart, the space dividing us feels heavy and fraught, like a deep dark chasm that's pulling me in.

"What should I do?" I ask.

His expression goes blank. "What do mean?"

"I mean should I leave?"

"Well that's up to you."

"Do you want me to leave?"

"Do you want to leave?"

"Of course I don't want to leave!" I cry. Tears once again prick at my eyes. "But I don't know what I'm supposed to do or say – what I can do or say to make this better. You tell me and I'll do it. If you want me to leave, then I will. I just want you to be happy, that's all I've ever wanted. And if my leaving will do that, then I'll go." I look around the empty space surrounding me, needing support, needing something to cling to, so I cling to the only thing I can – myself.

For a moment James just stares at the ground, then he looks up at me and shakes his head.

I shrug, exasperated. "No? No – you don't want me here, or no – you do?"

"For fuck's sake!" He slams his hand on the door frame, and looks away angrily. I daren't speak for fear of reprisal, and just like that I've had enough. So I make the decision for him but he's blocking my exit.

I walk toward him, gesturing for him to move, but he doesn't. He stands there, his stare intense.

I'm instantly weakened but I hold my nerve. "What do you want?" I ask again, my voice filling up the silence surrounding us.

His eyes move to my lips. My whole body starts to tremble.

He moves closer to me and puts his hands around my face, cradling it. I can feel the heat from his body flowing straight into mine and it's like the entire world has shrunk down to this one moment.

"You," he simply utters. "I want you."

Then he's kissing me, and this kiss feels different, more intense. Everything seems magnified. I'm aware of absolutely everything. Every single subtle move he makes.

He pulls me into the house, us stumbling awkwardly, but not once do his lips leave mine. He backs me up against the kitchen table and effortlessly lifts me onto it as if I'm made of air, and places himself between my legs. Then his mouth moves from mine, to my neck, his tongue searching over my skin, then he's kissing me again. His hands run down my back. My entire body's aching for him.

"I love you."

I pull back in shock. "You love me?"

His eyes flicker and flame as he traces my lower lip with his finger. "How could I not."

His lips are on mine again and we're kissing intensely. His touch becomes more urgent, frenzied. He pulls me closer. His hips are pressing hard into mine.

"I want you," he says hungrily into my ear and, for the first time, I can honestly say I'm hungry too.

"I want you, James."

He doesn't need a second invitation. He pushes my skirt up. I pull his t-shirt over his head, only breaking from our kiss to do so. My hands roam his smooth firm chest, the contours of his muscles defined with every movement he makes.

Everything about this is right. He loves me. I love him. And nothing else matters.

I trace my fingers over his stomach. A low groan emits from deep within him. I reach down to unbutton his jeans. He kisses me harder.

I want him so much. I feel like I've spent an eternity waiting for him, waiting for this, and I don't want to wait a moment longer.

And that's when the window starts to rattle.

James stops, startled, and glances around the kitchen. "What's going on?"

I look around. The whole room is vibrating now. A glass falls off the kitchen surface smashing loudly against the hard floor.

Then I feel it.

Something's forcing its way into my body and it's painful, really painful. I cry out.

James's wide eyes are on me. He looks afraid. "Luce?" He takes a step back.

I follow his stare, looking down at my body.

Oh no.

I'm changing. I'm losing solid form. I can see a sparkle beginning to escape from me. I'm going back to how I used to be. They've found me. They're taking me home.

Panic stricken, I look back up at James. His eyes are on full alert.

"Luce . . . what's happening?" he says voice shaky.

"They've found me." I sob.

"Who's found you?"

"The Elders."

"Who?"

"My family. They're taking me home."

"No." He reaches for me as I do him but our hands pass right through one another's. "No Luce! I can't lose you!" The fear as evident in his voice as it is on his face.

"I'm so sorry."

His hands are in his hair. "You can't go. I don't want you to go." His voice breaks. "It's too soon. I can't say goodbye to you."

"So don't say goodbye."

"Say what, then?"

"Tell me you love me."

"I love you," he whispers.

"I love you too. I'll find a way back to you, I promise."

I keep my eyes on his face, ensuring he's the last thing I see.

Suddenly I'm in a meadow, the grass green and lush beneath my old sparkly feet. But it's not home.

"Hello, Lucyna." I hear a voice I know so well come from behind me.

I spin around, startled. "Arlo?"

Chapter 16

No Going Back

Arlo stands before me, looking just as glorious as the last time I remember seeing him.

"Arlo," I repeat, this time more insistently. "What's going on? Where are we? Where are the Elders?"

"Lucyna," he says voice cold, detached. "The Elders sent me to retrieve you from Earth to inform you that you are no longer allowed back home."

"Oh."

His words sting me. He sounds so cold. So . . . inhuman. I know this is just his way but that knowledge doesn't make it hurt any less.

Then I realise this is how I used to sound, how I used to come across to all those suffering humans, all of those who were drowning in their grief and loss. And I instantly feel glad that I've changed to who I now am. But then the reality of his words hit me, pulling me right back down with them.

"I'm banished?" I stare at him, troubled.

"Yes." He nods formally, setting his golden hair shimmering around his face.

Banished.

I never even considered the possibility. Obviously I knew there would be consequences to my actions, but I was expecting an eternity stuck in Pure Land being kept away from all humans, being kept away from James. But never for a moment did I think they would banish me.

And suddenly I feel very alone.

I look into is bright green eyes. "Why are you here telling me this? Why not one of the Elders?"

"They did not wish to see you," he says holding my stare. "They requested I come to inform you. You are advised that you will still exist as you are, but you are no longer a Bringer or granted access to Pure Land. The privilege has been taken from you. It was taken the moment you chose to save the human's life."

Suddenly I feel very angry. I straighten myself up. "Why did you bring me here to tell me this?" I gesture around, wondering just exactly where it is I am. "Why not tell me on earth?"

"I was told not to leave you on earth in your prior state. I had to bring you back to your true form so you could see me." He holds his hands together in front of him. "It has taken us some time to find you, Lucyna. There was no trace of your essence once you'd changed."

Then I ask him the question I have pained over since it happened. "How did I change?"

He shakes his head. "We are not sure."

It's a long moment before either of us speaks. Then I say in a small voice, "So I can never again go home."

"No."

And that's it – final. The end of everything I know.

I'm panicked. I feel like I'm freefalling into a giant black hole. I have no home. What am I going to do? It's one thing to not want to go back, but another thing entirely to have the choice taken from me.

And then it hits me. Why am I even concerned with this? I can finally have what I want; I can return to earth and be with James. Of course I will miss Pure Land, miss being a Bringer. But really what did that hold for me anyway? Just a sterile, cold, empty existence.

I think of James at home stood there in the kitchen and the sense of urgency I now feel for him relinquishes any other thoughts I could have, and there's only one thing left for me to say.

"I want to go back to earth, Arlo," I state boldly. "Change me back to whatever I was before and send me back."

Surprisingly to me, his brow furrows and a look of unease sweeps his face. His action not tying in with who he is – what he is.

"Arlo?" I look at him confused.

He presses his lips together and smiles gently. "Lucyna," he says voice suddenly sounding harmonious and caressing, like a melodic song, no longer cold and hard. "I had always hoped it wouldn't come to this." He spreads his palms out. "I had hoped to somehow spare you all of this."

"What — what are you talking about?" I'm well aware of how shaky my voice sounds but I'm not currently in a position to be able to disguise it.

He closes his eyes briefly whilst drumming his fingertips on his forehead. "There are some things you need to know before you make any decisions about where you want to be . . . and who you want to be with."

My head is swimming with thoughts, questions. Disquiet bathes me and I instantly feel the need to get out of here because one thing I am absolutely certain of is that something is very wrong.

I take a step back, increasing the distance between us.

He smiles gently. "Lucyna, I'm only here to help you —"

"I don't need any help," I cut him off, trying to project sternness into my weak voice, attempting to make my intentions clear, even though all I feel is edgy and worried. "I just want to go to earth and be with James."

"I do understand how you're feeling," he says softly, fingering the lapel on his black jacket.

My eyes narrow onto him. "And just exactly how would you understand what I'm feeling, Arlo?"

He brushes his hair back, and stares at me with eyes full of regret. "I'm not who you think I am."

I'm having a weirdly vivid sense of déjà vu here, this being not too dissimilar to my conversation with James, except now it's me on the receiving end.

I can feel nerves creeping over me, so I steel myself. "And just who exactly are you?"

He doesn't speak for what seems like a long time but, in reality, it's probably only a matter of seconds. Anxiety quickly fills me up, and just when I don't think I stand the silence anymore, he speaks.

"I'm not a Bringer," he says voice firm, sure. "I'm an angel."

My eyes widen with disbelief. "What? You're an — angel?" I feel totally blind-sided. "But I don't understand. You can't be. We don't mix, angels and Bringers don't mix. We never cross paths, never . . . and you've always been with me in Pure Land, with me . . ." My weak voice

146

peters off.

Arlo sweeps his hand behind him, manifesting a bench. He sits down on it and motions for me to join him.

I shake my head. "No. I'll stay where I am."

His eyes fill with sorrow and I feel a huge twinge of guilt, obviously not enough to encourage me to move because I stay right where I am.

"I don't know where to begin," he says dolefully.

I cross my arms over my chest. "The beginning is usually a good place."

"That could take me a while," he chuckles softly, quickly drying up when he sees the unrelenting look of impatience on my face.

He leans forward, arms on thighs and gazes up at me. "I've never been a Bringer. I just made myself appear as one. I did it so I could be with you. I needed to be there to watch over you and that was the only way."

Instinctively, I tense up. "And why did you need to watch over me?"

He presses his hands together, palm to palm. "Lucyna, you have what you could call . . . a complicated past and I don't really know how to tell you all of it without —"

"Just get to the point, Arlo" I hiss, surprising myself at how incredibly harsh I sound. And I can tell he's surprised too, by the look on his face.

"Are you sure?" he asks calmly. "Are you sure want to know everything?"

His green eyes are fixed onto mine and I don't look away, can't look away. It's like we're locked in a game of truth or dare, and the first to look away is the loser.

I hold myself firm. "Of course I do."

"Even though there may be things you would rather not hear?"

"Yes." I gesticulate, impatiently. "Just tell me."

"As you wish." He spreads his hands out and rests back against the bench. "You used be an angel."

If I thought I'd been blind-sided before, this definitely champions it.

"I was an angel?" I can barely get the words out.

He nods. "Yes. We were close friends. And for a very long time we

147

resided together in Heaven, with all the other angels, of course." He glances at me knowingly before continuing, "And there are many of us, Lucyna. Mainly we are of God's initial creation, but sometimes a lower being will have served for the greater good and be given the privilege to rise up and be anointed as one of us. It does not happen often and when it does it is truly an honour of the highest degree." He leans forward. "And that's where Arran comes in."

"Who's Arran?" I manage to ask, even though my mind is such a jumble of thoughts I can barely focus.

"He's the angel you were in love with – and he loved you too, for a time," he adds, seemingly oblivious to my internal affliction. "Or so we believed, but unfortunately, unbeknown to the rest of us – to you – Arran was unlawfully revealing himself to humans whilst on earth, well only one actually, a human woman –" His eyes flick to meet mine. "It happens, immortals falling in love with mortals. It's rare but not impossible, as Arran proved – and as you well know." He gives me a pointed look.

I instantly feel ashamed and very uncomfortable. I look down, away from his enervating stare.

"Then one day, without warning, Arran told you he was leaving you, leaving Heaven. That he had fallen in love with this human and he was leaving to be with her." I look up, instantly meeting his solemn green eyes.

"You were devastated, Lucyna," he adds.

I sink to the floor, suddenly feeling very weighed down. When I look up, Arlo is sitting there in front of me.

"You tried to talk him out of leaving," he continues, his voice speeding up, "but nothing could change his mind. And to place cruelty upon cruel, he made the wish on you, forcing you to make him mortal and send him to earth so he could be with his human. As angels, Lucyna, when a wish is placed upon us we have no choice other than to fulfil it – and you fulfilled his wish. It destroyed you to do so . . . and he knew that." His eyes seek mine, locking onto them. He holds my gaze, projecting as much warmth as he can until I feel like I'm literally coated in it. "You weren't the same after that day. It was almost as if something inside you had died."

I feel numb. I bring my knee up to my chest and wrap my arms around it. I feel like I'm listening to someone else's story . . . which to me I am . . .

"Why don't I remember any of this?"

For a moment he looks caught off guard, but then he calmly says, "I took your memories away."

"You did what?" My voice hitches up a couple of octaves.

His eyes harden and focus off somewhere else, as though he's seeing another time, another place. "I only did what you asked of me," he says, his voice slightly raised. "You told me you couldn't bear the pain of losing Arran and you wanted me to take it away. You said you wanted me to erase your memory, remove everything and make you a Bringer so you would never again have to feel. I tried to reason with you, but you wouldn't listen. I told you I wouldn't do it, so you took it out of my hands and you wished it on me." His hard eyes refocus back onto mine, sending a chill shivering through me. "You did to me what he'd done to you."

His face is suffused with anger and, even though I know nothing of what I've done, I still find myself looking away, guiltily.

"And when you did that," he adds, a touch bitterly, "it was out of my hands, there was nothing I could do other than to fulfil it. So I erased your memories, turned you into a Bringer, and took you to Pure Land." He shakes his head. "Not my finest hour but, like I said, not my choice either."

I pull my other leg up to my chest and rest my head on my knees, avoiding his stare and gaze out at the grassy meadow that seems to roll on endlessly.

Everything is upside down and I have no idea what to think about first.

"I couldn't just leave you there, though," he says, his voice suddenly soft but so very intense, "no matter how angry I was with you."

And it's the intensity in his tone that makes me look up at him.

He moves closer to me and takes hold of my hand, staring down at it. And I instantly realise this is the first time Arlo has ever touched me. I follow his gaze, no longer seeing what he sees, now only seeing my old sparkly self. My ability to feel his touch no longer there, back to the old desolate way I used to be. And all I feel inside is complete and utter sadness, mourning the loss of what I so briefly had.

"You were my friend, Lucyna." He sounds determined. "I had to do something, so I did the only thing I could and I stayed there with you in Pure Land and passed myself off as a Bringer too."

I'm suddenly struck with a thought. I look up at him. "How did the Elders not know you weren't a Bringer. They must have sensed you were an angel – and for that matter, why didn't they question my sudden appearance?"

He smiles, a very regal smile, straightening his back as he does so. "I am an angel, Lucyna" he says in a condescending tone. "A higher being. We have great powers at our disposal. I can make myself appear as I wish." He sweeps his hand down himself with a flourish. "Make anything appear as I wish. Neither the Elders, nor any of the Bringers, would have ever questioned our appearance because, to them, we had always been there."

"And just how long have we been there?"

He bows his head. "Three hundred years . . . and it was three hundred years of plain sailing. I didn't even see what was happening to you until it was too late. I never saw it possible that he would come back into your life and –"

"Who?"

"Arran."

"Arran?" I say with confusion. "I don't understand? When did he come back?"

He keeps his sorrowful, green eyes fixed on my blue ones. "James is Arran."

And I'm fairly positive that for a moment, time actually stops as his words resonate through me.

"What?"

"It's Arran's soul that resides in James' body. He just doesn't know it – doesn't know who he used to be."

I pull my hand from his, ignoring the look of hurt on his face. "I don't understand," I repeat, voice trembling.

He sits back, resting on his hands. "When Arran eventually died in his mortal body all those years ago, he couldn't gain access to Heaven as a normal human soul would because his soul was cast as an angel – he may have had a mortal body but his soul will always remain the same. That's something only God has the power to change. And when Arran decided to abandon us, abandon Heaven, it meant he could never again access it." He presses his hand to his chest. "So each time his mortal body dies, he is instantly reborn into another, he can't just be left to wander earth as a soul. It's been this way for the last three hundred years and he will continue to do so for all eternity."

I sit in shock, struggling to comprehend what I'm hearing, unwittingly watching Arlo as runs his hand over his hair, mesmerised by the efficiency of his movement, following it until it finally finishes its journey resting back in his lap.

"And you're saying James knows nothing of this?" I ask not moving my stare, my voice sounding as empty as I feel.

"No." He shakes his head. "He has no idea. Arran's soul only reawakens at the point of death, but as soon as he's reborn he instantly forgets. That is how all rebirths work, even for human souls . . . well except they come to Heaven before rebirth." He lifts a hand and unbuttons his jacket. "And for the last three hundred years your paths have never crossed. And, as I incorrectly assumed, why would they ever? Out of all the soon-to-be seven billion humans on earth, it was very unlikely that you would ever meet. Well, currently, it would have been a . . . one in, six point eight billion chance to one, to be exact."

My head is buzzing with all this information. It's just too much. It can't be true. I don't want to listen to this anymore.

I jump to my feet. Arlo looks up at me startled.

"I don't believe you," I say resolutely, admonishing him with my hand. "I don't believe any of this."

He looks stricken. "Why would I lie to you?"

"How should I know?" I say bitterly. "Apparently you've been lying to me for the last three hundred years so . . ."

Anger skims his brow and he lithely gets to his feet. "Right. Fine," he

151

says in a controlled voice, re-buttoning his jacket. "You can just see it for yourself then."

He starts to move toward me.

"What are you doing?" I say, holding my hand up, taking a big step back.

He laughs softly, shaking his head. "Calm down, Lucyna. I just meant I'll return your memories to you, then you'll know the truth for yourself. I can also return you to your angelic form if you wish?"

"You can do that?"

He looks at me as though I've just asked the most stupid question ever. "Of course I can. All you have to do is wish it and it's done."

"As easy as that?"

"As. Easy. As. That," he affirms.

I think quickly. If what Arlo is saying is true, then is this what I want? Do I really want to know who I used to be? I must have been in an inordinate amount of pain to want to forget it and never feel again.

But then that also means I've spent the last three hundred years hiding from who I truly am.

I look at Arlo. He has his arms folded across his chest and the impatience is clearly stamped on his face.

I don't want to hide anymore.

"Okay," I say tentatively. "Change me back and return my memories, Arlo. I wish it so."

He comes over to me until we're a breadth apart, and cups my face with his hands. "Close your eyes," he instructs.

I do as I'm told.

I don't feel anything for a long moment – then I suddenly feel it.

My head is all warmth and fuzziness, my whole body tingling, and then a white noise rushes through my mind, filling every crevice. Doors that were once sealed shut are now opening, the memories flooding back to their rightful place.

Scenes begin to flash through my mind like an old movie, and I have to work quickly to catch hold of them.

Mainly I see Arran. His face fills out my mind. The lazy smile he used to wear on his lips, his light brown hair that always fell messily around his face, his dark, penetrating eyes . . . and that's when I see James. It's the eyes. They have the same eyes . . .

I can hear Arran's soothing voice so clearly, it's almost as if he's standing here before me now, telling me he loves me and he will until time ceases to exist. I remember how happy I was. Then I feel it, the pain I felt the exact moment he told me he was leaving me for her. Oh God, it hurts . . . it hurts so much – too much.

I feel desolate, alone, wretched. It's like I'm been crushed by it.

I see it all. I remember it all.

"Lucyna." I open my eyes to a very concerned Arlo, his hands gripping my arms, us both sitting on the floor. "Are you okay?" He shakes his head. "Of course you're not. I should have known this would be too much for you to take all at once."

I stare blankly at him, wincing as the memories continue to wash over me like a tidal wave. The pain is so raw, it's like a darkness taking me over.

"Say something, Lucyna. Please."

I steel myself, seeing how worried he is, and force myself to speak. "I'm okay," I say.

He moves to sit beside me and puts his arm around me, pulling me to him. "It's a lot to take. I should have warned you how overwhelmed you'd feel, especially with the memories I'd concealed. Even though they are hundreds of years old, right now, to you, they'll feel fresh. They'll very quickly dull, I promise you." He sounds so sure, so confident and I want to believe him.

I lean into him, needing comfort. Then I notice my body. I look just as I did when I was on earth. No more sparkle, just creamy white skin. I should be elated at the sight, but nothing can overtake this pain I feel.

"This is my fault," he says sorrowfully. "I should have handled this better. I shouldn't have just given you your memories back like that."

I glance up at him and he regards me warmly, his green eyes gazing down at me. But for some reason I find myself shifting back slightly, away from him. If it bothers him, he doesn't show it.

"No, Arlo, I asked you to do this. None of this is your fault. I'm the only one at fault here." I look down at my hands, feeling like I barely

153

know myself anymore – which is odd considering the barrage of memories I've just received back.

"No," he says sternly. "The only one ever at fault was Arran."

I can see it so clearly now. I can see why I was instantly drawn to James, why my feelings returned the moment I met him. My memories may have been buried, but my love was just hiding, waiting for his return. James and Arran may look and be different in so many ways, but the eyes clearly show they are one in the same person. The same dark, unfathomable pools I fell in love with all those centuries ago. And now, here I am, once again in love, once again in unimaginable pain.

"Lucyna?" Arlo squeezes my hand. I can hear the concern lacing his voice.

"I'm okay. Really," I add, seeing the look of doubt on his face. "I'm just trying to process everything."

He reaches his hand up and brushes my hair back. I quash my instant urge to move away, not understanding why I feel the need to do so.

Arlo is my friend, the only one who has cared for me unconditionally. It must be because I'm not used to him touching me, especially not in such a caring manner.

"I'm so sorry for doubting you, Arlo," I say sincerely. "And I'm sorry for everything I've put you through."

"There's nothing to be sorry for."

"Yes, there is. You've done everything I have asked of you. You've cared for me even when I didn't know it. I can never thank you enough."

He smiles warmly, then his face turns serious. "So what now?"

"What do you mean?"

He looks past me. "Well do you still want to go back to earth . . . back to James?" he asks the latter part in quieter voice.

I shift uncomfortably as a wave of anger pulses through me at the mention of his name. I never knew I could feel such furore, especially not in relation to him. But it's the thought of what Arran did to me that's spurring it on, the thought of seeing those eyes again. James and Arran are melding together in my mind, and there is not a thing I can do to stop it. That's when I know there's no going back.

"No. I don't ever want to go back there," I say vehemently, surprising myself at just the level of resentment in my voice. "I don't ever want to see him again."

"You can . . . well you can stay here – if you want to."

"And whereabouts is here?" I ask distractedly.

"Shangri-La"

I look at him and laugh. He's certainly got my attention now. "Arlo, be serious. Where are we really?"

"Shangri-La," he says again, stressing the words to really drive his point home.

"But Shangri-la doesn't exist," I say pedantically. "It's just a myth, invented by a human, a supposed realm for immortals. And if it did exist, then surely I would have known . . ." I peter off at his steady expression.

"It very much does exist," he grins, waving his hand around. "But only a chosen few know about it, know how to access it." He winks at me.

"So how do you know?" I ask, still feeling sceptical. "Why are you one of the chosen few?"

"Because I'm special," he chuckles and taps his nose with his long pale finger. "It really is a beautiful place. It will make a great home for us both –"

"Us both?" I say with open surprise.

His green eyes sparkle at me. "You didn't think I was going to leave you alone here did you?"

"Well I didn't expect –"

"I know you didn't expect, Lucyna." He smiles. "But I have already spent forever with you. I'm not about to ditch you now." He rises to stand and holds his hand out for me to take.

I waver, again not knowing why. All I do know is there's a reluctance coming from deep inside of me.

"Unless you don't want me to stay with you?" he adds, looking shyly down, his golden hair partly obscuring his perfectly sculptured face.

I look up at him, my only true friend, all I have left, and I brush my stupid hesitation aside. I smile brightly. "Of course I do," I say, clasping hold of his hand, allowing him to pull me to my feet.

"It's going to be great," he says happily, leading me along by my hand. "It'll be just like old times . . ."

I continue to smile, pretending to listen as he talks on, but I can't concentrate because right now all I can see in my mind are those eyes, those dark brown eyes.

And I know I'm doing the right thing by staying here but that doesn't stop the hurt and regret from steadily flowing through me like a poison.

Chapter 17

Guises

It hasn't worked.

All the pretending I'm okay, all the ignoring my pain.

No, it hasn't worked, not one single iota.

Arlo was very wrong when he said the pain would dull. It hasn't. Not in the slightest.

If it's at all possible, I'm actually even more miserable than I was the day I got my memories back. Which was what . . . two weeks ago, give or take a day or two? Time has become pretty irrelevant whilst I've been here.

For all I think about every single second, of every long day, is him.

And even though I may appear to the outside world – well Arlo as he's the only one I see – that I'm happy, with not a care or concern, the truth is I'm unhappy, sad, forlorn, mournful, afflicted and all of those things combined in one, to create the ultimate, most wretched misery you could ever imagine, that horrific it makes me want to hide away and lick my wounds for all eternity to come.

I wear this happy guise because I'd thought by doing so, by pretending I was okay, that it would somehow make it true . . . only it's not really working out that way. It was always going to be impossible for me to forget when the luggage of my past was hot on my trail.

And I can't tell whether the misery I feel is solely because of the pain Arran caused me all that time ago or because I miss James so much that been away from him is starting to cause me what can only be described as actual physical pain.

I'm not really sure what to do, well except for to continue on as I am. Which isn't looking too promising, all things considered.

I can quite clearly see why I had Arlo wipe my memories and change me all those years ago. I'd be tempted to ask him to do it again, if I didn't think that'd be the final straw for him when it comes to me.

I look up at the bright blue sky, watching it wink down at me through the green leaves that sit high above, the hammock I'm laid on swaying gently in line with the warm breeze. Then, without warning, an image of James kissing me flickers through my mind, the sight so clear, so intense, I feel like I'm going to explode from the agony that accompanies it. I clutch my arms across my chest, hoping to somehow compress the pain.

I miss him. So much. Too much.

My minds starts to drift, remembering the way he would touch me, kiss me, his smell, his laugh . . . his infectious laugh. I wonder what he's doing right now . . . if he misses me . . .

Stop it.

I made the decision to stay away and I have to stick to it. Going back to James would ultimately only lead me straight back to hurt. That's what Arlo says, and he's right, I think.

James is Arran. James is Arran. James is Arran.

I sit up in the hammock, swinging my legs over the edge and try to block my mind from my memories. Then an image of purple asters, just like the ones from James' garden, appears in my mind. I open my eyes up to see hundreds of them all sprouting out of the ground before me. Great, now I'm manifesting without even meaning to.

What was it he said they stood for . . . a symbol of love and patience?

And that's when I know it's no good. I can't go on like this.

I love him, I miss him and there's not a single thing I can do about it.

What's the point of being here wallowing in eternal misery, hiding myself away from love, when if I just give myself up to it, even with all the risks that accompany it, at least I'd finally be living, even if only for a short time.

What is life without love? A hollow empty existence and haven't I already done that one for long enough.

James isn't Arran, he's simply James, and he's who I want to be with. I have to go back. . . . no I want to go back.

Now I just have to find a way to tell Arlo.

I start, when I look up and see him walking toward me. Well I suppose now is a good a time as any . . .

"Asters . . . nice." He nods down at them. "I was looking for you. I've got something to show you." He turns and starts walk away as though it's a given I'll follow him.

"No, Arlo, wait . . . I need to talk to you."

He stops and turns back to me, a sudden curiosity stamped on his face.

I glance down at the trampled asters he's just waded through, stalling, feeling fearful for what I have to say.

"You're leaving aren't you?" he asks quietly, slowly. The disappointment evident in his voice.

I nod.

"You're going back to him?"

"Yes," I utter, sounding as guilty as I feel.

He says nothing, just glares at me, a look so icy it cuts right through me, a silence so strong it's practically deafening.

"And what about everything he's done to you?" he asks stonily.

I curl my fingers around the thick edge of the netting and shake my head, unable to meet his eyes. "It wasn't James that hurt me."

He grips his head, frustrated. "James is Arran, what do you not understand about that? And we all know what Arran was, what he did, what he was capable of." He sounds so condescending, so belligerent, that it enrages me.

I jump to my feet. "What Arran did!" I expostulate. "Not James. He doesn't know any of this. Nothing of who he was, what he did."

I so desperately want him to understand my decision, understand how I feel. I want him to be okay with it.

He turns and walks away from me and for a moment I think, that's it, argument over, but then he turns back.

"James is Arran, Lucyna, irrespective of what you may say or want to believe. He might not know it, but he is. It's in him to hurt you again. And he will, trust me. If you go back to him, it'll only be a matter of time . . . and do you really want to go through all of that again?"

I sit back down on the hammock. "No, but –"

"There are no buts when it comes to him, Lucyna. You know this better than anyone." He comes and sits beside me. "I only want what's best for you," he says gently, looking sideways at me with his vivid green eyes. "All I've ever wanted is for you to be happy. You're better off here with me where it's safe, where he can never hurt you again." He reaches over and pats my hand.

I can feel myself weakening to his words. I close my eyes and count to ten. Then I open them back up.

"I know you want what's best for me, but he is what's best for me. I know you don't understand that but I want to be with him."

He stiffens beside me, then abruptly stands, and when he finally looks down at me, I see a rage in his eyes so fierce it actually unnerves me.

"After everything I have done for you!" he suddenly bellows, his voice so thunderous it startles me. "And this is how you choose to repay me! By throwing it back in my face and returning to him. He destroyed you, Lucyna, made you so completely miserable you felt that you had no other choice than to change who you were so you wouldn't have to feel the pain that he left you with."

I scream. I actually scream.

Arlo looks visibly shocked and I know how he feels. Even now, I sometimes have no idea where some of these emotions come from.

I get to my feet. "I will not have this argument with you, Arlo. I'll do as I wish." I know how petulant I sound but I can't help it.

"But look at what happened to you because of him," he says scornfully. "You chose to become a Bringer, of all things, because of him." And the disdain in his voice shocks me, which I think is plain enough on my face, as he very quickly changes his demeanour.

"I'm sorry," he says urgently. "I didn't mean it the way it sounded. I just meant that he'd changed you and not for the better. You know this yourself."

I fold my arms over my chest and, feeling as sure as I look, say, "Arran may have changed me, but James brought me back to life."

"And what about me?" he remonstrates. "Me. The one who has cared for you, done everything for you. I've never hurt you . . . never abandoned you."

"I know," I say softly, quickly changing my tone, "and I am, and will

160

always be, eternally grateful to you, but it doesn't change the fact that I want to be with him. I can't just stay here with you out of some misplaced sense of loyalty."

Okay, so I'm not quite sure why I just said that and, honestly, that sounded a lot better in my head. But it's too late now, I can't take it back.

His face hardens. "So go, then," he says, his voice devoid of feeling, and turns away from me.

"I need your help." I cringe as I say the words but know I have no other choice.

"Don't you think I've helped you enough?" he says this without turning around.

"I know you have, and I wouldn't ask if I had any other choice . . . if there was any other way."

He turns around, and folds his arms across his chest. "And just what is it you now require of me?"

He knows exactly what I need, he's not stupid – he's just going to make me say it out loud.

I hold my nerve. "I need you to make me human and send me to earth."

He unfolds his arms and laughs hollowly. "And why would I do such a thing?"

I stare calmly into his bright green eyes. "Because you're my friend."

He seems to falter but then he shakes his head resolutely. "No, I won't do it."

"Please, Arlo."

"No."

I look at him steadily. "Don't make me do it."

"Don't . . ." He frowns. "Please, Lucyna, don't make me do this."

"But you're giving me no other choice!" I suddenly yell.

"You have another choice!" he yells back, angrily shaking his head.

We glare at each other for a long moment.

He pushes his hands through is golden hair. "Just stay here, please."

"No, I want to be with James."

"Then you are being idiotic."

161

"Maybe I am," I shrug, "but I love him."

He looks at me fiercely. "If you place this wish on me, then you will be on your own, Lucyna."

I sit down on the edge of the hammock.

I don't want to lose Arlo and I really don't want to hurt him, but I can't just stay here with him out of guilt.

"I'm so sorry," I say quietly. "I don't want to lose you but –"

"Wish it," he says cutting me off, voice hard, eyes like slits.

I brace myself, gripping my fingers into the netting and lift my head high. "I wish to be human and for you to send me to earth."

He glances down to the ground, and when he looks back up his eyes are different. Yellow. Bright yellow.

I feel a beat of alarm. Something's wrong.

Then everything seems to slip into slow motion.

My eyes move downwards to see all the asters surrounding me have all withered and died. The sky suddenly pulls in dark. And then Arlo utters those immortal words, and I know it's too late.

The next thing – pain, such pain. It's excruciating. I'm screaming. I know I am, I can hear it clear in my mind, but there's no sound coming. Just nothing. Blackness. Total and utter black, surrounding me everywhere.

I'm falling. Fast and hard.

Then -

Chapter 18

Forgotten

Oww, my head hurts. Really hurts. It's practically throbbing off my shoulders.

I'm aching all over and my mouth is parched. I'm so thirsty. I feel like I haven't had a drink in, well – a really long time.

I reach my hand up to my head. It feels all woozy and foggy – what is wrong with me? I can't even open my eyes because they feel so heavy and tacky.

Hey, hang on, what's that sound? It sounds like . . . water?

Where am I?

With a huge amount of effort, I wrench my eyes open and, squinting in the bright light, I somehow manage to lift myself up slightly, and I find myself face-to-face with the ocean. The frothy waves are washing up onto the shoreline before me.

What am I doing here?

I prod my brain for the answer but none comes. It's like there's a dense fog covering everything and I can't seem to penetrate it.

I sit myself up further and rub at my pounding head. Then I slowly glance around my surroundings taking in the beach spread out all around me. There's a couple of people further up walking a dog, then I clock a man quickly approaching from my right, jogging along the shoreline.

"Excuse me," I say, but my voice comes out scratchy and hoarse and he doesn't hear me. I manage to kneel myself up onto my protesting limbs. "Excuse me!" I say more loudly, waving my hand about.

Thankfully I catch his attention and he stops just past me and turns back, continuing to jog on the spot, looking at me questionably.

"Erm, can you tell me where I am?" My voice still sounds as rough as sandpaper.

He glances around and then back at me, a smile creeps onto his lips. "The beach," he says flippantly.

163

I rub my forehead, frustrated. "I mean which beach? Whereabouts?"

He peers at me curiously, still continuing to jog on the spot. "Bondi."

My stomach tightens, like a hand's just grabbed hold of it. Something doesn't feel right.

I sit back onto my haunches, my heart pounding. "Bondi?" I say my voice jumping about with apprehension. "As in Bondi beach in Australia?"

He laughs condescendingly. "Yes, as in Bondi beach in Sydney, Australia." He accentuates each word as though I'm the most stupid person he's ever met.

Bondi? Australia?

No that's . . . I don't know.

I throw my mind back as hard as I can, trying to catch hold of something, anything, but there's nothing, nothing at all, just an invariable . . . nothingness. Not a single tangible memory for me to grab hold of. It's like trying to wade through mud. Everything's all muggy and cloudy. My memories are out of my reach, almost as if I no longer own them, no longer have a right to them. Because no matter what angle or route I try to take in my mind, I keep drawing a blank, a big, fat blank.

Oh God, what's happened to me? Why can't I remember anything?

I feel a massive stab of panic.

"Heavy night, eh?" the jogger says jeeringly, grinning down at me, and I think it must be the look of absolute horror on my face, that changes his to concern. He stops jogging, comes over, and crouches down in front of me.

"Hey, you okay?" he asks, wide eyes peering at me.

My eyes start to sting and a big fat tear suddenly trickles down my cheek. "I don't know," I gulp, twisting my hands together in my lap. "I mean, I don't know how I got here."

A look of surprise flickers across his face. "Oh, erm, what? You don't know how you got here?" he echoes my words, as though he barely believes them.

I shake my head numbly as another tear rolls down my cheek. I roughly wipe it away. "I'm not sure what I'm doing here . . . I don't know how I got here."

"Oh, erm, right, well, it's okay, don't you worry." He pushes his blonde hair off his damp forehead. "I'll, erm, I'll . . ." I can see his eyes scanning around and then he fixes his sight onto something. "Just wait here a sec," he says, quickly rising to stand, "I'll just go get some help." He dashes off, leaving me alone.

I wrap my arms around my trembling body.

Less than a minute later, the jogger arrives back with a dark haired, very tanned guy who's wearing sunglasses, black shorts and a white polo shirt emblazoned with the word – Lifeguard.

The lifeguard crouches before me but the jogger stays standing, hanging a bit further back.

"Hey," the lifeguard says, "you okay?"

I press my lips together and shake my head.

"Here." He hands me a tissue he just pulled from his shorts pocket.

"Thanks," I mumble. I take it gratefully and wipe my eyes.

He pulls off his sunglasses, revealing the bluest eyes I've ever seen – well I mean, I think they are.

"I'm sorry," I sniffle.

"You've nothin' to be sorry about." He smiles, eyes warm. He sits down in front of me, crossing his legs.

"My names Fen. I'm a lifeguard – obviously." He grins down at his chest and I force a weak smile in return. "So, this guy here –" He thumbs over his shoulder glancing back at the jogger.

"Paul," the jogger affirms.

"Paul, right –" Fen the lifeguard says with a nod, then looks back to me. "– said you might need some help, that you're a bit confused, that you don't remember how you got here. That right?"

"Yes," I say in a lowered tone.

"Okay," he says, tucking his chin length dark hair behind his ears. His phone starts to ring and I jump at the sound. My eyes follow his hand to his belt where his phone is clipped. He switches it off without looking at it, all the time keeping his bright blue eyes fixed on me. "Were you drinking last night?" he asks. I see his eyes quickly sweep over my clothes as though his answer lies there. I follow his gaze down to my jeans and white t-shirt.

Was I drinking?

I push my hair back off my face. "I'm not sure – I mean I don't think I was . . . I – I can't remember."

"Right," he nods, "did you maybe have anything else, something a bit – stronger?" he asks this in a quieter voice.

"Stronger?"

"Drugs."

Erm . . .

"No, I don't think so . . ." I shake my head, leaving my brain feeling like its still swishing about inside. "Well, I mean . . ." I sigh and shrug helplessly, looking straight into his eyes. "I don't know."

"Okay." He rubs his forehead with his knuckles. "So can you tell me the last thing you do remember?"

I curl my fingers together, clasping hold of the tissue in my hand.

Taking a deep breath I close my eyes and try again. I push my mind back really hard, as far out as I can, but again all I draw up is a blank. Panic quickly rises in me.

I flick my eyes open. "I don't know!" my voice shoots out in terror. "I can't remember! I can't remember anything!"

I can see the shock reverberate through his eyes but he still manages to hold a calm, warm exterior. His look is so warm and so calming that for a split second I actually feel comforted. It doesn't last long when the present slams straight back into me.

"You're telling me you can't remember anything?" I can hear the tinge of disbelief in his voice.

And I don't blame him. If I was him I'd be the same. I'm me and trust me, I'm finding it pretty hard to believe.

I rake my fingers through my tangled hair. "No, I can't," I say feeling somewhat breathless.

I look at him. His brow is all furrowed. I can see his thoughts furiously flicking away behind his insanely blue eyes and I know what he's thinking. He's thinking I'm either an alcoholic, a drug addict or just plain crazy . . . or maybe actually all three combined.

But I don't feel crazy - slightly hysterical maybe, but not crazy.

166

"I'm not crazy," I hear myself saying, "I just can't remember." I cover my face with my hands, pressing the soggy tissue up against my cheek.

He inhales deeply. "I never said you were crazy. I just wanna help you."

I peer out from in-between my fingers to see him looking at me sincerely.

He pushes his hand through his dark hair. "Have you got anything with you, like a purse, a phone . . ." A quick glance around me answers his question. "No, okay." He drums his fingers on his bare knee. "Well, can you give me a number of someone I can call for you and we'll go from there?" He reaches for his phone.

I flick a quick glance over at the jogger, then back to Fen. They're both staring at me expectantly and I don't know how to answer.

I feel like my heads short-circuiting or it's possibly about to explode because the more I try to force the memories, the worse it gets, the higher my level of panic rises. I try to search my brain for a telephone number, reaching to the outer edges of my mind, but there's nothing there except for a vacuous void where my memories should have been. No telephone numbers, just absolutely nothing.

"I don't know any numbers." I can feel the blood pumping furiously through my veins and my face is getting hot.

A look of frustration flickers over Fen's face. He clips his phone back to his belt and folds his arms and stares at me. "Come on, you must know one, how about your mum's or –"

I shake my head furiously, forcing his words to come to an abrupt end. And as I look at his bewildered and frustrated face, I suddenly feel powerless and so completely and utterly vulnerable.

"I. Don't. Know," I say, my voice snapping and unable to avoid it doing so. "I don't know anything!"

"Okay, just try to keep calm," he says in a composed voice.

"I can't!" I cry. "How can I keep calm? I'm here and I don't know why I'm here, or how I even got here and . . . and . . ." I tail off breathlessly as the realisation drenches me. I have to bite my lip to stop from crying. My stomach is churning about in dread and my heart is beating so fast I feel like it's going to jump out of my chest as I comprehend just how

167

very bad this actually is.

Because the truth is even when I try to think of the most basic things about myself, nothing comes. It's like I know everything and absolutely nothing. I know this is sand here below me and that's the ocean over there, and that's a seagull hovering in the sky just there, and I know what a lifeguard is, but for some terrifying reason I know absolutely nothing about myself, not one single thing.

"I know you're scared," Fen says, his voice controlled, deep, "but you're gonna have to try and stay calm because I can't help you if you don't." I can see his hand clasped around a radio that's attached to his belt.

I close my eyes, taking a few deep breaths. Blood is beating in my ears and my heart is pounding so loudly I'm sure he must be able to hear it.

I open them again to see Fen looking at me with uneasy eyes. The radio is in his hand now.

"I'm sorry," I apologise, pulling my knees to my chest, wrapping my arms around them. My eyes are swelling with tears again.

I see Fen exchange a look with the jogger who's actually moved further away from me.

Fen moves round and sits beside me. "Look, what I'm gonna do is radio to my colleague and get her down here to cover my patch so I can take you to see a medic. I think that's the best thing to do. Is that okay with you?"

I rest my cheek on my knee and glance sideways at him. "Yes," I say.

"Good." He puts the radio to his mouth, pauses and looks back at me with questioning eyes. "What's your name?"

I tighten my arms around my legs and take a deep breath. "I don't know. I don't know my name." I push the air from my lungs and a stray tear trickles from the corner of my eye.

I see the shock reverberate through his face. "Bugger," he murmurs quietly.

Yeah, bugger. That just about covers it.

He puts his arm around my shoulder. "Don't worry," he says in a soft voice, patting my shoulder gently, "it's all gonna be okay. I'll make sure your okay." He puts the radio to his lips and starts talking quickly into it.

I sigh heavily and another tear breaks free, followed by another, then another.

And I know it's not going to be okay. How can it be when I don't even know my own name?

Chapter 19

Desolate

"So you're seeing Mark Rogers at two pm for some tests, is that right?" Dr Woods asks. His grey eyes are peering out from over the top of his glasses as he looks enquiringly at me.

I repress a sigh. More tests. Great.

"Yes." I nod.

"Good, good," he mutters. "Well I'll pop back afterwards to see how you got on." He pushes his glasses up his nose, gathers his papers up and shoves his pen into his jacket pocket. He gets up from the chair beside my bed and heads for the door.

He stops just shy of it and turns back to me. "You're gonna be okay, you know," he says in a well-meaning voice.

"I know."

"We're all here to help you. I'm here –" He pats his chest. "– anything you need, you just have one of the nurses beep me – anytime," he adds with a warm smile.

"Thanks," I say forcing a smile in return.

"See you later, then." He sweeps through the door which closes behind him with a thud.

I flop back onto my pillows and sigh loudly into the encumbering silence.

I'm sat on my bed in my room in St Vincent's Hospital. I've been here for six days. Mark Rogers is the neurologist who's coming to see me this afternoon, just in case you were wondering. I've seen him once before, on the day I arrived here. Dr Woods, he's the specialist who's been taking care of me since I arrived.

And well, Dr Woods and Mark Rogers, and several other brain doctors have all concluded, after a lot of tests and CT scans, that I'm suffering from some severe form of focal retrograde amnesia.

Amnesia, I know – great huh? The worst case they've ever heard of, apparently, which is comforting to know.

You see, after all the extensive tests they've done, they have only managed to discover what I already know, which is that I don't remember anything about anything.

Well what I mean is I know the sky is blue and the earth revolves around the sun, and that wall over there, well it's really bland shade of yellow. But when it came to them asking me what year it is or who the current prime minister of the country is, or well basically anything about myself – I couldn't answer because I don't know.

I know absolutely nothing about me, not my name or where I live, or how old I am.

Zilch. Zero. Nada.

I've come to terms with it, sort of. Well as much as you can after six days.

After that day on the beach, when Fen had radioed through to his colleague, he took me to see their medic who advised that he bring me straight to the hospital, and here I've been ever since.

Fen has been really wonderful to me. He was amazing on that first day. He stayed with me the whole time, keeping me company, waiting patiently whilst I had test after test done. And he's been visiting me every day since, bringing me things like magazines and chocolate, which is really kind of him because he doesn't have to. All I am to him is just some weird girl who rocked up on his beach, putting a dent in his otherwise normal working day, declaring to him that I have no memory of who I am.

And that's the really weird thing about my amnesia, you see, the doctors can't seem to figure out how I've come to acquire it. Generally it's caused by a trauma to the head of which I have shown no visible signs. And normally people who have amnesia lose a few months, a few years maybe, at the most, but it seems I've lost everything which rarely happens, if ever.

The only other possibility Dr Woods could offer was that an emotional trauma had triggered it. That can happen, as I've been told. Post-traumatic stress disorder, Dr Woods called it, when something so horrific happens to a person they block it out and their memory just kind of switches off. Dr Woods said he thought it unlikely in my case due to the extent of memory loss, but he didn't want to rule it out.

So he said, in quiet undertones, he thought it best that I had a 'physical' examination done.

I lay there whilst Dr Woods and the attending nurse did the examination, feeling sick to the pit of my stomach every time I thought of the many different possibilities of what could have happened.

And after what I can only describe as the most humiliating experience I've had to endure so far, Dr Woods assured me everything seemed fine. He said if something emotional had happened to trigger my memory loss, then it most certainly wasn't anything sexual because my hymen was intact, meaning I'm a virgin. And, if I'm as old as I look, that makes me a mid-twenty-something year old virgin.

Wonderful.

Another piece to add to the ever growing puzzle that is me.

Mark Rogers, the hippy neurologist in his brown cords, flowery shirt and long brown straggly hair, comes to see me at two, as arranged. We go into the family room which is a welcome change of scenery from the drab four yellow walls of my room. We sit at a table and do some tests where he has me drawing pictures from memory, recounting a short story that he reads to me, remembering fifteen words in a list, that sort of thing. The tests are pretty much the same ones as he did the last time I saw him, barring the physical examinations he did to my head and eyes. I don't see the point to it in all honesty. It's not like recounting words are gonna bring my memories back but I dutifully play along.

I remember exactly how his face lit up like a Christmas tree when he first discovered the extent of my memory loss. He was looking at me like I was the cure for cancer, and he could see the Nobel Peace Prize in sight (and yes I do know what that is; Fen told me about it the other day).

Mark said, in an excitable voice, that my case was extraordinary and that someone (I'm guessing him) would want to write a paper on me at some point.

I felt like slapping him.

He's a nice guy, don't get me wrong, but that was the last thing I needed to hear.

I know to him I'm just an interesting case that might boost his career, but to me this is everything, this is every memory I've ever made that's gone missing. All of them vamoosed, just like that.

Mark does tell me, though, what exactly it is that has happened to my brain. He says, in simple laymen terms, for some reason my warehouse of memories has shut down, the door is locked tight, for want of a better word. They're all in there and intact but they're hidden behind this hermetically sealed door and, unfortunately, I appear to have lost the ability to unlock said door. Or maybe, as he put it, for whatever reason I just don't want to.

I felt like telling him, if I could open it I would, but for some reason I held my tongue.

I've tried, believe me. I've raked through my mind until my head starts to pound and my eyes blur, and I can't take it anymore. But every single time I come up dry.

Dr Woods popped back in as he said he would. He really is a great doctor. He didn't stay long, though, as there really wasn't anything to say because the tests with Mark had identified nothing.

He did let me know the DNA swab the police took from me didn't show up any results in their I.D. system. You see, Dr Woods informed the police about me on the day I arrived, and the next day a female police officer came to see me. She took my fingerprints and a DNA mouth swab to see if I would show up on their files to help identify me. The fingerprints came back the next day with no results but I was really hoping the DNA would. Well, to be honest, I was pinning all my hopes on it. I did my best to hide my disappointment from Dr Woods when he told me, but I think he knew.

The press have also been notified about my 'story', so that's been running in the paper and it's also been on the local news.

It hasn't been big news, though, because on the day I was found, there was a bus crash and a lot of people died, so that kind of overshadowed my story, which of course it should. But I am praying that someone will see my picture and recognise me.

Fen comes at dinner time. He's snuck in a McDonalds meal for us both. We eat together and he tells me about his day and the waves he caught this morning – he went surfing before work which he does nearly every day. Apparently his day was pretty standard. You see, as he puts it, nothing has yet trumped finding me on the beach, which is a good thing, he assures me, as he'd be pretty busy with two amnesiac's to visit. My response – 'Ha, bloody ha'.

I like Fen. He's easy to talk to, he makes me laugh and he takes my mind off all of this. He gives me a sense of normality which is exactly what I need right now.

He's also taken to calling me Pommie. Apparently I don't sound Australian. No one could seem to place my accent, but concluded that if anything I sound English which, if I'm from England, makes things even more confusing as to why I ended up on a beach here in Australia. Obviously I don't know my name, and Dr Woods had said it would be a good idea to give myself one, help to start me off with some form of identity. I refused. I told him the only name I want is the one I had and, when I remember that, I'll let him know. No one knew what to call me, so Fen started calling me Pommie and it stuck.

So here I am all alone now. Fen left not long after we finished our dinner as he's going out with friends. I'm sat in the dark after another long day of tests, still no better off, staring out the window whilst the lights from the city glitter down below.

I feel so alone, so completely and utterly alone. And I don't mean physically. There could be a hundred people in this room and I'd still feel alone. This kind of solitude comes from deep inside and I have no way to fill it.

How can I not know who I am? How could I have forgotten everything about myself?

I need to remember. Something. Anything.

But what if I can't – what then?

I'm just praying someone comes for me. There has to be someone out there who knows me, knows who I am, where I come from. I can't just have appeared out of thin air. And all I need is one person, just one person to tell me who I am.

And if no one comes, then . . . well, honestly, I try not to think about

174

that because the thought scares the hell out of me.

I look into the window, my reflection gazing back at me. I feel like I'm looking at a stranger. Almost as if I've accidentally landed in this body that doesn't really belong to me, and the owner's going to turn up any minute and take it back.

I move closer to the glass. "Who are you?" I whisper to my reflection, my breath steaming up the glass. My eyes stare knowingly back at me as though they hold the answers to everything but refuse to tell.

I bang my fist frustratedly against my head, my eyes suddenly hot with tears. I withdraw from the window, get up from the chair and climb into bed, pulling the covers over me. I curl myself up into a tight ball as the loneliness presses into me silently, devastatingly, and I let the tears flow like I have done every night for the last six nights.

You don't have a soul. You are a soul. You have a body.

CS Lewis

Chapter 20

James

It's been six weeks. Well, forty-three days to be exact, forty-three excruciatingly long days since she vanished from right before my eyes. Funny, six weeks is actually longer than I had her in my life. It's crazy how I can be so in love with someone I've only known for such a small amount of time. And I know to some it might seem impetuous and foolhardy, but I didn't stand a chance. How could I not love her? She's amazing and beautiful, and quirky, and different, and . . . well you get the picture.

She saved me and I don't just mean on the night of my accident.

My life was pretty crap and I was fast heading down the road to Shitsville until the moment I saw her, then everything changed, it all just clicked right back into place. I started to feel normal again, like I used to before dad died, and I knew everything would be okay from there on out as long as she was around.

It doesn't matter to me who she is, or where she comes from, I just want her.

I know it might not make sense. Nothing about this whole situation makes any sense, but it doesn't change how I feel, and right now I just need her back here with me. I'm kind of finding it hard to breathe without her.

It's the not knowing that's driving me insane, not knowing where she is, if she's okay . . . if she's ever coming back.

The thought of never seeing her again makes my head feel like it's going to implode, so I try not to think about it. I have to stay positive. She said she'd find a way back to me, so I just have to hold onto that.

I will see her again.

When she first disappeared, I didn't know what to do — what I could do. I just stood there in the kitchen, paralysed, eyes transfixed on the spot where she'd been. I literally couldn't breathe. It was like someone had a tight grip on my lungs and was expelling every bit of air from them. I felt powerless. There wasn't a single fucking thing I could do. Every instinct was telling me I should look for her, tear the streets up searching, but I'm guessing where Lucyna's gone is not somewhere I have ready access to.

All I've done since is to try to keep myself busy with anything and everything, pretending to the outside world all is okay so I don't have to think about how much I miss her. Trust me, it's easier said than done. It's the night time that gets me. When I'm alone. That's when I feel it. When I feel all sore and empty inside.

I've had to lie to everyone about where she is. I said she's gone to visit her family and I suppose in a weird sort of way it's true – and, really, what else could I say, that she's a heavenly being and was taken back to Heaven?

Hmm . . . I think not. I'd probably end up been committed.

A couple of times I've woken up in the middle of the night, panicked, thinking it was all a dream, she was a dream, but my heart beats her name too loudly for her to have never been in it. She made me feel alive again and I'm not ready to let go of that just yet, or maybe ever.

And even though, once again, I wish I could hide here in my bed all day, I know I can't. I have another day I have to get through, a business to run.

I push myself up, swing my good leg over the side of the bed, and drag my potted leg over to join it. My feet touch the oak floor. Bloody hell that's cold. I should really get a carpet put in here, but Lucyna did say she liked the feel of the cold beneath her feet. She said it made her feel alive. Now I know her, I know exactly what she meant.

With a sigh I reach over and turn the radio on the alarm clock on, anything to fill up this silence. It springs to life with exactly what I didn't need.

'Show me the meaning of being lonely,
Is this the feeling I need to walk with?
Tell me why I can't be there where you are,
There's something missin' in my heart.'

Fucking Backstreet Boys.

I grab the clock, yanking the plug out of the socket and hurl it across the room. It smashes against the wall, shattering to pieces. And once again the room is silenced to deafening. I hobble over to the bathroom, slamming the door loudly behind me.

The shower does nothing to make me feel better. It's nothing but a bloody chore at the moment. I'm perched precariously on the side of the bath, pot covered with a plastic bin bag, trying not to get it wet. I swear the minute it's off, I'm getting a long, hot shower.

When I've finished, I clamber out of the bath, wrap a towel around my waist, rip the bag from my leg, and wipe the condensation from the mirror above the sink with my hand.

Jesus, I look like shit.

I reach for my toothbrush and, without warning an image of her appears in my mind. I close my eyes and try desperately to hold onto it. It's not clear. I can't see her as I used to. She's starting to fray around the edges. I rest my forehead against the cool glass, hoping in some way that will make it clearer. It doesn't. And it's too late; she's gone.

What if I forget what she looks like? What if one day I just wake up and I can't see her anymore?

The loss slams into me hard.

I feel so completely and utterly alone, and I have to hold my breath just to stop myself freaking out, because this is a different kind of loneliness. It hurts so much that my heart actually aches with physical pain.

Come on, James, focus. It's just another day. You've done forty-three so far, what's another?

I take a deep breath, pull back from the mirror and set about brushing my teeth.

When I'm done, I open the door leading straight into my bedroom, the steam following me out and . . . "Jesus Christ!" I yell, jumping in shock. There's a woman stood by my bed and she's definitely no woman I know.

"Not quite," she smiles lightly.

"Who the hell are you?"

179

"Isabel. You've no need to be alarmed, James." She lifts a calming hand. "I'm here to help you."

"Help?" I say agitated and confused. "What makes you think I need help?"

"Lucyna," she says.

"Lucyna? What about her? Is she okay? Where is she?" And the words just keep on tumbling out of my mouth.

She holds up a firm hand, cutting me off. "Lucyna's fine – well sort of."

Fear grips a tight hold of my stomach. "Sort of? Sort of!" My voice is starting to sound slightly unhinged. "What's that supposed to mean?"

"Don't worry, I'll explain all. But please dress first," she says, gesturing to me.

I glance down at my half-clad body and tighten the towel around my waist. I grab the t-shirt that's hanging on the radiator beside me. "Tell me," I say, dragging the t-shirt on over my head.

"She's in a hospital in Sydney –"

"Australia?" I say incredulously.

She nods curtly, her red hair falling across her face. She pushes it back. "She's fine physically. She's human now, but she has no memory of who she used to be, of anything . . . of you."

I rest up against the wall, my body suddenly weary, all my urgency halted. "How?"

She sits down on the edge of my bed. "From what I'm guessing she was made a mortal by Arlo and he took away her memories."

"Arlo? Who the hell is he?"

"Arlo is an angel like me – like Lucyna used to be, and well . . . also like you once were."

I laugh awkwardly. "What? I used to be an angel?"

She nods casually.

I feel nothing if not casual. Uncomfortable – yes. Casual – not so much.

I make a noise that was supposed to be another laugh but this time it comes out sounding strangled. Nothing's registering at her words. I mean you would think if I used to be something like that it would spark

180

some sort of recognition, wouldn't it?

I push my damp hair off my forehead. "You must have got it wrong – I can't have been an – an angel."

She regards me silently for a moment. "No, I am correct," she says, certainly. "You were Arran. You and I knew one another. You look different now, but you were definitely him."

"How?" I ask.

"You left behind your immortality to become a mortal three hundred years ago at your own request, so you could be with a mortal woman."

I'm starting to feel jittery. Circuits are firing off in my brain. And this conversation is making me feel distinctly uncomfortable. "Was Lucyna the woman I left to be with?"

"No." She shakes her head irritably. "Lucyna was an angel at that time too."

My brow furrows. "So you're saying I knew Lucyna all that time ago?"

"Yes." She hesitates. "Well you and Lucyna were together, but you left her to be with the human. And not long after you left Heaven, she disappeared along with Arlo. I have not seen any of you since, well until six weeks ago when Lucyna's essence registered with us on the day she changed form – from, surprisingly to me, a Bringer – to save your life."

I listen intently as she continues.

"I was sent here to monitor her, well the both of you – I must say I wasn't in the least bit surprised the moment I realised who you were, that she had saved you from that car wreck. Lucyna loved Arran immensely. And when she vanished again a few weeks ago without trace, I was concerned, so I have been searching for her ever since. There has been nothing, well not until yesterday when I fortunately became aware of a story being broadcast by the humans about a woman found in Australia recently with no memory of who she was – and low and behold it was Lucyna."

After hearing that you'd think I'd be shocked, stunned in fact, but with all I've heard and seen recently, I'm way past the element of surprise.

"How did she end up in Australia?" I ask this calmly, and God knows how, because I feel anything but.

"I don't know for sure but I believe Arlo may be somehow responsible."

"And this Arlo – why would he do this to Lucyna?"

Her face falls. "I have my own theory . . ."

I narrow my gaze. "And your theory is?"

She looks out of the window. "Inconsequential." Her tone is brisk. "The important thing is that I find him which I can't do." Her voice trails off and she is silent for a moment. She looks back to me. "It seems he doesn't want to be found and that he didn't want Lucyna to be found either as her essence is being masked. Her mind has been blanked of all memories. I can't see anything, it's as if there's been a wall built up in there and it's too dense for me to penetrate. The only way I'll know anything is if she'll allow me to try and release the memories locked in her mind. But she has to consent to this, and even then I still may not be able to break through because the magic Arlo has worked – if it is him, is strong."

I stare out the window at the cool clear day, my mind frantically working away, trying to figure this all out.

I take a deep breath and look back at her. "Okay," I say, crossing my arms over my chest, "so let me get this straight in my mind. You're telling me I was an angel called Arran, and me and Lucyna were together, but three hundred years ago I left her to be with another woman, and then she left Heaven with this Arlo, became a Bringer, found me – Arran . . ." shit this is confusing. ". . . disappeared again possibly thanks to Arlo, and has now turned up in Australia, human, with no memory of who she was."

The corners of her lips turn up. "Basically, yes."

I press my lips together. It all sounds so . . . hmm . . . confusing, mind-bending, a bit on the crazy-side . . . need I go on?

I suddenly have a thought. "Who was the woman?"

Isabel looks at me inquisitively.

"The woman, Arran – I mean, I –" I shake my head, "fuck, this is confusing! Sorry," I add when I realise that I just cursed in front of an angel. Isabel looks at me blankly and says nothing, so I carry on. "Who was the woman I left Lucyna to be with?"

"I don't know," she says indifferently, crossing her ankles. "It wasn't a matter I cared to look into. You made your decision, end of story."

Okay. So that's me told.

"Has it ever happened before, an angel becoming mortal?"

She purses her lips and nods formally. "It has happened, not many times. Arran was one of a few. We don't really spend time around the living to attach ourselves emotionally, but sometimes curiosity can get the better of us."

"You?"

She laughs, a genuine laugh. "No. I hadn't been to earth in a very long time, not until I was sent here to watch you and Lucyna. There's nothing here of interest to me."

I uncross my arms and rub my forehead with my fingertips. "Have you spoken to Lucyna?"

"No, I wanted to speak to you first. I didn't want to turn up there and scare her with this announcement. She's unlikely to be reasonable, as she's already feeling very scared and alone."

Isabel's words make me feel sick to the pit of my stomach. I can't bear the thought of her being there all alone and frightened, and also very fucking angry at who put her there.

"And I thought if you came with me —" Isabel continues, breaking me out of my pensive thoughts. "— it could be the key to help me unlock her mind. She might not be aware of it, but the emotional tie she has to you is undeniably strong, that's been proved once already. She may listen to you because I can't even attempt to return her memories without her consent."

I meet her eyes. "There would never have been a moment I wouldn't have come."

"Good." She rises gracefully to her feet. "Let's go, then."

I nod, but there something I need to ask her first. It won't make a difference to anything, but I have to know. "Isabel." I pause. She looks at me curiously. I clear my suddenly hoarse throat. "Did Lucyna know who I used to be when she saved my life?"

"No, she had no clue of who you were, who she used to be, or of your history together." She regards me warmly for a moment. "At that point she loved you."

"Because I used to be him?" I think out loud.

She flashes me a tight smile. "Maybe . . . partly."

Now I know I'm not so sure how I feel about it but I push it aside as there are far more important things to think about, mainly how quickly I can get to Lucyna. The rest I can sort out later.

I push off the wall. "Right, I'll just pack some clothes and get my passport –"

She laughs condescendingly, halting my words. "James, we're not travelling by human transport. I will take us."

Okay, so now I feel stupid for even speaking.

"But I'm going to need you a bit more mobile than that," she adds, pointing a finger at my leg.

Almost immediately I feel a warm tingling sensation running through my broken leg and hear a crack. I watch in astonishment as the pot crumbles to the floor. I look down at my bare leg in shock. The pain is gone. I bend it slowly. It feels fine, well better than fine.

"It's fixed," she says off-hand, like she's just glued a cup back together, or something trivial like that. "And put some trousers on. I don't think turning up to see Lucyna in a towel will help matters."

I grab my jeans off the chair by the window and pull them up under the towel, instantly realising the ludicrousness of the situation I'm in. I'm half-naked dressing in front of an angel. Hmm? I twist my lips, forcing the smile from my face, as I button up my jeans. It must be hysteria or something which, given the situation, I think is a perfectly reasonable thing to feel.

I push my feet into my trainers. "Okay, let's go," I say fervently.

Isabel comes over and holds her hands out. I take hold of them. "Close your eyes," she instructs, "and don't open them until I tell you to."

"Okay," I say, a touch apprehensively. Well, truth be told, I'm absolutely shitting myself but if it gets me to Lucyna, then I'm prepared to do just about anything. I close my eyes and open them straightaway.

184

Isabel sighs, impatiently.

I look straight into her green eyes. "Lucyna's not going to know who I am, is she?" I say, my voice sounding tinny as I suddenly realise the calamity of the situation.

She looks back at me regretfully. "No."

"Do you think you'll be able to get her memories back?" I ask, hopefully.

She smiles a tight smile. "I can't promise anything."

My heart sinks. I compress the pain down and close my eyes.

"Ready?" Isabel asks softly.

"Ready." I instantly feel a shuddering sensation run through my hands, up my arms, spreading throughout the whole of my body.

Within a matter of seconds I hear Isabel's whispering voice say, "You can open your eyes, James. We're here." She releases my hands.

Nervously I peel my eyes open and sway slightly on my feet, feeling unsteady. I press my feet into the floor whilst quickly casting my eyes over the moonlit room.

Isabel silently points over my shoulder and I turn to see Lucyna. She's asleep in bed. My heart nearly explodes with relief. Six weeks I've waited for this moment. Six fucking weeks. And now I daren't move.

I force my feet forward and, very nervously and very quietly, I tread over to the bed.

I gaze down at her. She looks just as I remembered, if not more beautiful. She's breathing deeply. The rise and fall of her chest is mesmerising, her face so peaceful, I'm almost afraid to wake her.

Carefully I perch on the edge of her bed and glance down at the book in her hand. She must have fallen asleep reading. I feel an instant rush of love for her. I gently pull it from her hand and reach back, placing it on the table by her bed. Then I brush her hair off her face with my fingers. "Luce, wake up, baby," I say quietly, cradling her face with my hand.

She murmurs in her sleep and turns her face into my hand, nuzzling it. I stroke the length of her nose with my thumb. "Luce baby, wake up."

Her breathing suddenly halts and her eyes flick open, bright blue and filled with panic. I withdraw my hand. She leaps backwards in her bed, her back pressed up against the wall.

"Who – who are you?" she says, wide eyes flicking from me to Isabel, then back to me again. There's not a trace of recognition in them.

Okay, so I wasn't as prepared for this as I thought I might be. I know I was aware she wouldn't know me, but Jesus, it really fucking hurts – A LOT – to have her looking at me like I'm a stranger. It's like a knife in the chest.

Pushing all my pain aside, I focus on her, focus on how she must be feeling right now. Pretty freaked out I'm guessing.

"Shh," I say gently, raising a calming hand. "It's okay, you're safe. We're here to help you get your memory back . . ."

. . . I hope.

Whatever our souls are made of, his and mine are the same.

Wuthering Heights – Emily Bronte

Chapter 21

A New Beginning

"Hey Pommie."

I look up from my magazine to see a smiling Fen coming through the door and my spirits instantly lift.

"Hi," I say, surprised. "I wasn't expecting to see you. I thought you were going out for dinner tonight for your mum's birthday?"

"I am. I had to come past the hospital on my way to the restaurant so I thought I'd drop this in for you." He hands me a battered looking book and sits himself down into the chair by my bed.

I notice he looks different. What is it? I eye him carefully, but I can't see anything specifically standing out. Understandably he looks a little smarter than usual. He's wearing black jeans and a fitted grey shirt. And his hair's tidier than he normally wears it. It's usually all mussed up. Actually, he looks quite handsome. I mean, I know Fen's good looking, I'd have to be blind not to notice, but tonight he looks, dare I say it, hot? Nerves flutter through my stomach at the thought. Okay, that was weird.

"Thanks," I say with a delay and begin to examine the front cover of the book. 'The Beach' – oh it's the one he was telling me about yesterday – and, no, he's not being ironic. Apparently it's really good and has nothing whatsoever to do with amnesiacs turning up on it. I'm reading a lot at the moment, anything I can get my hands on really. Well, it's not like I have much else to do and it's nice to escape off into someone else's fantasy for a while. It distracts me away from my own depressing reality.

"You didn't have to bring it now, though," I say putting the book down on the bed. "I could have waited till tomorrow. It's not like I haven't got plenty to keep me busy." I point towards the stack of books piled up on the table.

He shrugs. "It's no problem." He kicks his shoes off, puts his feet up on my bed, rests his head back on the chair and closes his eyes.

"Comfortable there?" I chuckle, nudging his foot with mine.

"Hmm, very."

"Hard day at work?"

"Yep." A lazy smile forms on his lips and he opens his eyes. It still surprises me just how blue they actually are. They're striking in contrast with his black hair and olive skin. They look almost luminous in this fluorescent lighting. "I had the early shift," he tells me, "then ended up having to stay late 'cause there was a problem with one of the boats." He yawns loudly. "Could really do with going home to bed but it's my mum's birthday, so what can you do?" He stretches his arms over his head. His shirt rides up and I find myself involuntarily glancing down. Wow, his stomach is really smooth and toned . . .

"So how's your day been?" he asks.

"Hmm?"

"I said – how's your day been?"

I realise I'm staring and instantly come to my senses. I see a flicker of amusement pass over his face.

"Oh, yeah, good," I smile.

He picks the remote off the table and turns the TV on. I glance back down at my magazine.

Actually that was a lie.

It's just been another pointless day of nothing. I've been here four weeks now, and after all the testing and neuro-psychotherapy sessions, there's still absolutely nothing happening in this stupid brain of mine. I've not even had one meagre, teeny tiny little memory resurface. So, yes, I still have absolutely no idea who I am.

The only memories I do have are the ones I've made since I arrived here. And the only good ones I've made are when Fen visits, which he does everyday, and has done since that day. We've become really good friends and, honestly, I don't know what I would do without him. I would never tell him this, mainly because it sounds so lame, but seeing him is the only good part of my day, the best part, in fact, because the rest of the time I'm miserable and lonely.

I know I need to start moving forward and I have been thinking about the future a lot lately. I can't spend the rest of my life like this, I can't keep hanging out for the past, hoping it'll return. I need to start living for now.

"You okay?" he asks. I look up from my magazine to find his eyes surveying me.

"Yeah." I close my magazine and chuck it onto the table. "Actually, I've been thinking."

He looks at me with interest. "About?"

"Well I've been thinking that maybe Dr Woods is right, you know, maybe it is time I start moving forward and I thought the best way to do that would be to – you know give myself an identity like he said – give myself a name."

"Aww, but I like 'Pommie'." He flashes me a cheeky grin.

I give him a wry look.

"I'm kidding!" He holds up a hand. "No, that's really great," he enthuses. "So, do you have one in mind?"

I nod but then instantly wish I hadn't. I suddenly feel shy and embarrassed. What if he laughs? What if he thinks it's a really rubbish name?

"So what is it?" he asks, pulling a packet of mints from his jeans pocket. He opens them up, pops one in his mouth and offers them to me. I shake my head.

"You know what, it doesn't matter," I backtrack. "I mean I'm not a hundred percent sure that I might go for it anyway, so . . ."

He gives me an inquisitive look. "Why won't you tell me?"

I look away from him, fully aware of how stupid I'm being and how I've now managed to make it more of a deal than it actually ever was.

I begin fiddling with my hair. "You might laugh," I say quietly, my eyes averted.

"Why would I laugh?" He crunches his mint. "It's not like it's gonna be something horrendous, like Gertrude or –" He claps a hand over his mouth. "Shit, it's not, is it?"

"No!" I laugh.

He chuckles and puts his feet down into his shoes, then he leans forward, resting his forearms on his thighs, blue eyes fixed on me. "You're gonna have to tell me now, 'cause I'm really intrigued."

190

I stare down at my long hair that I've started to plait. Why do I suddenly feel so shy around him?

He points the remote at the TV, switches it off, gets up from his seat and sits down on the bed beside me. I glance up at him and meet his eyes. My heart does this weird fluttery thing and my mouth suddenly dries.

This is getting really weird. What is going on with me?

"Would it help if I told you my name?" he says, pushing his hand through his dark hair.

"I know your name –"

"No," he butts in. "Fen's not my actual name."

I stop plaiting. Now I'm intrigued. "Okay," I say, raising an eyebrow.

He rubs his hand over his mouth. "Promise not to laugh?"

"I promise." I begin untangling my hair.

He eyes me suspiciously. I maintain steady contact, widening my eyes. "I promise," I emphasise, jokily holding my hands up.

He's quiet for a moment. "Osvaldo," he finally says, face deadpan.

I laugh.

"Hey!" He pokes me in the arm jovially. "You said you wouldn't laugh."

"Sorry," I say, trying to keep a straight face – unsuccessfully, might I add. "Wow, erm, Osvaldo, its erm . . ."

"Portuguese," he says dryly. "My mum's Portuguese. It was my grandfather's name."

Okay, so now I feel mean for laughing. "Where does Fen come from?" I ask, feeling tense, worried I've offended him. I tuck my hair behind my ears.

"My surname's Fenn, and it's what all my mates have called me since school – and anything's gotta be better than Osvaldo," he adds grinning, eyes twinkling at me, and I instantly relax.

"I didn't realise you were from Portugal," I say, but now I look at him I can see it.

"I'm not. I was born here, my dad's Australian but my mum's originally from Portugal."

"Ah, right. So can you speak Portuguese?"

191

"Fluent." He nods.

I lean forward, excitedly. "Ooh, say something to me in Portuguese."

"No," he says coyly.

"Go on," I urge.

He sighs, defeated. "Alright, but on one condition – you have to tell me the name you've picked for yourself?"

I purse my lips. "Okay. Deal. But you go first."

He chuckles, shaking his head. He fixes his insanely blue eyes on mine and says in a lightly accented voice, "Estou tão feliz que você veio em minha vida linda menina."

A shiver runs through me and my heart does this little flip-flop. "What does that mean?" I ask, my voice suddenly sounding hoarse.

"Nothing of importance," he brushes me off. "So, go on then, it's your turn and I promise not to laugh – unlike some people – scout's honour." He does a two finger salute.

And something flashes through my mind, like, I don't know – recognition – a memory – maybe. I close my eyes and try to grab hold of it – but no, it's gone. Dammit!

"You okay?" I hear the sound of Fen concerned voice.

I open my eyes. "Yeah, I'm fine." I rub my head. "I don't know, just when you did that – that salute, it seemed really familiar."

"What, like a memory?" he asks, looking hopeful.

"I don't know." I shake my head, frustrated. "Maybe I've had this conversation before or I've seen someone do that, or – oh I don't know – argh!" I rap my knuckles furiously on my head.

"Hey," he says soothingly, "don't try and force it. It'll come if it's meant too." He rubs my arm and I suddenly feel really irritated.

"It's easy for you to say!" I snap, instantly regretting my outburst when I see the look of sadness on his face.

What is going on with me today? Now I'm picking a fight with the only friend I have.

"I'm sorry," I say quickly. "I shouldn't have snapped at you."

"It's okay," he replies kindly.

I flop back against my pillows. My head feels like it's going to explode with frustration. I close my eyes.

"You should probably tell Dr Woods what happened," he says tentatively, in a soft voice.

"I will." I sigh. "Not that there's really anything to tell him but I'll mention it tomorrow."

We lapse into silence. I feel Fen shuffle on the bed and open up my eyes to see that he's turned away from me and is staring out the window.

I sit up and cross my legs in front of me. "So you were a boy scout, then?" I ask, wanting to go back to how we were before I ruined it.

He glances sideways at me, looking puzzled, but then his face suddenly clicks into understanding. "Only the Joey's. Didn't make it further than that. Discovered a surfboard, you see."

"Ah." I nod. "Shame, I bet you looked real cute in your little uniform." I laugh and tug on his sleeve.

"I look better in my board shorts," He grins cheekily and catches hold of my retreating arm.

My eyes are instinctively pulled to his and something passes between us. The air thickens. Everything seems heightened. I feel a pull to him I've never felt before and I'm lost for words. All I can do now is breathe. The smile drops from his face and we hold eye contact for several seconds before I finally break it. He releases his hold on my arm but I can still feel his touch there.

He clears his throat. "So, anyway, enough of you trying to distract me from the original convo." He turns his body around to face me, bending his left leg up onto the bed to rest it lightly against mine. "Tell me what this elusive name is?"

But now I'm finding it really hard to concentrate because all I'm aware of his that his leg is touching mine, and how he's so close I can smell his aftershave entwined with the scent of the beach. He smells safe and I finally realise exactly just what it is that's going on with me.

I meet his steady gaze and butterflies take flight in my stomach. I take a deep breath and concentrate on my words. "I was thinking, maybe . . . Lucy?" I bite down on my lower lip, waiting for his approval.

He tilts his head to the side and regards me for moment. My face instantly heats under his gaze. "I like it." He nods. "Lucy. Yeah, it suits you."

"You think so?" I say, feeling secretly pleased.

"Yup, I think it's perfect." He smiles and I realise that I'm actually struggling to breathe steadily.

I wonder if he can tell? Surely he can. I look down at my hands.

There is a silence for a moment between us. He's the first to break it. "I think you're doing great, you know." I look up at his words. His face is candid, sincere. "Better than I ever would. Picking a name is a real step in the right direction."

I blow out a breath, suddenly feeling aggrieved and very frustrated with myself. Hell, if picking a name is a step in the right direction, then that makes me just about the most tragic person in the world.

"You know what I think?" I say, rattled. "I think I'm tragic, Fen. I mean, look at me," I sweep my hands down myself, "I have absolutely no clue who I am and I don't know if I ever will. I live in a hospital because I don't know where my home is. I'm like some old lady that's lost her way –" My eyes are hot with tears. What the hell is wrong with me? And it's like now I've started I can't seem to stop, and on I ramble, " – and I can't stay here forever and I don't know where I'm gonna go, what I'm gonna do, and the thought scares the hell out of me, and the best I'm getting is what might not even be a teeny tiny glimpse of a memory. Great! Actually, no, it's crap and I'm a freak! And I'm all alone in this! I have no one! Absolutely no one!" I pause, breathing heavily. My face instantly flames with embarrassment at my outburst. I daren't look at him. "I'm so sorry," I utter, pressing my fingers under my eyes to catch the falling tears.

"You've got nothing to be sorry for. And you're most definitely not a freak." I glance up at him through my lashes. His face is turned away from me and he's staring out the window. I can't make out his expression. "And you're wrong, you know," he says after a moment, his voice deep, "you haven't got no one," he turns his head back to look at me and I'm taken aback by the intensity of his gaze, "you've got me."

And I suddenly feel very nervous. He lifts his hand and tucks my hair behind my ear. My heart starts beating like a jackhammer. I'm sure he must be able to hear it. He runs his fingertips down my jaw, his eyes

194

never leaving mine, then he takes my face in his hands, leans forward and kisses me.

And it's good. Really good.

He kisses me gently, his tongue touching mine ever so slightly. He tastes of mint. He runs his fingers into my hair and I start to lose myself in him. In the kiss. My body floods with feelings for him I hadn't even realised I had until now. I want this so much . . .

Then, without warning, I'm hit with a sharp stab of guilt, right smack bang in my chest. It literally knocks the wind out of me.

I pull away and push him from me, so hard he nearly falls off the bed.

Fen looks as surprised as I feel. I don't even know why I just did that. All I do know is that my face is prickling with guilt and I feel like I've just betrayed someone by kissing him, by feeling this way about him.

"I'm sorry," I say, breathless, my heart pounding, "I just –" I shake my head at a loss for words.

"Don't be sorry, it's me who should be sorry," he says, voice quickly switching to detached, eyes avoiding mine. "I shouldn't have done that. It's far too soon for you – for anything like that. I'm sorry." He stands up abruptly and walks over to the window, resting his arm up against the frame.

I stare at his back, feeling at a loss. What is wrong with me? I have this wonderful guy here who likes me and I like him, really like him, yet I push him away the minute he gets close. Maybe I'm right, maybe I am a freak

"I'm sorry, Fen," I say in a quiet voice. "I don't know what happened. I really wanted you to kiss me but . . . I don't know what's wrong with me." I shake my head, despairingly.

He turns and rests his back up against the window, crossing his arms over his chest. He looks at me and his tense features soften. "Nothing's wrong with you," he says gently, "you've been through a lot. It's understandable." He unfolds his arms and pushes his hands into his jeans pockets. "I should go, though." He jerks his head in the direction of the door. "If I'm late for dinner, my mum'll kill me." He smiles but I can tell it's forced.

195

I feel a shot of dismay. I don't want him to leave, not like this, but it's not like I can ask him to stay after what I've just done, and I bet he can't wait to get away from me anyway, and I don't blame him.

"Yeah, of course," I say, trying to sound light, twisting my hands in my lap. "And thanks – for being so understanding." I force a weak smile.

He shrugs lightly and pulls his hands from his pockets. "Bye, then," he says, holds his hand up in a half wave and heads for the door.

I stare at his retreating back suddenly feeling like I'm drowning. What if he never comes back? What if I never see him again? I really don't want him to go. *So say something for God's sake! Don't just let him leave thinking you don't want him.*

"Fen, wait!" I jump up off the bed.

He stops and turns back, eyes full of surprise. I walk toward him, my pulse quickening, my whole body trembling. I'm not really sure what I'm going to say, I'm just hoping something will come, fast.

I lift my hand up to his face and stroke his smooth olive skin with my fingers. He really is gorgeous and he wants me. Happiness bubbles up inside me and I somehow manage to keep the smile from my face.

"You're wrong, you know," I say tenderly.

His eyes flicker. "About?"

"That it's too soon," I trace my finger over his beautiful mouth, "because it's not."

A smile sneaks onto his lips. "You sure?"

"Very."

He takes hold of my hand and kisses it, then slides his arm around my waist and pulls me to him.

And this time when he kisses me I don't push him away.

It's deep and passionate. My head tingles with anticipation. I slide my arms around his neck. His hand trails down my back, sending electric sparks shooting through my stomach, heading straight toward my heart.

"Minha linda menina," he murmurs, his lips grazing against mine.

I move back to scrutinise him. "What does that mean?"

He smiles shyly. "My beautiful girl."

I feel all warm and fuzzy inside. I lean forward and kiss him again.

When we finally break away, he slides his arms around me, pulling me close to him. I rest my head against his chest, breathing him in, listening to his beating heart. I feel safe. Happy. And I shove that horrible prickling sense of guilt away that's threatening to engulf me. I don't understand it and I certainly don't want it.

After a minute, he loosens an arm from around me and he lifts it to look at his watch. He sighs heavily. "I'm really gonna have to go this time," he says looking down at me regretfully. "Tables booked for eight."

I look at his watch. Seven forty-five it says. "Hmm, you better get a move on," I say and release myself from him.

He catches hold of my waist and pulls me back. "I don't want to go."

I glance up at his face. "I don't want you to go either."

He holds my chin with his thumb and forefinger and gazes down at me with his beautiful blue eyes. God, I really could get lost in them, in him.

"Até amanhã," he says. I look at him quizzically. "Until tomorrow," he explains.

"Ahh . . . will you teach me some Portuguese — amanhã?" I say, my eyebrow raised as I try to mirror his beautiful accent. It doesn't come off so well.

He laughs. "Sure." He presses his lips to my forehead with an air of finality and releases his hold on me.

He pauses by the door, holding it open. "Amanhã, Lucy."

My heart does a little somersault. "Amanhã, Osvaldo."

He winks at me with those beautiful bright blue eyes of his, then retreats through the door.

I flop down onto my bed, my skin still tingling from his touch, a huge smile plastered on my face. I cover my face with my hands and simply concentrate on remembering the experience for a moment. Now that's a memory I'll definitely be holding on to . . .

Okay, it's no use, it's still there. No matter how I may try and pretend it isn't, that annoying little feeling of guilt is insistent on prickling away at me.

Why do I feel so guilty about being with Fen?

Unless ..... no, that can't be right, but wait, maybe – I mean it could be possible, possible that I have someone, someone like Fen who's out there looking for me, who misses me. Is that why I pushed Fen away, because my subconscious knows the truth?

I feel a rush of anger. Well, if I have, then where the hell is he, why hasn't he come for me? I've been in the papers and on the television . . . unless he hasn't seen the press about me. Oh, come on, who am I kidding, he'd have to live in a hole not to have seen my face somewhere.

Conversely, if I am right and there is someone, why has he just left me? Maybe he doesn't want me anymore.

I feel abandoned, alone. A lump forms in my throat and tears well up in my eyes. I swallow them back.

This is crazy! Why am I getting upset about an imaginary boyfriend I most likely don't even have? Stop being so stupid. I laugh out loud at the absurdity of it.

And I'm not alone, I have Fen, and he's most definitely the future I want.

Brushing my stupidity aside, I pick the book up off the bed Fen brought me and flick to the first page.

I'm three pages in, and I'm not taking in a single word because my mind keeps drifting to Fen. I can't wait to see him tomorrow. I close my eyes and remember how he looked just before he left and how it felt to have his body pressed up against mine, and how very sexy he sounded when he spoke to me in Portuguese . . . Minha li - Minha lind- oh, whatever he called me, 'his beautiful girl'. That's all I need to know. A shiver goes through my entire body. Oh and that kiss . . .

I think at some point I must have fallen asleep because I'm not in my room anymore, I'm in the most beautiful garden I've ever seen and there are these purple flowers everywhere. I sense someone behind me and turn to see a man. Even though he's only standing a few feet away, I can't make out his face. It's all blurry and unclear. But I know in his presence I'm safe. I feel happy and loved. He motions for me with his hand. I walk toward him until I'm standing right before him. I look up at his face but it's still fuzzy. He lifts his hand and brushes my hair off my face. His hand feels so real, like he's actually here with me now. I can feel his skin on mine and he feels like heaven. Wherever his hand touches, it leaves a delicious trail of warmth in its wake.

"Luce, wake up, baby," he says, his tone deeply melodic.

Mmmh, his voice blankets me . . . I feel so warm, so safe, and he smells familiar. What is that scent? Hang on – smell - how can I smell him?

"Luce baby, wake up," he says again.

That's when I feel the hand on my face and my mind instantly clicks in. I'm not dreaming anymore, I'm awake, and that voice I can hear – well it's here in my room with me right now. My breath catches in my throat as panic zips through me and my heart starts to beat wildly.

I don't recognise the voice. Something's not right. Why would someone be here in my room at this late hour except the nurses? And that voice most definitely does not belong to any of them. Instinctively I know something's wrong.

I flick my eyes open to find a man with dark hair, and even darker eyes, gazing down at me. And it's the intensity of his stare that unnerves me.

He slowly withdraws his hand away from my face and I'm sure I see a trace of sadness in his eyes, but I'm far too freaked out to register it properly.

I jump back in bed, practically climbing up the wall. Then I spot a woman standing in the corner of the room. I don't recognise her either. This only helps to raise my panic levels a good couple of notches.

"Who – who are you?" I say, voice trembling, eyes flitting between the both of them.

I see a look of shock reverberate through the man's face but his features quickly soften.

"Shh," he says, raising his hand. "It's okay, you're safe. We're here to help you get your memory back."

What?

Chapter 22

Remember Me

"What?"

"We're here to help you," the dark haired man repeats softly.

I notice how dark it is outside and my eyes immediately flick to the clock. Ten thirty pm.

"How did you get in here? No visitors are allowed in after nine and there's no way the nurses would buzz you in . . ." My stress level is rising along with my voice. "Who the hell are you?"

The dark haired man glances back at the woman standing in the corner and looks back to me, his gaze wary. "I'm James and that's Isabel," he says thumbing over his shoulder. "I'm . . . well, I'm your . . ." He shakes his head. "It doesn't matter who I am," he adds quietly, "but Isabel, well, she's an . . . well, she's here to help you and —" He pauses and takes a deep breath. "Isabel an . . . an . . ."

"I'm an angel," she says.

I splutter out a laugh. I'm looking at the both of them, expecting their serious faces to crack into humour any second now . . .

They don't.

"What?" I say incredulously. "You're seriously expecting me to believe you're —" I point at Isabel. "— an angel." I can barely keep the grin off my face or the haughty tone from my voice.

"Yes," she says stringently.

"I know it's a lot to absorb," James intercepts, his voice warm, steady, "but it is the truth. Honestly."

And right here and now I've decided that out of these two loons, I prefer talking to him.

He seems the nicer loon.

"So who are you then, the Easter Bunny?" I deride, my eyes fixed on James as I very slowly and very quietly slide off my bed.

James raises his eyebrow and I can see his mouth twitching with amusement. I can tell he's struggling to keep the smile from his face which makes me warm to him, slightly, and I mean only slightly because obviously the guy is as crazy as hell.

I stand tall trying to exude confidence even though my body feels like it's made of rubber. "Okay, so you both need to leave." I jerk my head in the direction of the door.

James stands. I see just how tall and broad he is. "Look," he says, hands spread, palms down, "I know how you're feeling right now. I've learnt a lot of things recently I never would have believed possible, but we are telling you the truth." He presses a hand to his chest. "You're gonna just have to trust me on that one."

I let out a half-hearted laugh. "Trust you? I don't know you to trust you. You two just appear here in my room whilst I'm sleeping and wake me up telling me she's –" I jab a finger in Isabel's direction. "– a bloody angel! Seriously, I want you to leave now." I point firmly toward the door, "and if you don't, I'm gonna . . ." I stall trying to think of a good enough threat that will get these two nutters out of my room, "– scream bloody murder!" My whole body is trembling as I sidle toward the door.

"Just wait a minute, please!" And I can only assume it's the desperate tone in his voice that makes me stop because I can't think of any other reason why I would. "I know I'm not handling this very well –" He puts his hands up and looks pained, "but if you'll just stay and hear me out, Luce, I can explain everything."

Time clocks off for a moment. I'm stock-still, wide eyed, mouth open.

Luce . . . Lucy? There's only one person who knows I was going to call myself Lucy and it's definitely not him.

"Luce?" I say my voice wobbling all over the place. "Wha- why . . . why did you call me that?"

He looks momentarily confused before his face snaps into understanding. "Luce is your name – well Lucyna's your actual name," he corrects himself, "but I always call you Luce."

My head's buzzing. Luce . . . Lucyna . . . Lucy. That can't be, can it? It could just be a coincidence, one hell of a coincidence, mind. But if it's not and he's telling the truth, that means he knows me. He could be the

201

key to my past.

"Lucy's my – it's the name I –" I pause, my hands fidgeting with thin air. I stare at James, seeing in him my glimmer of hope, my chance to finally access the past I've so desperately longed for. "Did – do you know me . . . know who I am?"

His expression softens. "Yes, I do." He pauses as though considering his words, then he says, "We were – are together."

I stare at him in shock. "Together? Like boyfriend and girlfriend?"

He smiles. It reaches all the way up to his dark eyes. "Yeah, you could call us that."

And my blood begins to boil, so hot I can barely contain all the rage bubbling up inside me. All I see is red. "So where the hell have you been for the last four weeks?" I yell.

James' face jolts in shock.

"I woke up on that beach on my own with no memory of who I am! I was all alone! Why haven't you come for me before now? Four weeks! FOUR BLOODY WEEKS!" I pause, chest heaving, my eyes hot with tears. Then I remember the nurses and other patients, and quickly rein in my anger.

The room is silent to the echo. Questions are uncontrollably spooling through my mind. James looks like he's not sure what to do and Isabel is stood there looking bored and untouched by my outburst. Finally I speak, in a voice now barely registering above a whisper, addressing James, "Why didn't you come for me sooner? Didn't . . . didn't you want me anymore?"

"Of course I wanted you!" He clutches his head. "You've no idea how much I've missed you." He comes around the bed toward me but I back away from him. He stops in his tracks, hurt etched all over his face, but I'm too consumed by my own grief to care. "I didn't know where you were," he says, his voice quiet, regretful. "And I'm so sorry you've had to go through all of this, Luce, really I am, but there was nothing I could do. One minute you were there, the next you were gone."

He fixes his pained eyes on mine and they're so intense I feel like they're burning into me, but even still, I can't seem to look away. "If I had known where you were I would have jumped on a plane and come here straight away, I swear to you."

And that's when I notice his accent. English. Like they said mine is. "Plane?" I repeat, confused.

"I . . . we —" He points between the both of us. "— live together at my house in London. We were together the night you vanished."

My anger once again takes over. "You're not making sense!" I tug at my hair, frustrated. "How the hell was I in London, and then I vanish and end up here in Sydney with no memory of anything? It doesn't make any sense!"

"I know it's confusing," he says hurriedly, his face taut, "but, Luce, you're different to other people."

"Different?" I exclaim horrified. A hundred scenarios of 'different' flash through my mind, none of them good.

"Okay, so different probably wasn't the best word." He smiles sheepishly. "What I mean is you're special, Luce, and in a very good way. But it's all a lot to explain, too much, and you probably wouldn't believe me anyway if I told you. That's why Isabel's here. She's going to try and retrieve your memories for you, if you'll let her, and then you'll remember everything for yourself."

I glance at Isabel. Her eyes are already on me and she nods in agreement with James. My mind is still racing. I begin pacing around in attempt to try to gather my scattered thoughts. I mean this is all just crazy. CRAZY. But, if one ounce of what they're saying is the truth, it means I can finally find out who I am.

I stop and turn to Isabel. "Just how exactly are you proposing to get my memory back — when all the doctors haven't been able to, and four weeks of intense therapy hasn't revived one single memory — just what makes you so special that you're gonna be able to do it?"

"I've already told you what makes me special," she says simply.

"Oh yeah, course!" I scoff and slap my hand on my forehand, "you're an angel."

She rolls her eyes at me. She actually rolls her eyes. "Okay, enough of this," Isabel says. She claps her hands together and everything stops. James stops moving. The look of stress that was furrowing his brow is now permanently fixed on his face. He's looks inert. And the room is so

203

still and serene it seems as if even the air has stopped circulating. The only things that are animated are Isabel and me.

My head is prickling and my every instinct is on high alert. My mind is telling me to sprint from this room but, unfortunately, my legs don't seem to be agreeing as they're not going anywhere.

"What . . . what . . . have you done?" I stammer.

"I've just frozen time – temporarily," she explains in a casual tone.

"Fr-frozen t-time? H-how?" My voice is shaking uncontrollably.

She closes her eyes briefly and shakes her head. "You know how, Lucyna."

"You-you're really an angel."

She nods.

"Is-is everyone frozen?"

She throws her head back and laughs. "No. I'm not that powerful. I've just suspended time in here, except for you obviously."

My eyes flick to James. "Is he . . . is he okay?"

"He's fine." She waves her hand dismissively in James' direction. "It's just like he's taking a nap. Anyway, to more pertinent matters, I am sorry to have scared you, Lucyna, but James wasn't getting anywhere. I did think you'd listen to him but obviously not – so I thought I'd cut to the chase and, instead, show you that I am who I say I am. Do you now believe me?"

My mind is frantically trying to keep up and I'm unavoidably distracted by the statuesque sight of James. I swallow hard before managing an answer. "Yes."

"Good," she says with a brisk nod of her head. "So, as James said, I'm here to help you try to retrieve your memories. We don't need to go into the whys and where-fors, it'll all be clear when you get your memories back – well if I can manage to get them back, but if it doesn't work then I will explain everything to you – is that okay?"

I nod slowly.

"Let's get on with this, then." She claps her hands together and James is instantly reanimated.

He looks confused. He opens his mouth to speak but Isabel cuts him off with a wave of her hand. "It's okay, James. Lucyna understands now

– don't you?" Her green eyes are looking pointedly at me, "and we're going to try to retrieve your memories, aren't we?"

"Yes," I whisper in my weak voice.

My eyes move to James. He keeps looking between Isabel and me. He is confused, to put it mildly, but he says nothing.

And now I can't take my eyes off him. It's like I'm seeing him for the first time. Isabel has proved beyond a shadow of a doubt what they've been saying is the truth. Which means he and I were together. He was my boyfriend. I must have loved him. And if Isabel can do what she says she can, then I'll remember that. And it feels . . . strange. He's really good looking, I can't deny that. But to know that very soon I will feel overwhelming love for this stranger standing in front of me is . . . well it's just plain weird.

"Lucyna," Isabel's voice pulls me back to the here and now, "let's get started, shall we?"

Reluctantly I pull my eyes from James to her. "What do you need me to do?"

She positions herself on the edge of my bed. "Sit down." She pats the space in front of her. Gingerly I climb onto my bed. James, seemingly coming to his senses, sits himself down in the chair.

"I need you to give me access to your mind," she says. "You grant me permission and I'll do my best to see if I can penetrate this wall that's been put up to shield your memories from you."

I feel a stab of panic. What if I don't like what I remember? I must have forgotten everything for a reason – mustn't I?

"How did I lose my memory?" I ask, my voice jumping about with apprehension.

"Someone stole it from you," she says in a calm, even voice.

"Who?"

She presses her lips together in tight line. "You'll know soon enough."

Her words do nothing to appease me or answer my question, but I find myself agreeing to do as she asks.

"Right," Her voice suddenly sounds very businesslike, "firstly you need to give me your permission."

205

I take a deep breath. "You have my permission, Isabel."

"Now give me your hands . . ." I place my hands in her already outstretched ones, "and close your eyes."

Before I do, I glance over at James. His eyes are fixed intensely on me.

"Lucyna, close your eyes," Isabel repeats, somewhat impatiently.

"Oh, yes, of course." I blink myself free and close my eyes, but not before I catch the heart-warming smile that appears on James' lips.

"Now, Lucyna, I need you to focus on that dense wall in your mind and push as hard as you can against it."

I go to the blackness I've been inanely fighting against for all of this time, and do as she says.

"Very good. Just keep doing that," Isabel encourages me. But now, the words I hear are not shared, they're inside my head.

She begins chanting in my mind, 'Memoria solvo . . . memoria solvo' over and over again.

I wait with bated breath for something to happen, and I wait, and wait.

Nothing's happening. There's no sudden return of my memories. Maybe it's me. Maybe I'm not doing enough. I squeeze my eyes tighter shut, scrunching up my face and shove all my mental strength at the wall. I feel warmth trickle through my head but it disappears as quickly as it arrived.

Isabel releases her grip on my hands. "It's not working," she says, sounding frustrated.

I open up my eyes, feeling incredibly despondent.

"Isn't there something else you can try?" James asks hopefully.

She glances sideways at him. "Maybe." She pauses, pondering a thought. "Well, I could try and use your energy to increase the power, James. But if I do, you'll be weakened and feel unwell for quite some time afterwards."

"Do it," he says without hesitation.

Compassion wells up inside me. "You don't have to do this," I say to him.

"Yes I do." He looks at me with those dark, unfathomable eyes of his and my stomach flips. "I want you back, Luce, and I'll do whatever's necessary."

I don't know what to say to that, so I say nothing.

Isabel gets up off the bed, walks around to the other side of it and stays standing. "Sit with your back to me," she instructs. I do as she says, so now I'm sat facing James, my legs crossed in front of me. "James, take hold of Lucyna's hands."

He pulls his chair up close to the bed and puts his hands out for me to take. I slip my hands into his. And the instant my skin touches his, my whole body ignites and I know we fit together. My mind may not know him but my body most certainly does, and it's telling me he is right. My skin is tingling and prickling. It's a powerful and overwhelming sensation. I lift my blue eyes up to meet his dark ones and I see how they carry my reflection. And more than anything I desperately want to remember, for James' sake as much as my own, because I know hidden somewhere in my mind are my feelings for him.

"James, Lucyna, close your eyes." Isabel's voice comes from behind me, breaking the spell. She places her hands around my head. Reluctantly, I tear my gaze from James and close my eyes.

"Now, James," Isabel says softly. "Focus all your energy onto Lucyna, think about how you feel for her, think of the happy times you shared together, and let those thoughts flow from you straight into her. And, Lucyna, I need you to do as you did before, focus on breaking through that wall."

Right, focus . . . focus. Break through that wall . . .

James does seem really lovely, nothing like the nut job I first thought he was. I mean, look at what he's doing for me. And I wonder how we were together. I think we must have been happy. He seems to like me a lot. Well, hopefully I'll know soon enough. Nothing seems to be happening in my head, though, just like before. I bet we look really weird, the three of us in this position. We probably look like we're doing some form of weird meditation.

"Concentrate, Lucyna!" Isabel's strict voice commands in my head. I feel like a naughty child that's been caught out daydreaming in class by the teacher.

I snap myself out of my reverie and slip my mind into gear, focussing all my energy on getting my memories back and, at the click of a finger, I feel it. The warmth I felt before is rushing through my head but it is more intense this time. And it's not only in my head, it's flowing all around my body, coming up through my hands from James. His hands tighten around mine. I wonder if he can feel it too.

Isabel begins chanting in my mind again. This time the words are coming quicker and an accent is lacing her voice, "Memoria Solvo. Memoria Solvo. Memoria Solvo."

I don't know why, but I too find myself too echoing her words, and my head instantly feels very hot and light. I feel sick. And that's when it happens. The wall starts to crumble and the memories flood into my mind.

And I know.

Who I am – was. I know James. I know everything.

My head is aching and my eyes feel heavy, but I force them open. James is the first thing I see. And the relief I feel at seeing him is immense, to say the least. I feel like I haven't seen him for an eternity.

"James." His eyes flick open and I see how drained he looks. "I remember," I say, and the relief that washes into his eyes makes mine fill with tears.

Isabel removes her hands from my head and I sense her stepping away from the bed. I launch myself into James' arms and he holds me tight to him. I bury my face into his neck and breathe him in.

I'm finally home.

"I thought I'd lost you for good," he says, his voice thick with emotion.

I lift my head up to look at him. His eyes are shining. "I'm so sorry." Tears are now running down my face. "I'm so, so sorry."

He holds my face in his hands, smoothing my tears away with his thumbs. "You've nothing to be sorry for." Then his hands are in my hair and he's kissing every part of my face, my lips, my cheek, my forehead, my nose, every inch of my skin covered with his touch. "God, I've missed you, Luce."

"I love you," I whisper. Then I suddenly remember Arlo. My thoughts escape me. "Arlo," I say bitterly. James looks confused. "I asked him to send me to earth and make me human so I could be with you and he went mad, but I forced him to do it, and I knew there was something wrong but it was too late, and then I was in so much pain and he must have taken my memory away and . . ." The words are just tumbling incoherently out of me.

"Ssh, Luce, calm down. It's okay." He smooths my hair with his hand. "Take a deep breath and start at the beginning."

I sit back onto the bed but keep a firm hold of James' hand, afraid that if I let him go I might lose him again. Then I start at the moment Arlo took me from James' kitchen and I recount the events leading up to this moment. Both James and Isabel listen intently as I tell my story.

Then I reach the hard bit.

"James." I fix my gaze on him. I know what I have to say, but I'm worried about how he's going to react to it. I take a deep breath. "There's something you need to know . . . about us . . . about you – our history together."

"I know. Isabel told me."

"About Arran?"

He nods.

"Oh." I look away. He squeezes my hand and I bring my eyes back to his.

"You love me – don't you?" I can hear the doubt faltering his voice.

"Yes, I do," I say, determinedly. "I love you very much."

"Then that's all I need to know." He smiles hesitantly.

I hold his gaze, willing him to see the truth I know he doubts. He's the first to look away. I don't push it any further. Right now I'm just happy to be here with him.

So, on I continue with my story. I'm just at the part about Arlo's eyes changing colour and the pain I felt when he changed me, when Isabel interjects. "We should go now," she says. "I'll take you both back to James' house."

I spin round to Isabel. "Leave? Now? But I can't! What about Fen?" My breath catches in my throat and a sick feeling washes over me like a tidal wave.

Fen. I can't believe I haven't thought about him until now. I can see from the corner of my eye that James is looking at me curiously thanks to my unscheduled outburst. My face instantly heats under his stare. I swallow down. "And Dr Woods and all the nurses," I add albeit a little belatedly, but hoping it will add the right effect, "I can't just leave without a word to any of them."

"But you have to," Isabel says firmly. "It's not a good idea to speak to anyone. Questions would be asked that you can't answer. It's best if we leave now."

"Who's Fen?" James asks with an inquisitive tone to his voice.

Oh no. What do I say? I don't think James will take the fact that only a few hours ago I was in Fen's arms kissing him very well at all. Memory or no memory. And really it's just not the time with Isabel here and everything that's going on. I'll talk to him later about it.

I plaster a smile onto my face and turn to him. I can see in his eyes he knows something's amiss. "He's my friend," I say in the calmest voice I can muster. "He's the lifeguard who helped me that day on the beach and he's been watching out for me ever since. He's been really good to me."

He pauses for a moment before speaking. "Right," he says with a nod and appears to let it go, saying nothing more on the subject. And I don't know if it's just because he's so drained or because he actually believes me. I glance over at Isabel and I know she knows differently. She says nothing.

So I'm back to lying to James again. Great. And the guilt I now feel is nothing compared to the guilt I was feeling earlier when I was memory-less. Now it's of epic proportions.

Arlo. This is all his fault. I can't believe what he's done to me. I thought he was my friend. If it wasn't for him I would never have met Fen and I would never have developed these feelings for him, causing problems between James and me. But is that what I would really want – to never have met Fen? I can't think about that now. The main question here is how did Arlo manage to take my memory? He doesn't have the power to overcome free will. Well, he must have, because he overcame mine. None of this makes any sense. But these are questions

I'll have to deal with later because right now I have to deal with the fact that Isabel wants me to up and leave without saying goodbye to Fen. He'll be worried if I just disappear. I can't do that to him.

I feel like the worst person in the world for saying this, but I have to do something. "I just can't leave without a word," I say meekly. "It wouldn't be right."

"Isabel's right," James assures me. "I know it's hard, these people are your friends, but it's not like there's any other choice."

I sigh, defeated. Then I have a thought. "Can I leave a note?" I look at Isabel hopefully.

Her brow furrows and she takes a moment before answering. "Okay. As long as you don't say who you really are or where you're going – then yes."

I climb off my bed and retrieve a pen and rip out a piece of paper from my notebook. I press the pen to paper and start to write . . .

Fen,

I have to leave. I'm so sorry to go without saying goodbye.

Thank you for everything. Truly. I would never have got through these last four weeks without you. I want you to know how much you mean to me.

Please don't worry about me, I'm fine.

I pause, hovering over how to sign it. I glance back over what I've already written and see just how ineffective these words really are. Then I suddenly recall Fen's earlier words to me - 'Estou tão feliz que você veio em minha vida linda menina.' This time around my vast knowledge of languages allows me to know exactly what it was he said, what he didn't want me to know at the time – 'I'm so glad you came into my life, beautiful girl.'

My eyes start to sting with tears and I'm glad I'm turned away from James so he can't see. I take a deep breath and close my eyes, keeping them at bay. When I feel safe enough to do so, I open them and finish the note.

Estou tão feliz que você entrou na minha vida, minha linda Fen.

Eu nunca vou te esquecer. Lembrar de mim.

Lucy
xx

I fold it over, sealing my pain inside, and stand it up on the table.

"Ready?" James says. I turn around to see him standing before me. Concern is lining his face. He looks exhausted. His skin is considerably paler than normal and I know it's all because of what he did for me.

Guilt spikes me again and I quell it. With a smile I reach over and take hold of his hand. His warmth floods me. He smiles down at me with tired eyes.

I take a surreptitious glance around my home of the last month. I can see Fen everywhere. I can't believe I'm just leaving him like this. There's an ache now rooted deep within me which I don't think will ever go. But I have James back now and that's all that matters.

"I'm ready," I say. "Let's go home."

Chapter 23

Bad Penny

We've been sitting together in the living room in silence, James and I, for oh . . . I'd say about twenty minutes now. Not one single word has been uttered between us since Isabel left on her quest to try to locate Arlo. She said it's imperative she finds him.

Me? Well the fact that Isabel thinks it's imperative to find him unnerves me undoubtedly, but I can't let myself think about him or why he's done what he's done. If I do, it'll open up a whole stack of questions my brain and my heart . . . well, mainly my heart, can't tolerate at the moment. It's trying to cope with enough, so to ask any more of it would be abject sadism.

James sighs heavily. His hot breath blows down through my hair, blistering over my skin. His arms tighten around me, pulling me closer. And even though we are close, about as close as two people can be, I know the issues sitting between us could span a distance the size of the Grand Canyon. He's bothered by our history. I can tell by every tap of his finger against my skin, by every deep breath he takes and every sigh he expels, that he's considering everything, considering us, considering me. He may as well have thought bubbles transmitting from his head.

But he's not ready to talk about it. Neither am I. Hence the silent reflection.

James' chest once again rises up as he draws another deep breath. I hold mine waiting to see if he's going to speak. He doesn't. I breathe out and wonder just how much longer this can go on for.

After a few more minutes of dead calm, I lift my head up and look at him, seeing his pallid exterior, the darkness sitting under his closed eyes. He doesn't look right. Isabel using his energy seems to have taken more out of him than it should have.

I reach up and gently brush his hair back off his forehead with my fingers. "You look tired," I say. "You should go to bed."

He opens his heavy eyes and looks down into mine. "I will in a minute. I just want to stay here for a bit longer."

I don't argue. I rest my head back onto his shoulder and press my body closer to him, comforting myself in his scent, and curl my leg up against his.

Hang on, wasn't that his broken leg?

"Hey," I say surprised, "your pot's gone."

"Hmm, yeah, Isabel fixed it before we came for you."

"Ahh, right . . ."

Silence.

He begins stroking my hair. "It was really hard without you here, Luce. I don't ever want it to happen again."

He doesn't need to say anything more. The undertone to his voice has said it all. I know we're going to be okay.

I hold back my tears and press my lips to his neck. "You won't have to. I'm not going anywhere ever again."

And it's at this exact moment I feel him. Arlo's here. How did I not anticipate this?

I pull away from James and turn to see him casually leant up against the wall across from us. He has a glow about him I've never seen before. And when his lips form into a smile, it does nothing to calm my fears about his reason for being here.

"Arlo," I say breathlessly.

"Hello, Lucyna."

"What?" James' confused voice comes from beside me.

"We should talk," Arlo says.

"Talk?" I say incredulously.

"Yes, talk."

"I don't want to talk to you."

I look of anger flickers over Arlo's face. "But I want to talk to you." His voice comes out measured, controlled.

"You heard her," James says in a menacing tone. "She doesn't want to talk to you, so why don't you just disappear back under whatever rock it was you crawled out from."

Arlo doesn't even bother to acknowledge James. His eyes are fixed on mine and, try as I might, I can't look away. I'm held in his stare.

"Who are you?" I ask.

Arlo looks confused. "You know who I am."

"No." I shake my head firmly. "I don't. The Arlo I know would never have taken my memory without my permission and dumped me off ten thousand miles away from where I wanted to be."

He presses his lips together and has the audacity to look forlorn. "I am sorry about that," he offers.

"Sorry!" I jump out of my seat. "SORRY! You stole my memory from me! And if it wasn't for Isabel I'd still be stuck out there now without a clue! How could you do that to me?" If looks could kill, Arlo would be dead to the ground right about now. If he was killable, that is. And my heart is pounding so hard it feels like it's about to burst out of my chest.

"I said I'm sorry." His tone is impassive, not really giving the impression he is. "But I was angry and it's not exactly like you left me with any other choice," he adds. "I couldn't just sit back and let you come here to him —" I see his eyes darken as he gestures angrily in James' direction, "and live in your little happily ever after, not after all the hard work I've put in."

I stare at him, frustrated. "Hard work?"

He chuckles softly, an earnest look capturing his face. "Do you still not see it, Lucyna?"

I feel angry, small, stupid and his calm confidence is unnerving me. I grit my teeth together. "See what?"

"He's in love with you." James' quiet voice comes from behind me.

Silenced, I glance down at James. His eyes are on Arlo. I follow his gaze over to Arlo whose expression is unreadable. But the moment my eyes meet his I see the adoration in them and the realisation comes screaming down on me.

I sink back into my seat. "You love me?" The words sound gloopy as they leave my mouth.

Arlo's features soften. "How could I not?"

I stare at him, dumbfounded. I grip my fingers into the plush sofa, suddenly feeling off balance. "But all this time and you've never said anything —"

"I wanted to but there was always something, or someone, getting

215

in the way." I see his jaw tense up.

"But–but," I rub my forehead, "why would you abandon me out there if you love me . . . I don't under–" And just like that I get it, like a slap across the face. I can't believe how stupid I've been. My whole body stiffens. "You did it to keep me away from James." Then a chilling thought occurs to me. My eyes snap up at him. "Did you have anything to do with Arran leaving?"

He says nothing. He just mirrors my gaze. But then he doesn't need to say anything. I can see the answer in his eyes.

I'm seething. White hot rage obliterates my common sense. "All of this has been because you *love* me!" I mock the word, wanting to sound as condescending as possible. But the instant it's out I know I've made a mistake.

Arlo's face hardens. His anger fills up the room. It's suffocating. I hold my breath waiting for him to erupt. Then I feel James' hand curl around mine.

"Don't touch her," Arlo says slowly, his voice cold.

James laughs, awkwardly. "What?"

I've heard that challenging tone in Arlo's voice before and I ended up in Australia with no memory. I panic. I know Arlo's capabilities and James is only human. For that matter, so am I. There is no way I can protect him. And even if I was still of my celestial form, I doubt I could measure up to whatever Arlo now is.

"It's okay," I say calmly. I slide my hand out from underneath James'. I can feel his eyes on me but I don't look at him. Instead I hold my hands together, resting them on my lap, and ask Arlo in an even voice, "So why are you here? What is it you want?"

"Hmm, let me think, what do I want?" He thrums his fingers against his chin. "What I've always wanted!" he suddenly snaps. "For you to notice me. For you to love me."

"I did." I take a deep breath. "I do." I try to say this with as much sincerity as I can muster.

Arlo appraises me with his eyes. "But not like you do him, Arran – James or whatever it is he goes by these days." He waves a dismissive hand in James' direction. "No, right from the start I was always Arlo the

216

best friend, Arlo the confidant. And I bided my time, thinking things would change, that you would one day love me in the way I do you and just when it seemed you were beginning to, that my time was finally coming, Arran showed up. And that was it. I became invisible. You didn't need me anymore . . . so I made it so you did."

"He hurts her in the worst way possible," James interjects, "so she turns to you, right?"

"Sharp, isn't he?" Arlo rolls his eyes in James' direction. "You think he'd have improved over the years – but he hasn't . . . and don't you mean *you* hurt her." Arlo's eyes narrow onto James.

"I just–I just don't believe this," I stammer, breaking into their angry stare.

Arlo raises his eyebrows at me. "Come on, Lucyna. I wasn't going to give you up that easily. I had to do something, but unfortunately it didn't turn out quite as I had planned. Instead of seeking solace in me, as I figured you would, you wanted to run away, to forget – to become a Bringer." He shakes his head and quietly chuckles to himself. "I certainly did not see that one coming. But then that's what I love about you, Lucyna, you never cease to surprise me, even after all this time." The way he's looking at me, with such intensity, makes my stomach curdle and it takes everything in me not to baulk.

"So I made the best of a bad situation," Arlo says, shrugging lightly, "and I lowered myself to that realm to be with you, but that you know already. I always hoped you would one day feel again, but really I was just so happy for it to be the two of us as before. Then *he* goes and turns up like a bad penny and spoils everything."

Arlo bends his knee and rests his foot up against the wall. He looks so casual standing there, like he's merely a friend who's dropped by for a quick chat, not a heavenly being with a hidden, not to mention very dangerous, agenda.

"I'd waited too long for you, Lucyna, invested too much time," he continues. "Losing you was never an option. So I arranged his little car accident. And he was supposed to die there and be instantly reborn into another human being as always. You wouldn't know where he was, problem solved, but then, for some reason, you were called to him. I

217

still don't quite understand how that happened because he should never have a Bringer. He can't return to Heaven, you know this. But I knew that night in the stadium there was something wrong, I could tell by your reaction. And if I didn't know better I'd think someone was working against me." He smiles wryly. "So I followed you, and there you were, saving him. Then Isabel showed up to keep tabs on you both and I couldn't do a thing. Seriously," he adds, addressing James, "if there was some way for me to get rid of you permanently I would do it, and I mean that, sincerely, from the bottom of my heart." He grins, menacingly.

"You're fuckin' insane," James spits.

"When love is not madness, it is not love." He taps his hand against the hollow expanse of his chest. "Pedro Calderón. Not that I'd expect you to know who he was." Arlo looks back to me. "So where was I? Ah yes, I had to leave you here with him —"

"Why are telling me all of this?" I ask.

He smooths his golden hair back. "I've spent a long time pretending to be someone I'm not in the hope you'd one day love me. That obviously hasn't worked, so I'm giving the real me a try."

I honestly have no idea what to say to that.

"Do you wish for me to continue?" Arlo asks.

I nod.

"Right, well I wasn't sure what to do with Isabel constantly around and, until I could figure it out, I thought I'd use his little friend Sara to keep things interesting."

"Sara?" James splutters, aghast.

"Hmm, yes."

James stands up. "If you've hurt her, I'll —"

"You'll what?" Arlo laughs, derisively.

My stomach drops hollow. I slowly stand up beside James. "Is Sara okay?"

He wafts a dismissive hand. "She's fine. All I did was magnify the girl's feelings for him, and I really didn't have to work that hard as she's already completely besotted with him." His face turns serious and his green eyes pierce straight into mine. "He did kiss her back that day, you

218

know, the day you caught them, and he'd have done a lot more if you hadn't have interrupted, no matter what he says."

James laughs. "Nice try." He turns to me. "Don't listen to him. He's talking shit, and you know it."

But Arlo's picked at a weak spot in me and that is what he knows.

"No matter, I know the truth," he hums knowingly, and winks at me. I feel like I've got bugs crawling all over my skin. "But that's the problem with you, Lucyna, you've never been able to see straight when it comes to him. So I was forced to resort to desperate measures to bring you back to me."

"What have you done, Arlo?" I rub my bare arms, suddenly feeling cold.

And for the first time since he got here, he actually looks uncertain. His armour chinks and I see a glimpse of the Arlo I used to know. There's a gap before he actually speaks and, when he does, his voice sounds tight. "I think you know."

I swallow hard. "Oh no, Arlo." I shake my head despairingly.

"He owed me from a long time ago. I once helped him out of a tight spot," he confides, trying to feign nonchalance, but I can hear the pride in his voice. "So I called in the favour to get rid of Arran the first time, but then I was all out of favours and you know he won't do anything for free so . . ." He shrugs, leaving his words hanging in the air.

I swallow down hard. "You gave him your soul."

He strokes his hand down his jacket. "Sold. Not given. And yes, amongst other things. And I got a good price for it."

And that's the exact moment when I realise that I've lost my best friend for good. I wipe the stray tear from my eye. "When?"

"Just before I brought you back – so I could bring you back."

I rub my temples. "Why would you do that?"

He looks at me sincerely. "For you, Lucyna. I'll do anything to be with you."

"Looks like you've wasted your time," James says, sounding surprisingly calm, "because you're never going to have her."

Arlo glances in James' direction, a blasé look on his face. "And who says so – you?"

219

"Yes." I can hear from the tone in James' voice that he's picking a fight.

Arlo laughs discordantly and raises an eyebrow. "Hmm, this could be interesting."

"No, James, this isn't a good idea," I plead quietly.

"You should listen to her," Arlo smarts, nodding his head.

James looks down at me. His dark eyes are blazing. "I can't just do nothing."

"Yes, you can," I say. "Go to Sara's, make sure she's alright. I'll stay here and talk this through with Arlo." Okay, so I have no idea exactly what it is that I'm going to say to Arlo, but I need to get James out of here quickly before Arlo does something to hurt him.

James looks at me, astonished. "I'm not leaving you here alone with him!" Then he makes a show of taking hold of my hand, the hand that's been nervously pulling at the hem of my t-shirt.

I see Arlo's eyes harden. The green in them quickly disperses, to be replaced with the bright yellow just like before. He rests his foot back on the floor and straightens himself up.

I have to stop this, now.

"James, please, you can't win this," I say.

"I know," he states angrily, "but there is no way I'm leaving you here with him, so we're leaving together." He turns to go, taking me with him.

I make to speak but I'm too late.

The energy in the room ramps up so high I feel like every hair on my body is stood on end. It all happens in a nanosecond. James' hand pulls from mine and I watch helplessly as his body flies at high speed across the room and smashes straight into the wall. I hear the sickening crack of his bones. He drops to the floor, debris cascading down over him.

"The only person leaving here is you, Arran," I hear Arlo mutter through my muted screams.

Chapter 24

The Art of Delusion

It's strange how a second can feel like an hour, and even stranger is how many thoughts can rush through your mind in that one second.

Stupid, irrelevant thoughts.

Like how James has only just got his pot removed, and how that's his favourite t-shirt he's wearing. And the picture frame that's laid on the floor, broken beside him, contains a photo of him and Max, the last one they had taken together before he died. He'll be devastated if it's ruined.

He hasn't moved yet. I know it's only been about two seconds since he collided with the wall, but he would move if he was okay, wouldn't he?

Should I panic?

Or maybe I already am, because something is tearing up in and around my veins, and I have this odd constricting pain in my heart, like there's a hand gripping hold of it.

But it doesn't seem real. None of this seems real. Maybe disbelief has taken me over and paralysed me, or maybe it isn't real. Maybe this is just a really, really bad dream.

My eyes wash down, shutting it all out. Everything's eerily silent, almost as if the world's holding its breath, waiting to see what's going to happen next.

I open my eyes.

No, it's real. He's still laid there on the floor, motionless, blood trickling from his head down onto the wooden floor.

Come on, James, move baby, you can do it.

Four seconds.

No, it's been too long now.

And in the snap of a finger, I'm running toward him, crying out his name. The words are tearing up in my throat.

Please, be okay. Please, be okay.

Then I stop.

I'm all but a foot away from James and I can't move. And it's not because I don't want to because, believe me, I want to. I'm trying but I've lost all control over my body.

"Sit down, Lucyna," Arlo commands.

And like an obedient animal, I do. I can't not. He's controlling my body, governing every move I now make.

I glance across at James. Tears spill from my eyes, running in quick succession down my cheeks.

"Don't look at him. Look at me."

My eyes involuntarily move to Arlo. He looks calm, impeccable. Not a golden hair out of place, not a sliver of emotion showing on his face.

"Please don't do this," I gulp back the tears, I'm unable to wipe away.

He sits down in the chair opposite me, relaxed, arms spread out across the back of the seat. "I'm sorry, Lucyna, but you always knew how this was going to go. I was never going to allow you be with him. You belong to me."

And then I'm filled with a rage I didn't even know existed. I feel like there's fireworks' going off in my head, firing about every which way. And all I know is that I hate him. Hate him. HATE HIM.

"I don't belong to you," I spit, venom snaking my voice. "You disgust me. I hate you."

He throws his head back and roars out a laugh. "Well, there is a fine line between love and hate, so I'm half the battle won." He shrugs.

I stare at him speechless. Does he have no feelings left in him at all? How can this be the Arlo that I've spent the better part of an eternity with? No, I can't accept that he's totally gone. There has to be some goodness left in there somewhere.

"Have you forgotten who you are – were - your very reason for being?" I implore.

"Have you?" he throws back at me. "If I remember correctly, you didn't think twice before turning your back on our home for your own selfish reasons . . . and on more than once occasion."

"That–that was different," I stammer.

"Was it?" He shakes his head. "I don't think so. You left home and changed all in the name of love, Lucyna, and that is all I've done. We're not so different, you and I. And that's why we belong together. I understand you better than you do yourself."

"I'm nothing like you! I would never do what you've done, become what you've become."

"Wouldn't you? Not even if it meant you could have the one thing you wanted above all else . . . not even if it meant you could save your precious James by doing so?"

I glance over to James. He's still not moving. Tears fill my eyes. I blink them back.

"No," I say, but even I can hear the doubt in my voice. "Please, Arlo, just let me get James some help." I look deep into his calm yellow eyes, pleading for compassion.

He looks past me. "No."

"James doesn't deserve this – this isn't about him, it's about me and you – he's done nothing wrong – he desperately needs to see a doc–"

"NO!" he roars, jumping up out of his seat. I flinch. "It's always him, him, him! What about me?"

"This is all about you!" I fire back. "We're here because of you!"

I stare at him hard, my chest heaving. I can see his jaw working angrily and his eyes look like they're on fire.

After a moment he sits himself back down in the chair and begins tapping his fingers on the arm rest. "Tell me about the lifeguard," he says.

My stomach tightens. "No."

"Do you want him to live?" He inclines his head toward James.

I sigh, defeated. "What do you want to know?"

"Are you in love with him – the lifeguard?"

I don't know how to answer this. I know he's tricking me in some way. There's a catch in it somewhere. And if I give the wrong answer, I could be putting Fen in danger too.

So I do the only thing I can, evade it. "He was good to me," I say. "He helped me when I needed help."

He chuckles. "But that's not really answering my question, though, is

223

it?"

I take a deep breath. "No, I'm not in love with him."

He raises his eyebrow. "I'm surprised to hear you say that."

I know I'm falling into his trap but I can't but help ask, "Why?"

He shrugs lightly. "Because it sure felt a lot like love when you were kissing him . . . or should I say me."

I feel sick. And dizzy. I stare at him, dumbstruck. "You're Fen?" I exclaim, finding my voice.

"Hmm." He nods. "That's what you need to realise, Lucyna. I'm always there. Wherever you are, I will always be alongside you. You can never get away from me." His lips curve up. "And did you really think I'd leave you out there all alone? What do you take me for? The only regret I have is that when we shared our first kiss, I had to be in the body of that dim-witted mortal."

My stomach turns over and, for a moment, I actually think I'm going to throw up. I feel wounded. And violated. I need to scrub him off me.

"How did you —?"

"Do it?" he interrupts.

"Yes."

"Easy. I can do anything I want now," he says proudly. He has this really smug look on his face which, if I wasn't human and immobile, I would really love to wipe off.

"I just 'borrowed' him for a while, well, his body. It was an easy way for me to stay off Isabel's radar and mask your essence at the same time, by being so close to you, you see. Every day I spent with you I could see your feelings growing for me. I always knew you loved me deep down."

"I didn't have feelings for you!" I rage. "I had feelings for Fen!"

"But I was him. And your kissing me told me everything I needed to know."

I laugh hollowly. "It told you nothing except that I was lonely and I was drawn to his . . . his looks. And if for one second I had known it was you, I would never have touched him."

He doesn't flicker. "I beg to differ," he says calmly. "You have feelings for me. You're just not ready to admit them to yourself yet. But that's

224

okay because we've got plenty of time for you to come to terms with them. I've waited this long. I can wait a bit longer."

I look at him with utter disgust and contempt. I can't believe I once thought this thing was my friend. He's so self-serving, so callous.

"I think you just manipulated the situation to your advantage, Arlo. I think you manipulated me into having feelings for Fen."

He actually looks like I've hit him really hard. "I didn't manipulate you. It's the one situation where I actually didn't have to do anything. Everything you did, Lucyna, you did of your own free will."

I know I would never have done anything with him freely, and I've had enough now. I'm done with his games. The more time races on, the less chance James has.

"Are we done?" I ask, ensuring to keep my voice firm and steady.

He looks at me confused. "Meaning?"

"Meaning – have you achieved what you came here to achieve or are we going to sit here forever and a day discussing your delusions? Because if we are, then please just put me out of my misery now."

He laughs loudly. It echoes around the room. "Yes. We are just about done. We can go now if you want . . . or do you want to stay and watch your boyfriend take his final breath."

My heart constricts. "Oh no, no, no, don't kill him," I say panicked. "Please. I'll do anything. I'll come with you wherever you want. Just don't kill him, please."

"Nice of you to offer," he muses, smoothing his hand over his hair. "But you were always coming with me. And he –" he points a finger, and glances over at James, a smile playing on his lips, "well, that's out of my hands. It's the blood that's been trickling into his brain that's been doing the trick." His eyes flash victory.

I stare at James, transfixed. "No," I whisper, my eyes blurring with tears. I blink them away furiously, angry they're blocking my vision.

He's been here dying right before my very eyes and I've not done a single thing to help him.

Hold on, baby. Please. I'm sorry.

"And . . . he's gone. Finally," I hear Arlo say. He doesn't bother to hide the glee in his voice. "So you see, Lucyna, you only have me left now. Looks like you're all out of options."

Chapter 25

Bloodied Hands

"Aaaarrgghhh!" Is that me screaming?

It must be.

"It's okay, Lucyna." I hear Arlo's dispassionate voice come from across the room. The sound is like hot needles piercing my skin. "The pain will pass soon."

Oh God, I'm being crushed. This is agony. Somebody help. Please.

I open my eyes and I'm looking at Arlo. He has his perpetual air of unconcern and calm. He doesn't look like he's just killed James.

James is dead.

Oh no. No. No. No. No.

I stare blankly ahead, tears flooding from my eyes.

"I'm sorry to cause you pain but it has to be this way," he says indifferently. "It's for the best. You'll see this soon."

I open my mouth but nothing happens. I'm empty of words. I'm hollow. I'm dead inside.

"We're leaving now," Arlo tells me. "I can't release the bind I have on you as I don't think I can trust you not to try and run. Not that you'd get far." He chuckles. "But best not to take any chances –"

And you'd think the next voice I hear would fill me with relief, but how can I feel relief when I feel nothing.

"Let her go, Arlo."

"Hi, Isabel," he says, seemingly unperturbed at her appearance. He gets up out of his seat. "Been a while."

"Not long enough." She smiles sweetly.

"Touché." He laughs. "So your here to save the day?" he adds with a sneer.

"And to take you home." She is watching him as a human being would watch a snake. As I would now.

He laughs again, louder this time. "Really? And you think you can do that?"

As he says this I see other angels appear. Three of them, evenly spaced around the room. I don't know any of them.

Arlo runs his eyes over them and raises his eyebrows. "Are you really sure you want to do this?" he says to Isabel.

"No, but there's no other choice. You're obviously not going to come willingly and I can't allow you to do this." She moves a hand in my direction. "So . . ." She leaves her words hanging in the air.

Then, in the blink of my eyes, the room is mayhem and I'm sat on the sofa, paralysed, in the middle of it all.

The energy in the room is so high it could light the whole city for a year. My skin is tingling from it. Arlo is really strong. His target is Isabel, and even though the other angels are all around him, he seems unfazed, able to keep them back with ease. I pray that Isabel is going to be okay.

But really all I care about is getting to James. I might be able to save him if I can get to him. It might not be too late. Because if I don't, he will be reborn and then I may never find him again. But even if I did, he wouldn't be James anymore. He'd be different.

Isabel manages to toss Arlo away from her, and the instant she does so he must have lost his focus because I can move. I'm up and off that sofa in an instant. Arlo doesn't seem to notice that his hold on me has gone or that I've moved, because he doesn't stop me.

When I reach James I drop down onto my knees beside him. I lean over and carefully pull him onto his back, laying him flat. His eyes are closed. There's blood matted in his hair and on his forehead.

I have to help him. How? CPR. I've never done it before. So, do it now. Okay. He's laid flat. Next tilt his head back. What is it, ten compressions? Fifteen? Anything for God's sake, Lucyna. Just stop wasting time.

I put my hands on his chest and begin CPR, not caring what's unfolding behind me.

"Six – seven – come on baby wake up – nine – ten." I stop pumping and blow my breath into his mouth, once, twice. His lips feel cold on mine. I wait a second. Nothing. I start pumping on his chest again.

"Come on James – three – you can't leave me here alone – six –

seven . . ." Tears are streaming down my face. I wipe them away on my sleeve. Tears are an added irritation I don't need. Right now, I need to concentrate on saving James. I breathe into his mouth again. Once, twice.

Then I hold my own breath.

Nothing.

"No! You're not leaving me!" I bang my fist on his chest. "I saved you once before. I can save you again!" I begin pumping harder down on his chest. "One – two – three, you're not leaving me, not after all of this. Not after everything I've gone through to be with you. Come on, James! This isn't you! You're a fighter! Fight, baby, fight! Nine – ten." I blow as much of my warm air into his lungs as I can. I stare at his face, willing him to breathe. "Breathe, James," I plead. "You can do it."

Nothing.

"NO!" I drop my head on his chest, gripping my fingers into his t-shirt. "Please don't give up!"

And then I'm angry. Angry with him for giving up, angry with me for letting this happen, angry with God for not stopping this from happening.

I beat my hands on his chest. "Wake up!" I cry. "Fight to stay! Don't let him win!"

I stare down at his unmoving face, my chest heaving up and down, the words cutting up in my throat and a sudden calm washes over me. I notice I'm crying again and my tears are dripping onto his t-shirt, spoiling it. I dry my face with my hand. Then I pull his limp body up onto my lap. I try to wipe away the blood on his forehead with my hand. It smears.

His blood is on my hand. I stare numbly down at it.

This is my fault. He would never have died if I hadn't been so selfish. If I had just left him alone in the beginning, Arlo would never have done all of this. He would still be alive now. James died because of me.

"I'm so sorry," I whisper as I trace my finger around his face. His perfect face. He looks so peaceful, like he's sleeping.

Did you know, James? Did you know you were going to die? You didn't cry out for help or say 'stop', or scream, or anything. You were just so silent. So quiet.

My eyes move to the picture of James and Max on the floor. I wipe my bloodstained hand on my t-shirt, and reach over and pick up the broken frame. I tip the shards of glass out onto the floor.

I study James' face in the picture. He looks happy. He was happy, before me, before I came and ruined his life. Before I ended his life.

This pain inside me is a burning agony filled with a sense of loss and regret which is never going to go away. I can't change any of it. I can't take it back. How am I supposed to go on living like this without him?

How did all those people I used to see when I was a Bringer do it? How did they go on? I press my arm across my chest trying to contain the wretchedness I feel. I can barely breathe. Nothing will ever make it go away.

Funny how when I was a Bringer, all I wanted was to be able to feel, and I remember how I used to wonder what was worse — to feel the agonising pain of loss or to have never felt it at all. At least now I know the answer.

And it's clear to me what I have to do.

I smooth James' dark hair away from his beautiful face and press my lips to his one last time. "I love you," I whisper.

I rest him gently back to the floor and place the photo of him and Max on his chest.

Then I rise calmly to my feet and walk into the still ongoing fracas, right into the direct line of fire.

Chapter 26

Live Forever

So this is what dying feels like.

It's nothing like I thought it would be. I feel like I'm being pulled through a wind tunnel backwards and at high speed. It shouldn't be like this, should it? Or maybe I'm being reborn. Maybe this is what rebirth is like. Of course, I won't die like a normal person – meet my Bringer, go to Heaven. I'm like James.

James.

Oh God, it hurts. It hurts too much. The sooner this rebirth happens the better. Then I won't remember anything.

Wait, didn't I do this before, choose to forget. Isn't that taking the easy way out? Am I a coward? Probably. I know it's harder to stay and fight but I can't do it, not without him.

Well I guess it's too late now anyway.

I knew the instant I was hit. I walked straight into the fight between Arlo and Isabel. The look in his eyes, the moment he saw that his bolt of energy aimed at Isabel had hit me, was poetic. I'm glad it was him that killed me. He'll feel that pain forever – unless Isabel couldn't overcome him and he finds me again. Oh God, what if he finds me and then I won't know it's him or what he's up to. Oh no, what have I done? I should have waited to see if Isabel was okay, I shouldn't have just left her or the other angels there with him. But if I had stayed and Arlo overcame them, I would still have been his. He would have taken me with him. Maybe it really is better this way. I had it right first time. Or maybe there was no right way. Honestly, I don't know and I don't care, I just want to stop feeling this way. Why haven't I forgotten yet? And what is that light? Where am I?

I blink open my heavy eyes.

I'm still in James' living room and I'm back sitting on the sofa.

Is this Heaven? Was I allowed back in after all? Have they forgiven me my misdemeanors and given me another chance? My heart lifts. If so, they couldn't have got my version of perfect more right. James' home. My haven. I feel so close to him here, surrounded by all his things. And they've got it spot on. Everything looks just like it used to before Arlo tore it all up. The only thing missing is James.

Bleakness wraps my heart.

"Luce?" It's the sound of a voice that I never thought I'd hear again. My heart nearly explodes with relief.

I spin around to see James sitting beside me. "James!" I breathe out in a flurry of relief and disbelief.

He smiles confusedly at me.

Are we in Heaven together? Really, it doesn't matter where we are. He's here. I feel like I'm going to burst with happiness. But wait, what if he's not real. What if he's just a figment of my very desperate imagination? I want to reach out and touch him to check if he is, but what if I do and he disappears. No, I'll just keep him here as he is for now.

I clasp my hands together. My palms are slick with sweat. Would I sweat if I was dead? My mind is trying to work it out but it's all too messy to make sense.

"You're both alive." I hear Isabel's voice come from behind me. "I've taken time back. About an hour or so."

I turn sharply to find her sitting in the chair Arlo was in.

"What?" is all I can manage.

Isabel looks at me like I'm an idiot. "You're both alive," she says slowly. "I reversed time to bring you both back."

I blink a few times.

James is alive. He's real. He's really here.

Complete euphoria floods me and I launch myself at him, throwing my arms around him. I feel his arms vice around me. I squeeze him as tightly in return

"Luce. I can't breathe," he gasps, laughing. I loosen my grip on him. I pull back, hold his face in my hands, and stare into his dark, dark eyes. I can't believe he's really here. I don't ever want to be deprived of looking at him again.

He smiles a lopsided smile and bites down on the corner of his lip.

232

He is beautiful. My heart is hammering against my ribcage.

"Not that that enthusiastic greeting of yours wasn't great," he says, brushing a stray tear from my eye, "but, erm, I'm a bit confused as to what the hell is actually going on here."

"Arlo killed you," Isabel says very matter of factly. "And then I, thanks to Lucyna, accidentally killed her, so I reversed time to bring you both back."

"You killed me?" I gasp as I nearly twist my head off my neck in my attempt to look at her. "I thought it was Arlo."

She presses her lips tightly together. "Nope. That was me, I didn't see you coming. I was too focussed on Arlo. Sorry. It helped though, you getting yourself killed, it distracted him for long enough for us to bind him."

Okay. Glad to have helped.

"Where is . . . Arlo?" I ask tentatively, sucking my breath in.

"At home where he belongs. He can't get back out. We've bound him, in a – let's say, 'restricted area' until we can figure out a better way to help him. Don't worry he won't get free. You're safe."

"Why did you bring us back?" I have to ask the question. "I don't mean to sound ungrateful," I add quickly, "because I'm not, honestly. I'm more grateful than you'll ever know."

She sits forward, bridging the gap between us. "I like a happy ending. What can I say?" She shrugs lightly.

"Thank you, Isabel, for everything you've done," James says, taking hold of my hand.

"Yes, thank you," I add, somewhat belatedly.

"You're welcome." She stands and my eyes follow her up. "I have to go."

"Isabel, can I ask – Fen, the guy Arlo used, is he okay – do you know?"

"He's fine. Damage control done. He remembers nothing as do the rest of the humans at the hospital. It's as if you never existed."

She smiles and winks at me.

I have to stop myself from laughing with relief. "It's been nice to see you again Isabel."

"Likewise," she smiles. "And just so you know, you've both been granted access back into Heaven . . . but I don't expect to see either of you anytime soon." She points an authoritative finger at James and me.

Before I get to thank her again, she's gone.

I rest back against James' chest. I can feel his heart beating against my back and his breath blowing down my neck, things I never thought he'd ever be able to do again. I block out all the horrendous memories and comfort myself in the fact there is nothing that can take him away from me ever again.

"So, you died," James says after a moment. His voice is rough and low.

"Yes," I answer quietly. I really don't want to get into this with him.

"What did Isabel mean when she said, 'it was thanks to you that she killed you?'" And there it is. He really doesn't miss a trick.

I shift uncomfortably.

He turns me round to look at him. "Tell me."

Surprisingly to me, tears spring to my eyes. "You'd died and I couldn't save you. I tried, but I couldn't bring you back. And it hurt too much. Then I . . . just kind of got in the way of their fight."

"How?"

I take a deep breath and look past him, staring at the wall. "I walked into the middle of it."

He sighs and holds my tear-streaked face in his hands, forcing me to look at him. "Why would you do that?"

"Because I couldn't bear the pain of losing you and I wanted it to stop."

"That was a really fucking stupid thing to do. You know that?"

"I know," I whimper.

He presses his forehead to mine, my tears running against his cheeks. "Promise me you'll never do anything like that again."

"I promise." I sigh. "Why can't we both just live forever as humans? Things would be a whole lot simpler if we could."

He laughs and moves back from me. "You're asking me that?"

I bite down on my lip, saying nothing. I know it's a stupid thought, but it'd be nice if it could be true.

"We might not live forever as we are, but you and me –" he points between us both, "we'll always be together. There's nothing to keep us apart now. And I, for one, think that's something to be very happy about." He wipes the tears from my face and smiles at me.

My skin burns from his touch. His hot breath is blowing over me, causing shivers to run freely down my spine.

"So, what now?" he asks. I can see his eyes are on my lips and I know exactly what he's thinking when he does that.

"I don't know." I shrug, feigning nonchalance. "We could go to bed, I suppose."

"Bed?" His eyes suddenly look really opaque.

"Sleep seems like a really 'normal' thing to do after everything we've been through tonight."

"Hmm, it does I suppose. But then normal's not so bad, I'd say."

He grins sexily and a bolt of desire zips through me. So I just have to lean forward and kiss him.

"You keep kissing me like that," he says drawing away from me breathlessly "and I don't think I'm gonna be able to make it out of this living room with you, let alone up to bed."

I climb up onto his lap. "I can live with that," I murmur, as I pull his t-shirt over his head and feel his hot body press up against mine. "I can live with anything so long as I have you."